TEMPLE
ARIANNA
∽ AND THE ∽
SPIRIT OF THE STORM

ROBBIE BALLEW
STEPHEN LANDRY

The Temple of the Storm Series:

1

ARIANNA

A fierce storm raged as my mother, Solph, cried, and my father, Carine, paced back and forth in the hall outside.

He's told me the story so many times I can recite it by heart. He wanted to be in the room with her, but something was wrong. My birth was not going as planned. Maria, the midwife, had asked him to wait outside.

My father swore that a bolt of lightning struck the house, that in that moment of blinding light he was sure the house would catch fire. But fire never came. There wasn't even a crash of thunder to follow the lightning. Without warning, the storm -- and my mother's screams -- had come to an abrupt halt.

My father rushed into the room and took me in his arms. He said there was a spark of electricity in my eyes. That all the force of the lightning had been bottled up inside me, and that's where my powers had come from. The powers I've spent years learning how to control. To suppress.

That's where my father always ended the story, but no matter how many times he told it, I could see him choking back the tears.

Hiding the pain. He wanted to tell me what happened next, but he never had the strength.

My father never told me the end of the story, but Maria did. She said it was my right to know. When my father rushed into the room he was so overjoyed he didn't even notice at first. He was filled with joy at the love that had entered his life, yet was unaware of the love that had left. When he finally saw her, he fell to his knees. Maria was afraid he might drop me by accident, but he never did. He laid me on my mother's motionless chest and crawled into the bed, cradling us in his arms. There he stayed, weeping late into the night.

He always believed it was all connected; My birth, her death, and the drought.

My father used to tell me about the world as it had been. The deep gorge that ran past our village with a trickling stream at the bottom was once a roaring river. The dusty, withering crop fields were once lush and green. The abandoned buildings that now sat boarded up at the center of our village were once a bustling marketplace.

I couldn't help but feel it was all somehow my fault. The drought had started on the day I was born. As far back as I can remember, my father spent more time searching for a way to bring back the rain than he had at home with me. Even when he was home, he spent most of his time poring over old books and scrolls.

I still have flashes of memory from when I was very young. Turning the pages of those ancient books, though I couldn't understand the runes and inscriptions. My father reading to me about myths and legends as I fell asleep. The memories are always triggered by the smell. Everything I remember about my father is encapsulated in that dusty smell.

There's one memory that stands out to me more than all the rest.

I was playing in the dirt, no more than four years old. My father crouched down next to me and smiled. I remember having mud all over my face.

"No matter what happens, Arianna, you must never let anyone else determine your path in life. You have the spirit of the storm in you, my little songbird. Embrace it, it is what makes you who you are."

His words still echo in my thoughts, in my dreams, all these years later. I might not have been able to understand them at the time, but I always knew they were important.

My father rose to greet Mayor Talze, a very fat man, and a handful of village leaders. I stood, not as a child but as a dreamer.

I remember seeing a wilted tomato plant nearby. Tomatoes have always been my favorite, though they rarely come in the ration packs. I tried to pick one from the plant, but it fell the moment my clumsy fingers touched it and splattered on the ground. The insides were all brown.

"Don't wander too far, Arianna," I could hear my father call after me.

"It's getting late, Carine, this had better be worth it," the Mayor said.

"It will be," my father promised.

"There's been grumbling among the workers at the mines, you know. You continue to take a share of the rations, but…"

My father cut the Mayor's cold voice off, "But once I've found a way to end the drought, there will be no more need of rations.

All those workers toiling away in your mines will be free to go back to their old lives."

One of the village leaders grumbled something I couldn't understand. I wasn't listening with anything more than a child's natural curiosity.

My father continued, "I have found some compelling evidence to suggest this drought has been brought on by magic."

My father had been telling me this for years. He had practiced this speech I don't know how many times. I never expected the village leaders would respond with laughter.

"Magic, what are you talking about?" One of the village leaders interjected. "You are an even bigger fool than Talze has told us."

The Mayor held up his hand and the elders quieted all at once. "Magic hasn't been practiced outside the Royal Academy in decades. Don't you think King Drevon would know if one of his own mages went rogue?"

Mayor Talze lowered his hand to his side and took a small piece of candy from his pocket. He placed it in his mouth with such belligerent joy as the others watched with hungry eyes.

"It could have been a Casar, a Firya, even a Satyr," my father reasoned. "Look at the sky! The clouds have never left, but the rain refuses to fall."

"What purpose could such a curse possibly serve?" said another one of the village leaders. "It's affected the other kingdoms just the same as ours."

By this time I wasn't paying much attention. I heard the Mayor begin to speak of the mines again. The same lecture I've heard him give a hundred times since then. How it had brought the village together. How it promised work for one generation after another.

Despite my father's pleas, no one was actually listening to what he had to say.

My attention was on the edge of the forest that bordered the crop fields. I swore I saw a pair of beady eyes peer out and then vanish. The eyes caught my attention and I toddled toward them. There was a guard patrolling the tree line, but he was walking the other way now. Maybe I could get just close enough to see what the eyes belonged to.

My father and the Mayor, just within earshot, continued to argue.

"You think because your daughter was born an elemental you know more about magic than the rest of us." I paused when I realized the Mayor was talking about me. Even at such a young age I knew I wasn't like the other kids, that my powers were special. I also knew that until my father could afford to send me to the Royal Academy of Magic I was forbidden to use my powers.

"Do you even know if such a curse is possible?" Even as I inched away I could hear the Mayor's dismissal.

"No, I don't," my father answered, his voice diminished.

"And do you know what it would take to reverse such a curse?"

"No, I don't. But that does not change the fact that it must be done! We must send out an expedition to find the truth!"

"We've heard the man's case. I think it's time to put it to a vote. Who would like to send a group of our finest elves on a perilous journey through Satyr infested forests…"

I was almost too far away to hear the rest as I approached the dark woods.

"…to break the curse that may or may not have been placed on our land?"

There was no response as the sun set and complete darkness fell.

I was in the woods. Alone. Farther than I had ventured before. I could barely see my own hand in front of my face. I was about to cry out for help when I heard a still, soft voice whispering inside my head.

Stay calm, child. I will guide us.

A ball of blue light formed in my hand, lighting the trees around me. I hadn't meant to use my powers, it had just happened.

As I stumbled across the roots of trees into the night I could feel chills run down my arm as if Emu, the goddess of the woods had invited me in.

I could hear a trumpet sounding in the distance. The guard must have seen me wander into the woods, but that didn't bother me. I was an explorer - like my father; determined to discover all there was to see.

I imagined all the strange and wonderful friends I might meet. As a child, the forest looked like the most magical place in existence. I pushed through the last of a sparse underbrush into a clearing and stopped short as a creature stepped out from behind a tree. The creature was wearing rough, leather garments. Its legs were covered in fur and it had hooves for feet. As I looked up in the dim light I could make out a face that seemed almost elvish, but there was something off -- it was familiar yet far away.

I held out my hand to show the ball of electric light to the creature. Maybe it wanted to play? I tossed the ball toward the creature, but it hit the ground much too soon. It bounced and rolled and came to a stop at the creature's feet.

The creature bent down to examine the ball of light. I could see its face more clearly now. Gentle, curious, but with large, twisting horns coming from the top of its head. Was this a Satyr? It was so like the pictures I had seen, with fur covering the backs of its arms and long, twisting fingernails that looked more like claws. But at the same time it wasn't like the pictures at all. The paintings of Satyrs in the Mayor's house were terrifying, and had sparked more than one nightmare in my young, impressionable mind. But this creature wasn't scary at all. He seemed friendly, more than anything else.

As I stood studying my discovery, I could hear footsteps rushing through the forest behind me and voices calling out my name.

My father stopped several steps behind me. The creature looked at my father, their eyes locking for several seconds, though it felt like a lifetime. They shared what I could only describe now as inquisitive glances before the creature turned and dashed away.

"Arianna, never do that again!" My father fell to his knees and wrapped his arms around me.

He was more determined than ever after that day.

That night my father pinned a map of our country up on our wall. He had spent weeks working on it, hand drawing every part of it and making sure it was all to scale. The Cyndarin Mountains to the east, the dwarven kingdom of Vaeger to the west.

He had even included the islands of the Magi and the lost continents many believed didn't exist. Much of my father's map was based on books borrowed from Fennox Castle, other parts were remade from tomes and grimoires he had found or bought from traders.

My father had drawn dozens of interesting locations on the map and was always adding to it. There was one spot in particular that always called out to me. My father would point at it and tell me that was where the curse had started. That he ventured there once hoping to find some clues but found it all in ruins. He called it the Temple of the Storms.

I made him promise to take me one day.

ARIANNA

As the years went by, my father became more comfortable leaving me home alone for longer stretches of time. It became clear to me that he would never be able to send me to the Royal Academy of Magic. Instead, I would have to learn how to hide my powers. I wished I didn't have them at all.

Maria looked after me while my father was gone, along with several other children from the village whose parents worked in the mines. I believed with all my heart that the work my father was doing was more important than the mines, but the other kids didn't agree. They teased me and often tried to goad me into losing my temper and using my powers. They succeeded more often than not.

No matter how hard I tried to control my anger, it would flare up before I could stop it, then fade away in an instant after I had shot a bolt of lightning into the ground or against a wall. I tried not to aim my outbursts at the other kids. My father always told me if I were to accidentally hurt someone there would be terrible consequences. Using magic without permission from the Royal

Academy of Magic was punishable by death.

Maria liked to teach us about the wide world while she watched over us. Some of the parents said it was a waste of time. Since the Satyrs had come out of hiding in search of food after the drought had started, the forest paths were no longer safe to travel. It wasn't safe to leave Manse Village, much less the Kingdom of Idril. Even some of the heavily guarded caravans of rations from the capital city of Fennox-Calil didn't reach their destinations.

Even so, Maria insisted it was important for us to learn what else was out there. To our west lay the dwarven kingdom of Vaeger, populated by the Casar. Maria told us they had long ago adopted a governmental philosophy known as democracy, whereby leaders were elected by the people in a popular vote. This was different from Idril, where the King's Council was made up exclusively of members of the royal families. Even in the villages, the governorship was a birthright passed down from father to son.

Maria told us there had once been talk of bringing democracy to Idril, but those ideas had been laid to rest after the drought started.

In the icy mountains to the north lived the Firya, who looked much like us but with short, rounded ears and pale, white skin. They had no formal government at all, but lived under a primitive system of tribal rule, similar to the elves who lived in the Southern Wilds beneath us.

Those elves were often referred to as South-Dogs, since they weren't technically a part of Idril, but had no kingdom of their own. The Southern Wilds were such a harsh and unforgiving place that those who lived there had been forced to become fierce, aggressive warriors. Their skin had become dark and leathery from exposure to the unrelenting desert sun.

"Is Argentis a South-Dog?" I asked Maria once. Argentis was a knight who had come from the capital to help Mayor Talze around the village. I had always thought he was different from the other knights. His temper was almost as bad as mine.

"Yes," Maria answered. "Best to keep your distance if you know what's good for you."

At age eight I found a small cuima, a fox-like animal with blue fur and a white stomach, long ears, and a tail that was colored black. The cuima was injured. It had come out of the woods limping towards what was left of our farm. I took the creature and cradled it. At first it seemed afraid of me, but as I matched my gaze with its own we became connected in a way that can't be explained.

I took the cuima home and kept it in my room. I hid it from Maria while my father was away. In my room, I treated its legs with red herbs that I had picked on the south side of the village. For several weeks I snuck food from the dinner table, feeding and nursing the cuima back to health. Before long it was even playful again and accompanied me outside as I went to gather herbs again.

Near the mouth of the stream, I saw the Mayor's son, Chass, fishing.

"You aren't going to catch anything," I told him. He was an older boy, about twice my own age at the time, but even then I could tell he was odd. All the other kids his age were working in the mines or apprenticing under someone in the village. A few had even gone to the capital to become squires. Chass, on the other hand, was fishing in a dry creek.

"I know," he chuckled. "It just helps me clear my head

sometimes."

"I didn't realize there was anything in your head to begin with," I teased. He turned to look at me, and furrowed his brow when he noticed the cuima, who had grown so much already her ears were up to my waist.

"What have you got there?" he asked. He had such a formal way of talking. I supposed that came from being the Mayor's son. His clothes were different, too. While the rest of us had to wear the same dirty rags for weeks at a time, he seemed to have a different outfit every time I saw him.

"She's my familiar," I told him, raising my chin proudly.

"Oh, right," he said, "every witch needs a familiar."

I stomped my foot indignantly at that last remark. "I'm not a witch, I'm an elemental. There's a difference."

"Right, right, I forgot," he said.

I scrunched up my face to look as mean as I could manage. "And I'm not afraid to use my powers if you tell anyone about her!" I said.

"Don't worry, kid," he answered with a wink, "your secret is safe with me." For as different as he was, I couldn't complain too much. At least he was nice. He would often come and play with me when Maria was too busy and my father was away.

"So what's her name?" he asked.

I looked down at the cuima, who was panting by my side. "I don't know," I said. "I haven't thought of a name yet."

"Really?" he asked. "That's odd. You must not really care about her, then."

"No, I do care!" I shot back. "I'm just..." I paused. To be honest, I wasn't sure why I hadn't given her a name yet.

"Scared you'll lose her?" Chass suggested.

I looked down at her giant, glistening blue eyes. I sat down cross-legged and scratched behind her ears and she licked my face.

"You're afraid if you get too attached it'll be that much harder when she gets taken away."

I hadn't thought about it like that before, but I knew it was true as soon as he said it. I had gotten so used to having things taken away from me that I had put up guards without even realizing it. Here I had something I could truly call my own, something that could make me really happy, but I was too scared of losing it to let myself get attached.

"Emery," I said. "I'll call her Emery."

I arrived back home late. Maria was waiting.

"Did you really think you could hide her forever?" she asked. "She'll be as big as a horse within a year."

I clenched my fists and felt the power of the lighting building in my fingertips. "I told him not to tell anyone!" I yelled.

Maria was smiling, and I noticed she was putting a plate of red meat on the floor.

"Scraps from Talze's big council meeting last night," she said. "Courtesy of your friend Chass."

The next day my father came home. I heard him arguing with Maria before she left.

That night he sat on the side of my bed and I knew what he was going to say.

"We can't afford to share our rations with a creature from the woods," he said.

"But Chass can bring us extras from --"

"Arianna," he cut me off, "we can't rely on anyone but ourselves. I know Chass means well, but there simply isn't enough food to go around."

"But daddy, I love her!" I pleaded.

He closed his eyes and sighed. "I know, sweetie. But our house is too small. She needs to be free to run and play. It's for the best."

He carried her off into the woods first thing the next morning, and didn't come home again for several days.

"We all have to make sacrifices," he said as he left.

I stayed up late reading from scrolls my father had found in the crypt of an old king. One scroll told the story of a Casar named Vel, a blacksmith, who labored on his greatest masterpiece. The scroll was written in an ancient tongue my father had been studying while on his adventures. I had learned to read it, too, by studying my father's notes, though he didn't know that. It made me feel close to him when he wasn't home.

Vel had lost his wife, his son, his home, and his old forge to a band of raiders who demanded he make them swords and armor. He fled with nothing but a few raw materials. Running from his pain. Running from his enemies.

It was on the edge of the Chasm of Fire that he found a small village. For a while he found peace. The locals had called him mad, believing his unorthodox methods would cause him to be cursed. Vel made a new forge that stood on the inside cliff of a volcano, a fire mountain. Harnessing fire from the melting crust of the planet Vel forged not a sword or shield but a relic.

It was the first of several he made, vowing to seal away the spirits of the world, to harness the power of the storm for his vengeance. Vel chanted in Casar tongue, day and night. He worked on his relic even as floods of magma erupted, threatening to destroy what little he had left.

Each and every day for years he sang and chanted, never eating, never sleeping. Vel hammered as loud as thunder; the echoes could be heard across the world. Every breath he took was filled with smoke and despite the discomfort of his home and the isolation, he continued relentlessly to forge.

"Spirit of rain, spirit of thunder, spirit of lightning! Come to me!" Vel would chant, holding his hammer high above his head before slamming it down. By the time the first relic was almost made, Vel's body had begun to give, nothing more than an empty husk, a Casar that refused to die.

According to legend, his spirit left what remained of his mortal coil and Vel turned into a blood dragon. It was in that form that he continued to forge away inside the heart of the volcano until three relics were made.

Without knowing I had already snuck into his study my father read me the story. He told me that he believed the relics were real, and that someone must have found them and used them to trap the spirits. That's what had started the drought. He told me that one day he would find them and free the spirits.

"Can I help you, daddy?" I asked. "I can use my magic!"

He smiled, but I couldn't help but feel there was sadness in his eyes. "So you could," was all he said.

"I think it's my destiny to be a hero like you," I said with a yawn.

He stroked my hair gently. "The things I do are dangerous," he said. "I love you too much to risk losing you."

Maria and my father weren't the only ones I heard stories from. In the village was a storyteller, a bard that came from Fennox Castle several times a year. The bard, an old man with a great gray beard and shaved head who ate and drank three times his weight would tell us tales of the Satyrs. The dangerous and vile creatures that lived in the woods.

"Satyrs have teeth as sharp as daggers, jaws made of steel. Wearing the skin of their victims, they lure unsuspecting children into the dark woods. There, they hang them from a tree, drink their blood, and chew on their bones!"

I nearly choked on the milk I was drinking. My father had earned a few extra coin on his latest adventure, and decided to treat me to a special dinner at the tavern.

He reached over and patted me on the back. "It's just a story," he said. "There's nothing to be afraid of."

"It's true, all of it!" the bard insisted as he came up to our table. "It was once, when I was a young man, I encountered such a beast. I watched helplessly as it devoured two of the kingdom's strongest mages, then came for me. I swung my sword like a pickaxe, and, lucky for me, I hit gold," he said with relish.

"Go buy yourself a drink, old man," my father said.

"I'm afraid I can't do that," the bard said as he turned out his empty pockets. "It seems I've bled myself dry."

"I don't have any extra," my father insisted.

"Then give me some of your food!" the bard demanded.

"There's only enough for us," said my father.

"Do you know who I am?"

"A drunken fool," my father answered without question.

"I have traveled day after day from Fennox Castle to share my guidance and wisdom with your daughter, your village, and from what I've heard you have refused to work in the mines," the bard was leaning forward, his hand down by his dagger. "You don't work a day in your life and you think you deserve something so precious?" He reached down and scooped a small red fruit off my plate. It was a rare treat that I had been saving for last. My father stood up.

"Put that back."

"What are you going to do?"

My father protested again. I could feel an energy swirling up inside of me as my father looked me in the eyes. Sparks of magic coming to life.

You can end this! Show that old fool what you are capable of!

"Take this," my father said, handing over his plate of food. "You look like you might fall over." My father smiled at me, taking the fruit away from the bard and handing it back to me. I felt calm. The raging voice faded once more into the background.

The bard sneered down at me and said, "I guess we don't get to see any fireworks today, after all."

The spark inside of me wanted to spread, to lose control. I remembered my training. I counted to ten. I began visualizing my bedroom, my books, my clay statues, the artwork I had drawn on the wall with chalk. I visualized my stuffed Rusco in my arms and my father sat down beside me.

The bard took the plate and walked away, joining the other knights from the kingdom and the geld who had come to claim the tax on what little money we made from the mines and the few businesses that still managed to stay open.

As angry as the bard made me, I was always fascinated by his stories. Especially when he talked about our king. King Drevon was the kindest, bravest, and most noble elf that had ever lived.

In one story he would be on the front lines defending a village against a raid from Firya in the north, and in the next, he would be in the streets of Fennox-Calil personally handing out rations in the poorest parts of the city.

There were some who said his policies were too aggressive and heavy-handed, but my father always insisted that he had the kingdom's best interests at heart. He was always willing to do what was necessary for the good of his people, even if it wasn't the most popular decision. I asked my father once if he had ever met the king.

"Not yet," he told me, "but I will. He's going to help me finish my mission."

By age twelve I had started working in the kitchen at the Mayor's mansion. Chass was always coming around and playing jokes. One time we were preparing a giant banquet for some visitors from the capital and Chass convinced me to help him sneak a batch of spicy peppers into the stew. He laughed for hours about how they had all tried so hard to keep their composure while politely asking what was in the recipe. I was just sad I couldn't be there to see it myself.

Over the years I'd found different ways to keep myself occupied during the weeks and months my father would spend away. I would venture into the woods or explore abandoned buildings in the village with Chass.

The day I turned fifteen was when my world fell apart. My father promised he would come back in time for my birthday, but he didn't. He would never come home again.

Chass and I were playing a game with some of the other village kids. We had two makeshift nets set up on either side of a field, and had to kick an old leather ball into the other team's goal.

I intercepted the ball then quickly broke off from the group and had a free shot at the goal. That is until Erie dove feet first to kick the ball out from under me. I tripped and rolled several times before landing flat on my stomach.

"Cheater! That was a foul!" I yelled. The other kids continued to play, following Erie's lead and ignoring me. I slammed my fist on the ground and let out a throaty growl.

Electricity arced from my clenched fist. The magic was gaining control. I stood and squared off. A ball of lightning formed in the palm of my hand and I pointed it toward Erie.

Let's teach that bully a lesson!

The words echoed in the back of my mind as if coming from far away. I'd trained for years to suppress my temper, but sometimes it would strike so fast I didn't have time to stop myself.

Chass jumped in the line of fire. "No!" I heard him yell. The blast caught him in the chest, turning his training armor black as pieces of it tore away like charcoal.

"Chass! You idiot!" I yelled.

Not again! My eyes grew wide and I clasped my hands over my mouth. I could still feel the temperature that had risen in my fingers. I felt horrified at what I had done. I ran over to Chass as he stumbled from the ground back to his feet. The other kids were staring now but I didn't care. I just wanted to make sure Chass was okay.

"I'm sorry, I didn't mean to… I was just…"

"You're welcome," Chass said, wheezing.

"What?"

"I just saved you from being reported to my father, again."

Whatever remorse I had been feeling dissipated at that moment.

"My hero. What would I ever do without you?" I asked, making certain he couldn't miss the sarcasm oozing out of every word.

"On second thought, maybe I will report you after all."

"Don't make me blast you again," I said, shaking my fist. The two of us smiled. It was one of the last times I would smile for a very long time.

A trumpet blasted in the distance.

My head bolted toward the sound.

"My father! He's returned!" I exclaimed. I sprinted away as Chass limped along behind me.

I heard him yell, "Wait! Something isn't right." But I ignored him.

I arrived back at my home just in time to see two elves hauling a cart which was covered over by a blanket. Underneath the blanket was what appeared to be a man's body. Mayor Talze ambled alongside. I froze. Chass caught up, out of breath.

"Father, what's going on?" Chass demanded.

"It was the Satyrs. By the time my men found him, it was already…

…too late."

ARIANNA

I'm not sure how long I stared at the cart, my eyes glossed over, my mouth ajar. I couldn't believe it was my father's body. I couldn't. Several guards stopped me from getting too close. As one tried to hold me back I broke free only to be grabbed by another.

I struggled against him and my fingers found their way into a small gap in his armor, just inside his elbow. I felt a shred of torn fabric underneath. Had I ripped it by accident? No, it must have already been that way. I could feel dried blood on his skin, a tell-tale sign of a fresh cut. The knights were always injuring each other in their sparring matches. There wasn't an actual war on, so the thugs had to take their aggression out somehow.

I dug my fingernails into the cut, and the knight howled and pulled away. Another shred of the fabric tore away in my hand, and I could feel the runes embroidered onto it. Probably a simple protection spell; apparently not a very good one, though.

I took another step toward the cart, then fell to my knees. I knew the truth, whether I wanted to admit it or not. And the truth was that I was too broken to keep fighting.

Chass wasn't far behind me. I could hear him arguing with his father, arguing with another one of the knights who followed behind the slowly forming crowd. I wanted to scream. I wanted to ignite the electricity I felt turning and growing inside my body and set the world around me on fire, but I couldn't.

I had years of my father's lessons, my father's words. Even in his passing, he was reaching out to me, telling me to maintain control. If I zapped a guard I would be thrown into prison, or worse.

"Take the body to Esther, he'll be able to do a full report and we'll send it off by raven to the capital. I never thought I'd see the day the wretched beasts would take one of our own," Talze said to no one in particular as he waddled his ever-expanding frame over towards me. "I will handle the preparations for the funeral myself. I know this is going to be hard for you, Arianna, but…" he continued speaking but his voice faded away as I found myself unable to focus on his words.

Eventually, the mayor and his men all left, and the ominous cart was rolled away. I was left alone, falling into the void that had been torn open inside my chest.

I heard a rustling noise behind me. It was Chass, still standing by my side after all this time.

"Arianna, I'm so sorry. I…"

He was moving his hand toward my shoulder. I cut him off.

"Don't touch me."

CHASS

I sat down in the grass behind Arianna. She knew that I was there, that was what mattered. I had always tried to be there for Arianna, whenever I could. Like Arianna, I knew what it was like to never know your mother. I also knew what it was like to have a father who spent more time with his work than with you.

As a child I used to idolize Carine. I could listen to his stories for hours. I always dreamed that one day I would get to explore the world, just like Carine. But when my chance came to go to the capital and become a squire, I couldn't go through with it. I was never quite sure what it was that held me back. The world just seemed like such a large place, and my world was so small.

I hadn't left the village since the drought, when the Satyrs made travel through the woods too dangerous. The towering stone walls of Fennox Castle were nothing more than a distant memory from my childhood. It was as though they were a part of a reality that couldn't be accessed from the reality I lived in. There was no bridge from here to there. I was stuck.

Part of me wanted to stay behind to make sure Arianna didn't. She had so much power, so much potential; she had the opportunity to become something truly great, and I didn't want to see her waste it. The older I got the more I saw that her father was doing more harm than good by trying to keep her safe. She could have been helping break the curse. He could have trained her from the day she was born for that very purpose.

Then again, I couldn't really blame him. The more I came to think of Arianna as a sister, the less I liked the idea of her being put in harm's way. That was the whole reason Carine had worked so hard to break the curse on his own: so she wouldn't have to. He wanted her to have a better life than the one he was forced to live.

Still, the question remained, if she had been with him when the Satyrs attacked, would he still be alive?

We had been sitting in silence for several hours when Maria approached.

"Esther has finished his examination of the body," she said. "Arianna, if you want to be with your father, now is the time."

Arianna didn't respond, and for a moment I wondered if she had even heard.

"The others say you shouldn't see him like this," Maria continued, "but I think --"

"I want to see him," Arianna said, interrupting her. "I want to see what they did to him."

I rose and extended a hand to Arianna to help her up. Without acknowledging my offer of assistance, she pushed herself to her feet and started walking toward the mortuary. I stood for a moment, unsure of what to do, until I looked at Maria and she nodded for me to follow after Arianna.

The already eerie quietude of the abandoned buildings was even more pronounced as we made our somber trek to visit Arianna's father. We passed into the outskirts of the village and just beyond the cemetery I could see the old mill that had burned down a few years ago. Only Arianna and I knew what actually happened to it.

"We never told your father about the old mill, did we?" I asked with a chuckle. We used to jump from the second-floor balcony onto the rotting hay below. Once she tried to jump from the third floor, but went too far and almost landed on a rusty old plow.

She paused and looked out at the mill with a straight face. "No, we didn't," she said flatly.

"I thought you were a goner, for sure," I said. "If you hadn't --"

"I didn't," she cut me off. "She did."

"What do you mean?" I asked. I had never heard her talk about her powers like that before; like they were another person.

"I don't know how to explain it," she said. "It's like instinct took over and I was blasting the wall before I knew what was happening."

The force from her blast had been enough to redirect her fall and send her crashing safely into the hay, but it had also set the mill ablaze. We had rushed into the nearby woods before anyone knew we had been there, and didn't come out till we'd circled clear to the other side of the village.

Without another word, Arianna started walking again. I had been hoping to lighten the mood with the memory, but it seemed the fun, playful Arianna I had known before was nowhere to be found. I couldn't imagine what she must have been going through. Her entire world had fallen down around her, and at only fifteen I wasn't sure she would have the strength to get through it.

This was just another reason why it was better that I had stayed behind. Carine's quests had always been dangerous. This had always been a possibility. If he had managed to break the curse, or at least figure out how to do it, that would have been one thing. As it was, could we really say it had all been worth it?

He had spent years following his obsession, and now that he was gone there was hardly anything to show for it.

As we approached the mortuary I decided it would be best if I waited outside. A few minutes after Arianna went in, my father came out. He seemed so lost in thought that he didn't even notice me leaning against the fence around the side of the building. I didn't mind one bit.

ARIANNA

I entered Esther's mortuary and smelled the burning incense in the air.

"And when you examined the body, did you, by chance, find anything unusual?" Mayor Talze's voice sounded like a snake. He stopped when I entered the room.

"I want to see my father," I demanded, standing straight and tall.

Esther opened his mouth to respond but Mayor Talze stepped forward, speaking with less of a hiss and more of a causal, almost jovial tone, "Ah, Arianna! We were just discussing the preparations for your father's funeral. Unfortunately, Esther has not yet had the time to dress your father's wounds. Perhaps, my dear, you should come back at a later time."

His words were so unexpected I almost didn't know how to respond. I didn't know what to say, but I knew I wasn't going to back down, either. "I want to see my father," I repeated. I directed the words towards Esther without giving the Mayor a second glance.

"Honestly, child, you don't want to remember him this way," Mayor Talze persisted. "Now if you'll excuse me I have business I have to attend to." He turned toward Esther and spoke again under his breath, "you will of course, notify me if you find anything out of the ordinary?" His voice had that hiss again as Esther shook his head and told him that he would, of course.

As the Mayor left the two of us alone, Esther smiled at me that same, pitying smile the rest of the village had been giving me since I was a child.

"What did he mean by that?" I asked

"I don't know. And I don't like it. He is right though, about one thing. You don't want to remember your father like this."

"I want to see my father," I demanded once more. One last time.

Esther must have heard the determination in my voice, as he silently escorted me back into the morgue.

My father's body lay uncovered. Deep lacerations were visible through his torn, bloody clothes. I walked towards him, choking back the tears.

"I have never actually seen a victim of a Satyr attack before," Esther said. He was pointing down towards the small cuts across my father's arms and wrist. It looked like the Satyrs had been carving runes into him as if he was some kind of sacrifice. "But I did not expect the cuts to be so clean as these. I would have assumed…"

"I would like a moment alone with my father, please." I didn't want to hear Esther explain any of it to me. Quietly, he left.

I stood over my father's body for several moments, forcing

myself not to cry. There were so many things I wanted to tell him. So many words left unsaid.

"You could have worked in the mines, you know," I started. "It would have been a simple life. We could have found a way to be happy. I can't claim my own ration pack until I turn eighteen, you know that right? Until then I guess I'm going to have to work in the mines." I was almost laughing, "I think I'm going to hate it even more than you would have." I paused and took a deep breath.

"I want to make you proud, I really do, but I don't know how. I want to finish what you started, but I've pored through your journals, studied all the old stories. There is nothing there! Why did you have to leave? What was it you were searching for?" I slammed my fist on the table. "We're no closer to ending the drought than the day you started!"

A spark of electricity jumped from my clenched fist to a wound on my father's body. The spark danced up the length of the wound and sealed it so not even a scar remained. I looked down in bewilderment.

I had always kept my powers suppressed because I thought they could do nothing but harm. I never knew they could heal, as well! Hovering my hand over another gash, I willed another spark to stitch up another wound.

For the first time in my life I let my powers loose and set to work healing the rest of my father's body. In that moment, I felt closer to him than I ever had before. I knew I would never be able to bring him back to life, but knowing that I was the one who dressed his wounds for the funeral gave me a sense of comfort like nothing I had ever experienced.

As a wound on his arm healed his clenched fist loosened,

revealing a crumpled piece of paper. I grabbed it and took several tries to unfold it as my fingers trembled. It offered the promise of answers. I knew whatever was written on this page were the words I had waited my whole life to hear.

It was blank.

I fell over and crumbled apart. As the tears fell from my face to the table, one hit the paper and, amidst the moisture, hidden letters faded into view. I wiped a tear from my cheek and rubbed it over the paper, revealing the full text:

"READ THE BLANK PAGES"

CHASS

As I waited for Arianna to finish paying her respects I looked out over the village cemetery. Manse had never been a wealthy village, and most of the graves were marked with simple stones, or not marked at all. That is, most of the graves outside the mausoleum where my own family's remains were interred.

I knew that Carine would be laid to rest next to his wife, in a far corner of the cemetery where the rough-hewn headstone he had chiseled out himself stood out among the pauper's graves. My own mother's grave was marked with an ornate marble statue that was likely the most expensive single object in the village.

I began to wonder if Arianna would be coming back out at all, or if she had fallen asleep at her father's side. I moved around to the front of the building, debating on whether or not to go in and check.

Just then, she barreled out the front door and nearly plowed me over! She stood back and gave me a confused look, as if she was surprised to see me there. I almost wondered if she even remembered that I had walked all this way with her.

I noticed she was clenching something in her fist. "What's that?" I asked.

"My father's last words!" she shouted as she took off down the dirt path.

After a moment of bewildered hesitation, I started off after her. "What does it say?" I asked as I ran behind her, but she never looked back. If she did say anything, I didn't hear it.

We didn't stop running until we reached her house. I went inside to find her in her father's study, already hard at work pulling books off the shelf, flipping through the pages, and laying them out on her father's desk.

"What is it?" I asked.

"Invisible ink!" she said, more excited than I had seen her in a long time.

"What do you mean?"

"Invisible ink," she repeated, holding up a journal to show me two blank pages. "All these years my father's been hiding his real discoveries with invisible ink!"

"His real discoveries?" I asked, skeptical. "What do you think he found?"

She paused, as if suddenly remembering something, then pointed in the direction of her bedroom. "There's one on my nightstand," she said. She went back to searching the books on the shelf, and I realized she meant for me to get the one from her nightstand. I went to her bedroom to retrieve it, and when I came back I found her gently dabbing a wet cloth on the pages of one of the journals.

As soon as I came in, she dropped the book she was working on and grabbed the journal from my hand. I looked at the one she had been wetting just as hidden words came into view. It told the story of Vel, but a slightly different version. This time, Vel successfully entrapped the spirits in his relics, and unleashed their power to level an entire village in vengeance.

I looked up as Arianna started reading out loud from the journal that had been on her nightstand.

"Arianna, I've left this journal out so it will be the first one you find. If you are reading this, it means I am dead, and it is your turn to carry on my mission."

She looked up at me, then back to the journal to continue reading. "I'm sure it will take you days to go through everything, but in brief, here is what you need to know. First, the legend of the storm relics is true. I don't know who is behind the curse, but they must have found the three relics and used them to capture the spirits of Rain, Thunder, and Lightning."

I moved to look over her shoulder as she read. There was a sketch of a tiny shrine sitting atop a snow-capped mountain range. "I am convinced that the Thunder relic is hidden deep within the Cyndarin Mountains, though I have not yet found any clues as to the location of the Rain Relic. As for the Lightning Relic, well, let's just say that's what started me on this journey in the first place. There is something important you need to know, Arianna…"

Her voice trailed off, and she stepped away to read the rest in silence.

After several long moments, she tore the page from the journal. Electricity sparked from her fingers and the torn paper burst into flames. She dropped it into a trash bin and the fire spread to other crumpled pieces of paper left behind by her father.

"Wait! What did he say?" I asked.

"Everything," she answered. "He told me everything."

CARINE

Arianna, I've left this journal out so it will be the first one you find. If you are reading this, it means I am dead, and it is your turn to carry on my mission. I'm sure it will take you days to go through everything, but in brief, here is what you need to know. First, the legend of the storm relics is true.

I don't know who is behind the curse, but they must have found the three relics and used them to capture the spirits of Rain, Thunder, and Lightning.

I am convinced that the Thunder Relic is hidden deep within the Cyndarin Mountains, though I have not yet found any clues as to the location of the Rain Relic. As for the Lightning Relic, well, let's just say that's what started me on this journey in the first place. There is something important you need to know, Arianna.

You are the Lightning Relic.

I don't know how it happened, all I know is that the night the curse was enacted, the Spirit of Lightning must have found a way to break free before it was trapped inside the relic, and chose to channel itself into you instead. You alone can free the spirits, and end the drought once and for all.

I've tried to protect you from this fate for as long as possible, but the truth is I've always known the day would come when you would have to sacrifice yourself to save the kingdom. I can only hope that you have the strength to do what must be done now that I am gone, because I did not have the strength to let you.

ARIANNA

Chass and I spent the rest of the morning poring over the journals together. I did my best to push the dizzying weight of my father's revelation out of my head and focus on the task at hand. We had to break the curse, no matter what the cost. My father had been too weak to do what needed to be done, and I knew that Chass would try to stop me, too, if he knew the truth. But I wasn't weak. I knew that I would have the courage to go through with it, when the moment came.

We pulled out a handful of pages that outlined my father's plans to assemble the relics at the Temple of the Storm in the ancient ruins of Castle Kakara. It was there that the curse had been enacted, and only there could it be broken.

We took the pages with us to the Mayor's mansion, hoping he would send us off with a squad of his best men, and all the funds we could possibly need to complete our quest.

Inside we sat on a bench made of ivory, lavishly decorated with carvings of animals. I started running my hand along the edges, tracing the shape of a bird with my fingers. Sometimes I forgot this was where Chass had grown up. Behind us was a graphic mural of a ferocious Satyr attacking a caravan of elves in the woods. As I stared at the mural I saw my father's face in all the elves pictured. For the first time I could remember, I felt relief when Mayor Talze entered through a side door.

"Now, children, what can I do for you?"

He motioned, inviting us to follow him into his office; another room even more extravagant than the first. As he meandered around an imposing desk he plucked a candy from an ornate glass dish and delicately placed it in his mouth as he sat down. The chair creaked under his weight.

He looked us over and his eyes narrowed when they landed on the papers we were carrying. I handed one over to him.

"My father knew how to break the curse," I said. "It's all right here."

Chass and I sat down as he looked the pages over. We were both nervous. Fidgeting.

The Mayor tossed the pages on the desk. "And what would you like me to do about it?" he asked.

Chass and I exchanged confused glances. "To help us find the relics," Chass said. "We can end the drought."

Mayor Talze twiddled his thumbs and clicked his tongue. His eyes were sweeping through the corners of the room as though deep in thought, trying to find the right words. After several agonizing moments of silence he looked back and forth between the two of us.

"Tell me Chass. If we were to share this information publicly, what would be the people's reaction?"

All of that waiting, and this was his response? The answer seemed obvious.

"They would be ecstatic," Chass answered. "They would finally have hope that they can return to their old lives."

"And perhaps not be stuck toiling away in the mines?" the Mayor clarified.

"Exactly!" I chimed in.

"Well, that is good news, isn't it?" He paused for a moment. His cheeks puckered slightly as he continued sucking on the candy from before. "Perhaps a little too good to be true."

How could he say that? All of the proof was clearly laid out in my father's journals!

"What are you saying?" Chass asked, incredulous.

"What happens when the people get their hopes up and it turns out not to be true? Or maybe it is true, and we simply are not able to break the curse? What happens when we fail?"

Both Chass and I looked down at the floor. Unsure of what to say, how to answer. Talze continued, "The people would be devastated. They would lose what little hope they did have. They would simply give up. The mines would fail, and our entire way of life would crumble overnight. And it wouldn't hurt just us. The entire kingdom depends on our metals right now. Our mines are a source of pride. A beautiful thing in a world full of disaster."

"So you're just going to let your people starve?" I growled through gritted teeth.

"The drought has devastated the entire kingdom. But here, in our little village, through hard work and my generosity, we have managed to survive. Our future hangs in a very delicate balance, and it is my duty to make the difficult decisions that will maintain that balance. I know my way is the hard way, but it is the right way."

"Are you saying you won't help us?" Chass asked.

"No, I will not. And furthermore, I forbid you from ever speaking of this again."

I felt my anger rising. I stood and marched out of the room before I lost control.

Chass followed quickly behind me but stopped in the doorway when his father called out to him.

"I know you don't understand now, son, but someday this burden will be yours."

Chass turned to look his father in the eyes.

"You're right, I don't understand. I've spent my entire life living in luxury while everyone around me went hungry. And I didn't understand. But now I think I'm starting to."

That evening I sat slumped on the edge of my bed sobbing. A clang from the kitchen startled me back to reality.

"Maria?" I called. I hadn't seen her all day, but it was possible she had to come to check on me and decided to prepare some dinner for me while she was here. There was no response.

I heard a steady, rhythmic thumping sound: the distinct noise of vegetables being chopped. Only it was much slower than when Maria or I did it. Whoever this was, they were clearly not a trained cook. I leaned against the door frame and saw Chass struggling to keep a bunch of green onions together as he diced them.

"Careful, don't want to lose a finger," I said. Chass jumped and nearly dropped the knife.

"Don't scare me like that and I won't." I gave him a faint smile. It was the most I could manage. He returned it, gentle understanding in his eyes.

"Stolen from my father's secret stash. I thought you might be hungry."

"Thanks." I wiped my eyes and walked over to the counter. I took a deep breath and let out a long sigh. "I just can't believe after everything it's all over."

"What if it isn't?" Chass asked. I stared at him, expecting him to say more. He just continued chopping as if his words had meant nothing. As if he hadn't just given me hope.

"What do you mean? Your father said…"

"I know what my father said." He set the knife down and instinctively licked his fingers before making a soured face. Onions never were his favorite.

"Then what else can we do? If he won't help us…"

"We don't need his help. We don't need anyone's help." He wiped his hands on a towel, then threw it over his shoulder. "We have everything we need right in your father's journals." That was his big plan? Really? I grunted and moved toward the table. I needed to sit.

"Everything? All my father ever found out was that one of the relics might be somewhere in the Cyndarin Mountains." Of course, that wasn't the only thing my father found out, but I wasn't ready for Chass to know the whole truth. I wasn't ready to face it myself.

Chass followed me to the table. I had never seen him this determined about anything. In fact, I had never seen him want anything this badly. He had always been one to do what others expected of him. Especially when that 'other' was his father.

"Well then we'll find the other relics along the way." He was standing over my shoulder now, but I couldn't bear to turn and look at him. I could hear him breathing, gathering his thoughts. "Look, once you know the truth about something like this, you can never go back."

"And once we leave the village without your father's permission he will never let us come back." I knew it was the truth. There was nothing more we could do. Chass knelt down beside me, his hand on the back of my chair.

"Then we never stop searching. The kingdom is only so big. The curse has to be broken. So what if it takes us fifty years?"

I scoffed, finally turning to face him. "We'll be dead in a ditch like my father long before that."

Chass stared at me with a piercing gaze. I turned away and started picking at a splinter on the side of the table.

"I'm sorry. I didn't mean…" I started to apologize.

Chass stood, towering over me and casting an oppressive shadow across my entire world. "So when do you start at the mines?"

Chass and I stood side by side amongst a crowd of mourners around an imposing funeral pyre. Mayor Talze stood with his hands clasped together in front of him, clearing his voice.

"What can we say at times such as this? It is a harsh and brutal world that we live in. It is not the world that many of us remember from our childhoods, but it is the reality we face today. Carine gave his life in pursuit of a better world. May we honor his memory by doing what he would have wanted: Not dwelling on our loss but rather picking ourselves up and working harder than ever for our children, for our kingdom, so that they may inherit a better life!"

The crowd mumbled in agreement and slowly began to clap.

I stood in shock and looked towards Chass, but his eyes were clenched shut.

Liar!

I couldn't stop myself…

Tell them the truth!

I took a step forward and yelled at the top of my lungs, "That is not what my father would have wanted!"

Chass grabbed my arm. "Not now," he whispered. I shook him off.

"Every one of you knows that my father believed we could end this drought, this way of life, through magic, not by suffering in the Mayor's mines so he could stay fat and lazy!"

"Arianna, know your place!" Talze hissed loudly.

"My father found the way to end the drought, but Mayor Talze doesn't want you to know that! The spirits of the storm have been captured and locked away! All we have to do is find them and release them! I say we put it to a vote."

Talze cleared his throat and looked over at me, smiling.

"Arianna is right. It is our tradition to vote on such important matters. Who here is willing to travel through Satyr-infested forests and over snow-covered mountains to retrieve these theoretical relics which will supposedly break the curse that some powerful magician has placed over our land?"

There was no response from the crowd.

Talze looked at me with a subtle smirk, "Anyone?"

Silence.

ARIANNA

I was floating somewhere in the void between worlds; in infinity. I listened and heard a voice call out. It sounded almost like an echo of my own.

"Come," it said, guiding me through the nothing that went on for far too long. Blue light began to fill my vision. Perhaps I was screaming. I had no way of knowing as I became surrounded by clouds and bursts of thunder and lightning. The voice continued and I began to feel like the only reason I was alive was because the voice compelled me to continue living.

I could feel the pressure rise around me. If I was in my mortal body I was sure I would have been in pain, crushed by the rising storm. A cold wind blew from above me toward my feet and I became a mountain. For a moment I completely lost my form and became the clouds. Rain, snow, and shadow became my flesh, weaving gently around waves of wind that became white bone. A pair of dark blue hands began to take shape, then legs formed and I fell to my knees, catching myself on cold stone as I stared up at the mountain that I had been moments earlier.

"What do you want with me?" I cried out, aware now that I had formed a mouth of some kind.

"What are you?" said the voice.

"I am Arianna, daughter of the great Carine," I answered.

"No…" the voice answered. Suddenly I was surrounded by shadows of Satyrs and other monsters. A golden dragon flew toward me.

"Kill it," the voice demanded.

"No," I said, trying my best to turn away from the army that was advancing all around me. Some of the Satyrs looked like they were made of the same clouds that had given me life.

"Now! Kill them before they kill you!" the voice demanded again.

I was falling. Back in the sky again. I could see the army, the dragon, the entire kingdom below me as I fell for what felt like forever. Once more into infinity as I became the storm itself raining down upon the world. As I was about to hit the ground I saw a reflection of myself.

I awoke with a start to the sound of chopping coming from the kitchen. At first I thought it might have been Chass again, but the chopping was too rhythmic, too precise. I arose to find Maria preparing vegetables that were on the cusp of going bad.

"After last night I thought maybe you could use something nice to start your day," she said.

"Thanks," I said, yawning and stretching. I sat down at the table and started writing down my dream. Something told me I shouldn't forget it. My father had told me that my mother was a strong believer in dreams, so I kept a small journal close at hand to record them. The journal had been a gift from my father. At the moment it was nearly full, and I felt sad knowing it would take a long time before I could buy something to record my thoughts again.

"Daughter like father," Maria said, noticing my scribbling.

"Maybe," I tried to smile but failed. I still couldn't.

"It will be okay. I'm going to put a word in with the Mayor and see if we can't get you working in the kitchen," she said.

"I don't want to work in the kitchen," I replied.

Maria fell silent. I felt terrible. I wasn't trying to sound like I was ungrateful. I didn't want to work in the kitchen, but I didn't want to work in the mines either. I wasn't sure what I should do.

"Your tools arrived by courier this morning, I've already brought them inside," Maria said. "The foreman also said that you can take your time coming in just don't be absent. They said your father was a great friend and send their condolences."

"How nice," I frowned.

I took a bite of a carrot, making sure not to eat the small part that was starting to mold. Maria had already packed my things for the mine in a brown satchel. One of my father's. I felt guilty using it and made a mental note to switch everything to a basket before I left. I could hear a songbird singing just outside the window, and for a moment it seemed like the world hadn't ended, after all.

CHASS

After breakfast I went out to the training field to warm up before my daily sparring session with Argentis. Since I had missed my chance to become a squire in the capital, my father insisted that Argentis train me himself. As much as I hated it, it was the one bit of consistency in my life.

It was the one responsibility I couldn't shirk, no matter how badly I wanted to. If I ever tried, Argentis would let me have it the next time he saw me. I was not particularly strong or athletic, but if not for these training sessions, I would likely have ended up as fat and lazy as my father.

There was something therapeutic about fighting. Being so focused on my opponent that the rest of the world disappeared for a few, brief moments. And today more than ever I needed the reprieve.

By the time Argentis arrived, I had already worked up a good sweat. With the never-ending cloud cover hiding the sun, it didn't get as hot as it used to. Still, it was too hot to be comfortable in my cumbersome training armor.

Argentis was accompanied by another of the knights from the capital, Eldrad. They likely planned to spar after Argentis was done with me. Argentis trained harder than any of the other knights. I had always heard that South-Dogs were violent and aggressive. Argentis was no exception.

For a South-Dog to become a Knight of Idril was itself a miracle. He worked harder than anyone to prove he was worthy of it.

Without a word, Argentis stepped up to the weapons rack and grabbed a staff. I took a staff, as well, and we squared off at the center of the training field.

Argentis struck first. He always did. I couldn't rely on my strength to overpower him, so I had to use speed to get the advantage. I parried his attack and spun around behind him. I managed to get a hit on his side before he had time to spin around.

Getting a hit in against Argentis was easy enough. The problem was, he could take a lot of hits. His training armor was dented and scuffed from years of abuse. It was rare to see him in his real armor, and when the knights did all come out in full armor it was almost impossible to tell them apart. The standard armor for Knights of Idril was tinted blue from the cobalt, which was the most common metal found in Idril.

Most of the ore we pulled from the mines could be used by the blacksmiths here in the village, but the cobalt had to be shipped off to the capital to be processed. Handling it in its raw form had driven more than one hapless miner to insanity.

Our duel continued for several long minutes. The more I ducked and dodged, the harder it got to catch my breath. Argentis was slow, but he was persistent. There was never a moment of hesitation between his attacks. He broke through my defenses more than once just by sheer force.

At one point he swung his staff wide and I took a jab at his stomach, but he took hold of my staff with his off-hand at the last second, pulled me in, and kicked me square in the chest. I tumbled backward and rolled several times before landing flat on my stomach.

As I pushed myself to my feet, I noticed for the first time Arianna on the sidelines watching. She was clenching her fists and seemed to be holding herself back from intervening in our skirmish. I gently shook my head in her direction, and she seemed to let off some of the tension.

I turned back to Argentis and he tossed me my staff.

"Our enemies won't go so easy on you," he said. "If I were a Satyr, you would be dead already."

I was quickly running out of stamina. If I was going to beat him, I needed to exploit his biggest weakness: his temper.

"If you were a Satyr," I shot back, "you might actually know how to fight!"

With a growl, he charged at me. I was able to step to the side and sweep my staff under his feet, sending him spiraling across the ground. As he pulled himself up he shouted, "Bold words from someone with the ambition of a snail!"

"True," I said, "all I want is to be better than you, but that's hardly worth bragging about."

He charged again and this time I managed to get in a jab across the side of his face. If not for his helmet the impact would have broken his jaw, at least.

He turned back to me as blood dripped onto his chest-plate from beneath his helmet.

"The only reason you are not starving on the streets is because you are Talze's son," he growled. "Anyone else would be hanged for refusing to train at the capital."

"Better to be invited to the capital and refuse than banished to a backwater village like you."

Without warning he unleashed an onslaught of attacks that sent me stumbling backward, struggling to keep my balance as I dodged and parried each one. When he finally made contact, the staff impacted my arm so hard that it cracked with a spray of splinters. He snapped the staff the rest of the way over his knee and tossed the two broken halves across the training field.

I expected him to stand down after that, but instead, he came at me with his bare fists. I responded with my staff, knocking him in the arms, torso, or legs with just enough force to push him back, but still he continued to advance.

Each impact of my staff sent a wave of pain through what I was certain would be a nasty bruise on my arm. When I had finally had enough, I sent one last jab into the center of his forehead, and he staggered for a moment before falling to his knees.

I left him there on the field, and stumbled toward Arianna so she could help me get my armor off. As she worked on loosening the arm-plate where I had been hit, she said, "You know I don't like watching you fight."

"Then why do you do it?" I asked.

She pulled me around to look in my eyes and the sudden jerk made me wince. "Someone has to make sure you don't get yourself killed."

"I am glad you have so much faith in my abilities," I said. Just then I noticed the basket of mining tools on the ground behind her. "Aren't you supposed to be at the mines by now?" I asked.

She sighed and looked back at the tools. "The foreman said I could take my time coming in."

"Well don't take too much time, or my father will start sending an armed guard to escort you every morning."

"I'll just call you to fight them off for me," she said as she pulled off the arm-plate and examined my bruise. "That is, if you think you can handle it." She poked at the bruise and I recoiled in pain.

"Ow!" I said as I swatted away her hand. "You really need to get going."

"Wow, you're eager to send me into the mines, aren't you?"

"No, it's not that it's just…" I wasn't sure exactly what it was. I didn't want to see her working in the mines at all, but I was more afraid of the alternative. My father could be a harsh man. "Just don't let them send you into the cobalt mines, alright? That stuff can mess with your head if you don't know what you're doing."

"Fine, I'll go," she said. "Let me at least get this cleaned up for you, first. I think I've still got some hortorum back at the house."

ARIANNA

The mine itself wasn't the worst. What might have once been a mountain had turned into a giant hole in the ground and every year it was getting deeper and deeper. From top to bottom it was nearly half a mile. From the surface you couldn't see the bottom in the dim, cloudy light.

I stepped off the elevator and into an underground tunnel. The newer sites were still buried below the ground, lit by dwarven fire. I carried my basket full of tools: A pickaxe, a small shovel, an iron hammer with a dozen spikes of various sizes. For the most part I would be using the pickaxe. Picking apart pieces of the cavern walls and throwing anything of value into one of many carts that were threaded all around.

The elevator stopped hard and opened, creaking as it did, and I stepped out. The mineshaft was empty around me. Somehow I expected more people. I rounded the corner and slammed into something cold and hard. I stepped back to get my bearings and found myself staring at the pale blue armor of a Knight of Idril.

From this close, I could see the runes engraved all over the armor. I immediately felt a presence that surrounded me in fear. Something like a fire burning around me that made it hard to move, hard to react. I couldn't even summon the energy of the spark to my fingers.

RUN. You can't kill it. You have to escape.

My basket fell to the ground, spilling everywhere. I turned as quickly as I could but a second knight emerged from the shadows.

The two knights pushed me back. Back towards the elevator just as it rose out of sight, leaving only an open shaft. My foot landed on the edge and I began to slip. Just before I fell the first knight grabbed my arm, clamping down hard enough to cut off all circulation. He turned and tossed me back into the mineshaft.

As I stumbled, struggling to keep my balance, I noticed another elevator shaft at the far end of the tunnel. I could just see the chains being pulled upward, and I knew an elevator cart was about to pass through. I ran for it as fast as I could. I could hear the heavy footsteps of the knights behind me, but they didn't seem to be in any hurry to catch me.

I reached the shaft just as the elevator came into view, and managed to dive over the short railing as it rose past the tunnel. As soon as the elevator reached the surface I burst out, pushing past a group of miners who were waiting to go down, and ran straight home.

Back in the light of day, the encounter almost seemed like a dream. Like I had just hallucinated the imposing knights. Had they sent me into the cobalt mines as some kind of cruel joke? No, the dull, lingering pain in my arm told me it was all real.

When I reached the house I found Chass was still there, letting Maria tend to his other wounds. Without acknowledging them I threw supplies into my father's satchel, including the map my father had drawn, which I carefully took down and folded.

"Arianna, what's going on?" Chass asked.

"Pack your things. We're going."

"What? I thought you said it was too dangerous?"

I answered his question by pulling up my sleeve revealing the hand-shaped bruise, still bright red and purple from my attack.

"Turns out it isn't safe to stay here, either."

6

CARINE

I still remember the day I first met your mother, back when we were both working for the Survey Corps. We were from two separate villages, on two separate survey missions, united by chance at an inn just over the border in Vaeger. I was on my way out, Solph was on her way back home.

I had just settled into my room after a long day of traveling. I was coming downstairs for a drink when I saw her dancing in a blue cotton dress. In that moment I forgot how to walk, to breathe, to do anything but love. Our eyes met and she gave me a smile that could have calmed the fiercest storm.

I wish you could have seen that smile, Arianna. She could have helped you control your powers far better than I ever have.

As I write this you are only eight years old, but already I can see her smile in yours. Every day you grow more like her.

Every day I dread the thought of losing you like I lost her.

ARIANNA

We decided to leave immediately, before anyone had time to stop us. Before we had time to stop ourselves.

I expected Maria to resist, but instead she pulled out a satchel of rations she had set aside for us. "This should last you a few days," she said. "After that, you'll have to hunt and scavenge what you can."

She pulled my father's bow and quiver of arrows down from where they hung by the door. He had taught me how to hunt, though we rarely caught anything. I wasn't a bad shot when it came to practicing on a stationary target, but I wasn't sure I could catch enough prey to stave off starvation.

Chass never hesitated to leave with me and I was grateful. We split up to pack our things and regrouped at the stables. He told the stable maid that the two of us were going riding that evening and would be back by nightfall.

We rode as fast as we could through the forest, hoping to reach a clearing before nightfall. The Satyrs rarely came out during the day, but at night the woods would be crawling with them.

Everything in the forest around us was poisonous or dying. The trees still burst from the ground, old and alive but they were dying, too. All of them. The forest brush was forcing itself to grow. Most of the leaves were red, brown, yellow, while few managed to stay completely green.

As the wind blew through the trees I felt at ease, as if my father's spirit was guiding us.

We found a safe place to set up camp and ate just enough of our rations to keep our stomachs from growling. We took turns keeping watch through the night, and made sure to be ready to get going again at first light.

Maria had promised to cover for us, but there was no telling how long she could keep the Mayor from finding out we had left. We didn't even know if he would send anyone after us or not.

I pulled out my father's old map and examined it. Now that we were safely away from the village, we needed a plan for where to go next.

"You have no idea which direction we need to go, do you?" Chass asked.

"I do!" I answered back. Truth was I didn't. I knew just as much as he did.

"My father mentioned the thunder relic being hidden in the Cyndarin Mountains, that's where we start. After that, we head north toward Fennox Castle and ask the King for help finding the rain and lightning relics," I answered.

"Which mountain?" Chass asked.

I stood and looked to the east. We were on a slight hill, and I could just see the peaks of the Cyndarin Mountains over the treetops. I pointed at one in the northern part of the range. "That one."

I knew it was the right one. It looked just like my father had drawn it.

While we waited for enough light to feel safe entering the forest, I practiced creating small balls of blue light with my fingertips.

I was starting to get good at it. Throwing them at targets, however, would take some getting used to.

Chass did his best to guide me. He suggested I practice with my bow and arrows to find a way to better aim my lightning strikes. He was a better teacher than I gave him credit for. Patient, unlike those that he had been forced to learn from.

I tried to imagine what it would be like to take a lesson in magic from Argentis. Just the thought of his gravelly voice yelling over my shoulder caused a sense of fear and anger to well up inside me. A spark of lightning surged through the arrow I had ready, and the shock of the spark made me let it loose. It whizzed through the air, sparking with blue light, and exploded into a cloud of bark and wood shavings when it hit the tree I had been aiming at.

We both stared wide-eyed as smoke poured out from the newly formed hole in the tree.

"That was dramatic," Chass said.

CARINE

Arianna, you may remember Cypress, the old mage who used to visit Manse from time to time. I never told you, but he was the reason I decided not to send you to the Royal Academy of Magic.

He had been an instructor there, before the curse. He told me the others refused to believe that the drought had been brought on by magic, and so he had left to seek truth on his own. He also told me that the majority of the mages there were charlatans. They practiced illusions and trickery, and would be ill-equipped to help you control the powerful magic you possess.

Normally mages who renounce the Academy are put to death, but King Drevon himself took sympathy on Cypress' quest and gifted him a special medallion, sealed with the King's rune to grant him protection on his travels.

I also never told you why Cypress eventually stopped visiting. I suppose you are ready to hear that story now.

Together we had gathered funding for an adventure to the North. It was almost a year later before we were able to actually embark on our quest.

I questioned whether the journey would even happen, paranoid that Cypress had used me as an unwitting accomplice to cheat the kingdom out of silver. For an older man he was quick with his tongue, and quicker with the staff and sword he carried. I asked him once, "Why does a mage carry a sword?"

He answered, "Because sometimes a quick thrust is better than a quick spark. Less noise; less of a mess too if you know what you are doing." Cypress was a dangerous man.

Inside the mountain pass we ran into a group of bandits.

"Those creatures will not be of use," said Cypress. "Kill them."

I could see the fire burning in his eyes, in his words, he spoke in an ancient tongue. A dead language brought back to life, filled with rage as each word growled from his lips, his tongue.

"Capture them, kill only if you must, we don't need more blood on our hands," I said.

"And wait while they regroup and come for vengeance?"

"They will not, not if you show them what true power is." I was pleading for the lives of the bandits when Cypress let out a howl and a shadow appeared around him growing out and under the bandits. Like staring into the void. The bandits hung in midair, just a little off the ground. Cypress raised his arm and it was as if some veil on reality had been lifted. Each bandit had a shadow snake wrapped around their neck. Invisible without magic. A noise like crickets could be heard all around us, a sound that was growing and growing until I closed my eyes. The bandits were laying down, unconscious on the ground, not one of them dead.

"Just a little trick of the light," Cypress said.

The great passage was without light. I relied almost entirely on Cypress for any sense of direction. We were walking through a small tunnel when I felt a spike jut out from the floor. I could hear small gears turning. As I reached down and felt one of the spikes I could feel an engraving. A warning to venture no further. Dozens of spikes, dozens of warnings carved on each along with an intricate pattern and dozens of different languages. Each a part of a trap, each individually engraved.

Carefully, we turned one corner to the next through the pass until we reached a wall. Pressing on a stone followed by a soft hiss our eyes were flooded by the rush of the sun. We kept low as we came out into what we could only assume was New-Ceuran.

The soil was dry, hot, cracked. It looked like a dried seabed between dozens of high mountains. Near the center were the bones of a giant beast, a giant shark that stretched across the land hundreds of feet. The forgotten body of a leviathan.

In some areas the brown crust of the world began to take on a dry red hue, alarming at first it soon became something of a relief to see the small changes in color. From where we came out we could see hidden below the bones a small temple. If viewed from above it would have looked like a star. The home of the spirits.

"Not what I expected," said Cypress.

"Is the curse really this powerful?"

"This is no curse. This is hubris, abandonment. There are no spirits, no Satyr, no living creatures left in this place, this is a ruin." Cypress was blunt and his words cut deep. Our journey had been for nothing. I almost broke down and cried right there but I still had to journey home. I couldn't show any more weakness than I already had.

"Did you expect a grand and glorious adventure?" Cypress asked.

"I'm looking for answers, not an adventure," I answered.

"Taking on the curse, taking on the sins of this world, this is what is to be expected. A dried-up corpse and cracked bedrock. A ruined temple and more questions than answers," Cypress tilted his head down and closed his eyes. Opening them again they had a blue light visible around them.

"Do you have any idea what it is we are looking for?" he asked.

"Answers."

"Yes, but what form do answers take? Should we assume they will speak directly to us, that they will make themselves known when we find them? Or do we have to continue to look? Even through the brightest light, we may not be able to see what is right in front of us." Cypress was being cryptic as usual.

"Answers, old man! What are you looking for? What do you see?"

"I see the world as it once was, fish swimming in the sea, whales, sharks, rays, even the spirits as they once were," he answered. As his eyes faded from blue to gray and back to normal again I began to see more wrinkles on his skin.

"What is happening to you?"

"It is a price. Magic requires sacrifice. That is the toll," he said and pointed towards the temple before waving his hand. "We are not alone."

And for a moment I saw the world as he had.

The ghosts of the past, shadows standing before me.

We have been told a great many things about our past, most of them haven't been told the same way twice, our history, the history of our world and all we know is only a part of the truth. The rest is for us to discover for ourselves.

Inside the temple, I had to force myself to stay conscious. My attention returned away from the visions of the past and towards the future I was working towards. I could hear the screams of Cypress behind me.

Hundreds of draugr rose from their graves as we began exploring the temple's inner sanctum. We found what we were looking for, what Cypress had been seeking. Not an answer to the curse that plagued our land but a weapon. A weapon that could destroy the Casar, the Satyr, the Firya, and would allow our kingdom to expand across the borders. It was a solution, but not the solution I had been searching for.

Mustering all of my strength I pulled out my sword and went back for the old man. The gates to the shrine were wide open and for a moment I felt lost. I could feel my stamina dissipating as I slew one, two, three of the reborn dead. Cypress had a strong will to live, even fatigued as we were. I found him still fighting for his life. I swung again, left to right and back again. Saved not once but twice by magic. Cypress was a great ally to have in battle.

Nodding towards me with a smile, Cypress motioned for me to go after the artifact. An ancient relic forged during the first age, it was a box covered in runes and engraved with the shapes of Satyrs on the front. We were two men fighting for our lives, fighting for our world.

We couldn't fight the horde that was coming. The magic in the shrine was too much for the two of us to take on our own. Cypress, drenched in blood, fell and rose back to his feet again. He glared at the draugr, eyes glowing yellow as he began to cast another curse.

"Are we escaping or what?" I yelled.

"Not without the artifact, the grimoire inside can change the world."

"Is it worth our lives?"

"It is worth everything!" A wave of yellow energy erupted around Cypress as the ground began to crack. The entire temple shook as the Draugr turned to dust.

"That will have bought us a few minutes," he said. Cypress was badly injured when he grabbed the box and opened it. Inside was a grimoire that he handed over to me. I opened it for just a moment. Inside were images of the Casar, Satyr, images of machines, weapons powered by fire and whale oil. Others powered by magic. It wasn't a grimoire as much as it was a book of chaotic creation. Dozens of the images were filled with warnings. The shadows appeared again. I saw the temple as it once was. A figure stood before me, their hands raised while three guards stood in front of them. They held rifles in their hands. Rifles that shot sparks of lightning. I raised my fist and shouted at the figures to disappear.

"Hidden across our world is the magic to make the impossible," Cypress said.

"This is not how we win," I said.

"This is how we create a new world! Our kingdom, our people are dying, with this lost technology we can control the future."

"The Casar, even our own kingdom, have already started using gunpowder. It's too dangerous! Entire villages have burned down developing weapons like this," I screamed.

"And many more will perish before the end, is it not survival of the strongest?" Cypress answered my screams with hollow words. The mage I had come to trust had used me as a pawn to help him travel. I was a hired gun, no better than a mercenary...

and if I brought such terrible secrets back with me I would be no better than a thug.

I had seen this happen before. A man so broken and desperate after losing everything to the curse he thought violence and war were the only answers. I didn't have the strength of will to stop it then, and a lot of innocent people paid the price. I wasn't going to make the same mistake again. I wasn't going to have more innocent blood on my hands.

More draugr had emerged from the ground all around us. The only escape was over a steep ledge into a canyon behind us, or back up the cliff from which we came. I jumped and grabbed hold of a branch, managing to pull myself up to a ledge without letting go of the grimoire clutched to my chest.

"Go!" Cypress called out as he was being overwhelmed by the undead monsters. "Save yourself! Use the grimoire!"

Just as he turned to look up at me I tossed the cursed book over the edge. He watched as it flew into the canyon where no living soul would find it again, and I saw his face move from fear and confusion, through the anger of betrayal, and finally into an understanding resignation. He stopped resisting the draugr, and they pulled him down into the solid earth. His body moved through the dry, cracked ground as though it were quicksand.

I forced myself to watch, though every fiber of my being screamed at me to look away. Cypress deserved at least that much respect. Just before his head sunk into oblivion I saw his lips move. His words were too quiet for me to hear, but I understood them just the same.

"You've doomed us all."

ARIANNA

My father's journals were filled with stories of sadness, of death, and yet despite all of it he always kept searching for another way. I remembered the old elven mage, Cypress. I remember asking why he hadn't come back with my father after the two of them left. I remember my father lying and telling me that Cypress had to venture back to the capital on urgent business.

How many lies had I been told? How many truths had my father hidden? I was reading stories of a man I never really knew and yet... I did. Everything I knew was still true, but there was more to the picture than that. He was a broken man. A man who sought answers. A man who would never stand for such destruction or war. It was one thing to save the world and another to destroy it. I think even if it meant sacrificing our entire kingdom to save the world beyond our borders my father would let us die. No, actually, I believe he would have searched all his life for another way -- just as he had.

Chass and I woke up early. We were starving. Our rations had

ROBBIE BALLEW AND STEPHEN LANDRY

already run dry and we were running out of clean water to drink. We had barely been gone a few days. We were resting atop a hill in an open field when I saw it, less than a mile away: a colorful garden surrounding a small house.

"Well, that's odd," I said.

"That garden… it's flourishing. I don't think I've seen that much green in… ever." Chass was just as amazed as I was.

"Let's go check it out," I said as I guided my horse toward it.

"I don't think that's such a good idea. We need to keep moving."

I stopped and turned back to him. "Whoever lives here has clearly found a way to work around the drought. Maybe they will be willing to help us!"

"We already know how to end the drought. What do we need help for?"

"I for one would like a hot meal before we starve to death."

"Which is exactly why we have to keep moving. The more ground we cover during the day, the better."

"You're scared, aren't you?" I teased.

"No, I'm just concerned for your safety, is all."

"The more allies we have in this fight, the better. Come on, what is the worst that could happen?"

"For one thing we could be murdered and eaten alive by a creepy hermit in the middle of nowhere," Chass said. I ignored him as we moved closer to the house.

"Trust me," I answered.

I had read him parts of my father's journal. Trying to keep the two of us on the same page felt important. Neither of us should hide anything from one another if we were going to be traveling together.

Well, everything except the fact that I held the Spirit of Lightning inside me and would inevitably have to sacrifice myself to free the spirits and break the curse. I knew if I told him that he would be even more worried for me than he already was. He might even try to talk me out of finishing the mission. At least that's how I justified not telling him the truth.

When we reached the house, we were mesmerized by the multitude of colors in the garden. Filled with green vines and accented by exotic blooms of red, purple, and blue. Rose bushes rose several feet in the air with thorns three inches thick. It was hypnotizing.

"Just let me do the talking, okay?" I said after we dismounted our horses and stood in front of the door. We both jumped when a strange voice came from behind us.

"Oh, don't worry. I'm sure I'll do enough talking for the three of us. I haven't had guests in years!" A gray-haired hermit, hunched over with age, immediately pushed past us and opened the door. Both Chass and I stood there, our eyes wide open, wondering how and where the old man had come from. There was something oddly familiar about him. A distant memory from my childhood...

"Come right in, dinner is almost ready," the hermit said, turning to us and smiling. As I looked into his eyes, recognition flooded in.

"Cypress!" I exclaimed. He gave me an affirming nod.

"Wait, but, I thought..." Chass stammered. "The Draugr..."

"Ah, so Carine told you about that, did he? Well, I survived! The good parts of me did, anyway." He looked me straight in the eye. "I don't blame your father for doing what he thought was right. He taught me a valuable lesson that day. I'm not the same man I was."

Inside the house was a cluttered mess. Colorful painted papers with sketches and clay sculptures of animals covered every inch of what was a wooden table sitting on top of moldy books. Little pieces of paper with runes were nailed between every doorway and small nets filled with giant plants hung from the rafters with green vines hanging down further. Parts of the floor were torn up where a small garden had been planted and plump red tomatoes were growing inside an entire closet.

I picked up one of the small clay sculptures. It was a wolf. It had a scowl on its face so detailed I could count the teeth and individual patches of fur. It looked just like the real thing only shrunken and discolored. The only reason it was recognizable as clay were cracks on the back of the hips.

"You can have that, or not, I think I've made quite a few of those," Cypress said from inside his kitchen. His house was strange. Bigger on the inside, it seemed, or maybe it was some type of illusion.

"Come, sit," he pointed towards a table already set for three.

"You knew we were coming?" I asked.

"I know a lot of things, and other things I don't. Is that so strange?" he said, taking a large bite from a potato. We both sat down and looked at our plates tentatively.

"So if you're not the same person you used to be, then who are you now?" asked Chass. The hermit looked at the two of us and swallowed his food. He gave us a serious look.

"That's what I came out here to find out, now isn't it?" he answered, taking another bite of his food.

"How have you been able to make your garden grow?" I asked, taking a bite from a cooked tomato.

"Lots and lots of compost. Waste not, want not, I always say."

"Wait, you're telling me we can reverse the effects of the drought with garbage?" Chass said, his mouth full of food.

"Oh no, who said anything about ending the drought? No, that took years and years of magic. Magic that takes a heavy toll. It is a temporary solution, at best. Your way will be much faster."

"How do you know we're trying to break the curse?" Chass asked, putting his guard back up.

"Perhaps," the hermit looked over from Chass to me, "a little songbird told me." I perked up as he continued, "But your quest is useless anyway. Only the king knows where to find the relics of rain and lightning." At that moment I looked away and bit my lip. Cypress narrowed his eyes at me, as if trying to read my reaction. He didn't know the truth, did he? He couldn't possibly. "And he will never allow an audience with a couple of peasants such as yourselves."

My heart sank. That was one of my greatest fears. My father had fought for years for an actual audience with the king and yet never once had it worked. "Surely, there must be something we can do, we have to break the curse!" I exclaimed, making a fist under the table. I was tired of being helpless.

"You are desperate, aren't you?" Cypress asked. "What do you expect to get out of it? Fame? Fortune? Free admission to the Royal Academy of Magic?"

"Of course not! I just want to finish what my father started and end the suffering of my people!"

"Oh, a selfless act of love. How touching. In that case, I might be able to help you."

"How so?" Chass spoke up.

Cypress finished what was left on his plate and swallowed, standing up and walking over towards a brown desk, barely held together by a few rusty nails. Inside it looked like the hermit had kept nothing; nothing but a key.

"Like Carine, I too was searching for the truth behind the curse." He placed the key inside the lock and twisted it, struggling for a moment as if it wouldn't quite budge. He smiled when it finally clicked and opened.

"I failed in my mission. I let my greed and ambition get in the way of my search for truth, and I have resigned myself to spending the rest of my days in solitude as penance for my mistakes." He pulled a talisman from the chest and handed it over to me. "Show this to the guards at the gate, and they will know that I was the one who sent you." It was beautiful and carved with a special rune, the king's seal. It even had weight to it as if made of pure silver.

"Now go Aria, you are our only hope."

I looked up at Cypress, but he was gone. It had all disappeared. Cypress, the cottage, the garden. There one moment and gone the next instant. Even the food we had been eating. The two of us sat there for a moment, confused. Unsure of what had just happened. The only proof that it had been real was the talisman in my hand.

"He called me Aria."

"I thought that was strange. No one's ever called you Aria before."

"My father did. Aria, his little songbird."

"So what does it all mean?"

"The deep magic!" I exclaimed.

"The what?"

I ran back to my horse and jumped up on top of it. Chass was slow but right behind me. I was more motivated than ever to find the storm relics and complete my father's mission. The talisman was the key, the hope I had been searching for. With it we would be able to speak to the king and save the kingdom.

"The deep magic! It guides all of our destinies. My father must have connected with it somehow. He must have used it to convince Cypress to help us! How else could he have known we were coming?"

"Okay, I have no idea what you're talking about, but if your father has some way to communicate from beyond the veil, why not just talk to us directly?"

"I don't know, maybe it doesn't work like that?"

We continued to ride and I did my best to explain. It took a few tries but I finally managed to make him understand. Like the veil my father saw in New-Ceuran that connected him to the past, deep magic connected our world with the spirit world and beyond. It was a magic greater than that which we all possess, deep magic was the aether that ran over all of us, giving us the ability to connect with one another even after death.

It was pure. Unadulterated. Neither good nor evil. Deep magic was all around us constantly guiding us, pulling us apart, pushing us together. Right now it was guiding me towards the mountains and the temple of the thunder relic. Deep magic was the red thread of fate that bound us together whether it was yesterday, today, or a hundred years from now.

ARGENTIS

I stood in Talze's office, appalled at his disgusting smile of grim satisfaction after hearing my report. I didn't care for my talents being wasted on bullying a little girl, but the fat pig had ordered me to do it, and obeying his orders was the whole reason the king had sent me out to this backwater dump.

"You were right, she's playing right along," I growled.

"Getting her out of town was the easy part. Now we have to make sure she stays out of our hair for good," the mayor replied. Eldrad came into the room behind me with a report of his own.

"Two horses are missing from the stables. Chass must be with her."

"Idiot," I said. That kid was always causing far more trouble than he was worth. It was a miracle I hadn't snapped his neck years ago.

"That is unfortunate," the Mayor responded. "Go, find him and bring him back to me. I don't care what happens to the girl."

CARINE

A beam of red light swept across my face. I was still having nightmares, visions of the veil, but that wasn't this. A doorway in my mind seemed to burst open; a rage. I felt powerful. I was going to win. A strange power coursed through my body. The power of a gemstone. A small relic but not the one I was searching for. It gave its wielder an incredible boost of power. I felt it running through my whole body from my neck to my shoulders and down my chest to my legs. I even felt it run through my arms and into the tips of my fingers as I clutched a greatsword with two hands.

Feeling like I was drowning I cried out in anguish, swinging against my opponent as a means to control it. I had to move. It was the only way the power wouldn't overwhelm me, and if I was going to survive and make it home I couldn't fail, I couldn't hesitate. Every move was life and death. My vision blurred before focusing. I felt like I had the vision of a Shrike searching for a meal.

A Casar warrior stood before me holding a giant ax. My sword found its mark, and he fell to the ground, the color of his blood expanding across the sand. I never should have come back here.

'Here' was a graveyard, the veil, formerly New-Ceuran. The remains of the leviathan and temple were repurposed. Turned into an arena. Away from the kingdom it was a place raiders had come to fight; duels to the death against other warriors and monsters. Creatures, aberrations created by dark magic that shouldn't exist.

This was my fault. I should have known Cypress had others following in his footsteps, searching for the grimoire. I was at least glad I managed to hide the cursed book before they could find it. Perhaps bringing me back to this hellish place was the deep magic's way of making me pay penance for Cypress' death. This arena was my dungeon and if I survived I would be granted salvation. Ten matches. That was all I had to advance.

Ten matches for my freedom…

I fell into this mess when I rescued a guild merchant named Gideon who had trapped himself inside the ruins of an old dam. Most of his wares were destroyed but he had collected enough accessories to trade in one of the northern villages. I should have turned around and gone home.

I had already been away from my songbird for weeks and had found nothing of value, nothing to stop the drought, nothing to trade for food or supplies. I had to change my focus and begin in a new direction. I couldn't stay gone any longer. All my heart longed to be home.

Gideon hired me as a bodyguard. It was good coin. He offered me enough to fund my next trip and keep my songbird safe. It should have been easy but nothing easy ever really is. Gideon sold me out while I slept. Traded me to an agent of the Lahari Cult that followed a dark grimoire. They were the ones who had taken over New-Ceuran, rebuilt it from the ground up and flooded it with aberrations. They changed the name. I heard many of them chanting it as we moved forward. They called it the Churn.

I cursed the wagon that brought me in. They had carved out the pass and opened it up wide enough for a road. I wasn't sure if it had been two days or three. The agent of the Lahari had kept me drugged. Thought it was safer and he was right. I was determined. When we emerged into the light we were surrounded by other agents and aberrations. A small parade of new champions for the Churn.

Many of the aberrations looked like smaller dinosaurs. Ancient beasts that roamed the land millions of years ago. Their fossils had been dug up all over Idril and in every part of the known world. Their much smaller descendants still hunted the wild parts of the world. It seemed black magic had been used on these aberrations to return them to their ancestor's size.

I was a slave for a week before they decided to put me in the arena. First against a couple of bandits that had tried to steal from them. I recognized one as someone whose life I had been able to spare before. He recognized me as well, not that it mattered. A gash across my arm is proof of that.

After winning I was rewarded with a hot meal and wine. I accepted the meal but refused the wine. They weren't going to win me over. The Lahari cultists were rotten. Rogue mages wanted dead by the kingdom. Had Cypress actually been one of them or just loosely associated I couldn't be sure but it was obvious they weren't thinking in the best interest of anyone but their own kin. After three battles I was rewarded with a gemstone. The gem was an experiment of theirs. A powerful weapon that made the wielder stronger, faster, powerful. They put me up against a captured Casar, throwing both of us into the pit and watching with wine in hand as we fought.

"We don't have to fight, we can turn on them, fight them together," I said.

"The last two that tried that were fed to the aberrations and eaten alive."

"I have this gem, it makes me stronger. I can rush them."

"You won't have time, I've seen them summon the dead in seconds."

"So you've given up?"

"I'm playing their game, between you and me I like the odds that I walk out alive," said the Casar.

"If we continue on like this no one will survive."

"So be it, none of us get out alive."

I would be lying if I said I didn't enjoy the look on their faces when they were surprised I won. By the second week I had gained enough of a reputation fighting day after day that they called me 'Praetor'. And as Praetor I was given my own quarters for the night, access to food, water, wine, and though I turned them away... women. All of it was wrong. Every day I searched for a way to escape. Someway, somehow I had to get out and go back to my home.

I staggered to my feet, winded. Three weeks had passed and I was face to face with an ogre. The beast looked like a giant man with a nose like a hog and large tusks that came up above its upper lip. It had long black hair and looked like it had lived a long life before being captured and brought to this hellhole.

I tried to speak to it. The ogre. I told it my name. That I refused to fight. The Lahari cult had mastered control of the veil over the temple grounds. That was their advantage. Here on this hallowed ground they could summon the dead. The ogre refused to listen. Afraid of the Lahari, not of me.

It swung a massive sword the size of a man against the ground against me. It was slow. It moved like it was underwater. It was too easy. The fight ended when I threw myself forward through the air and landed on its arm, removing the ogre's head from its shoulders in one smooth stroke. The Lahari wasted no time bringing the match to a close. Clapping as they summoned a dozen dead warriors around me. They didn't attack. They awaited the command of their masters who ordered me to lay down my sword.

After that victory they started giving me fewer fights. The more I went into the arena, the closer I got to winning my freedom. They much preferred parading me around like a prized pet as long as possible.

It was several weeks later when an opportunity presented itself.

"Time to leave," said a young prisoner named Ethra.

"We can't," I answered.

"We can, but only the two of us. I have a way out." He had come from a long line of thieves and had been picking the lock on his cell with a bump key he had hidden under his skin.

"You're new, you aren't going to make it past their Draugr, they have the entire temple on lockdown."

"I have a plan," Ethra said just as he opened his cell door.

"What is that?"

"I have the famous Praetor on my side," he said, opening my door. "Also I know the quickest way to the armory without running into trouble."

Ethra wasn't lying. It had been years since I had put my trust in anyone outside my own village. He led us to the armory without any trouble and I grabbed the gemstone along with a sword while he took two blades carved from the leviathan's bone. The armory itself was huge. Filled with a variety of weapons like swords, staves, maces, even whips. Anything and everything for the entertainment of the Lahari.

"Just what I came here for," he smirked.

"You wanted to steal some swords?"

"No, that gem in your hand, promise me that once we are safe you will sell it to me. I believe I've saved your life so we can call it a fair trade."

I looked at the gem. It was fair. Ethra had saved my life but this was a weapon, not something I could just give away or put into the hands of the wrong person. Plus, with it I might be able to bargain my way into a meeting with the King.

"We can't leave, not yet," I said.

"What do you mean? Our opening is closing, I've been studying this place for days," said Ethra.

"We can't leave without taking the other slaves with us," I explained.

"We can't afford to rescue anyone else."

"Then I'm not going." I closed my fist around the gem and laid my sword against the edge of the armory table.

"They won't outrun the aberrations, the Draugr, the Lahari, I'm sorry."

"If they can't run we'll carry them, we can't leave anyone behind."

"Look, you've won, what, five, six matches out of ten? You might actually have a pretty good shot of winning all ten but what do you think happens next?"

"Salvation."

"Salvation isn't the same thing as freedom. The gem, the battles, they're testing you. Seeing how much you can handle before they start the real experiments. They'll turn you into one of their aberrations. There is a reason no one outside the great rift knew of this place. No one escapes, no one leaves."

"I'm not leaving others to that fate if I have the chance to save them."

"We'll have a better chance of saving them once we're on the outside. Please, I need you to trust me on this."

I wasn't happy, but I could see his logic. I just had to trust that he would return to save the others once he found his own freedom.

Our escape went nearly as planned, but the little bit that didn't made all the difference. We could see our final egress into the outside world when the Draugr came for us. I don't know how the Lahari caught wind of our escape, but somehow they did.

Ethra threw himself into the shadows, striking only when he could hit them without being seen, while I acted as a shield, defending him from the bulk of the attack while bodies piled up in front of me. We were almost out when the Lahari summoned an aberration to come for us. It seemed to have been forged from the blood of the great leviathan itself.

It was a battle of life and death. I dropped the gem and felt the rush of power fade from my grasp. My blood-lust faded and reality came back into focus. Red eyes leered towards us. The aberration stomped heavily toward us, its jaws threatening to shred us to pieces with every chomp.

Ethra staggered. He fell and quickly scurried across the ground in search of the gem.

"We have to go!" I shouted.

"We can't leave without the gem!" he shouted.

"Is it worth your life?"

"It is worth the life of every slave in here," he replied, and I finally understood. The gem was the key to rescuing the others.

He finally found it and snatched it. It looked heavy in his hand. The power coursing through his veins seemed too much for him to handle.

He tried to run, but it was too late, the burden of the gem too heavy. He fell to his knees and the aberration took him in its jaws. With what strength he had left, he tossed the gem in my direction.

I took hold of it and ran. The aberration was temporarily abated as it chewed its prey, and with the gem in hand I easily powered through the last few draugr between myself and freedom.

Outside the mountain pass, I discovered a group of soldiers from the kingdom waiting, led by a powerful mage. The mage revealed to me that Ethra had been sent by the king himself to uncover some weakness inside the Churn. The Lahari were a rising threat within the kingdom that needed to be eliminated. I gave them the gem that Ethra had sacrificed his life for. They thanked me for my trouble with five hundred coin, and told me to never speak of it again.

I had hoped this might be my chance to earn an audience with the king, but the mage wouldn't hear of it. He told me the king was far too busy to meet with every peasant who did a good deed.

I watched from a nearby ledge as the mage unlocked the full

potential of the gem, raining fire down upon the Churn and reducing it to rubble and ash. I had no doubt it killed every living thing inside.

It seemed strange that no one would ever pass through the Churn again, like the whole thing had been imagined. One nightmare was gone, but with the deaths of my fellow slaves, a new host of nightmares began.

I have lost too much to this curse already, and I am afraid of what sacrifices it will demand of me before this is all over. It is a terrible thing, losing those you love… but please remember, hold onto what we have, what we had, and always press forward.

And never leave anyone behind.

·10·
ARIANNA

I jerked awake as something brushed against the back of my tent. Probably just the wind. I had fallen asleep reading more of my father's journal. He was more of a fighter than I thought. The things he went through to come home. The dangers he had warned me about as a child. It was frightening but real.

It was Chass' turn to keep watch. I could see his silhouette against the campfire; now barely more than a few stray embers. Chass' head was slumping down. He slipped and almost fell off the log he was sitting on before jumping back awake. I started gathering my things, getting ready to take over and let him get some sleep.

I saw Chass jump to his feet and unsheathe his sword, but before I could scramble out from my tent a second figure emerged from the darkness and grabbed him from behind.

"Arian - -" his voice turned into a muffled cry.

I rushed out of my tent, grabbing a small dagger by my side. The first thing I saw was terrible claws digging into Chass' cheek.

A Satyr. Part man, part goat, almost completely covered in fur from the neck down, with horns curled around the sides of its head. The same creature that had killed my father. Was I staring at my father's murderer? It turned towards me, yanking Chass around with it.

"Stand back," its voice was deep.

I moved into a defensive stance.

"What do you want with us?" I shouted.

"This is the Mayor's son, is it not? A very valuable hostage, indeed."

"Let him go!" I demanded, making my voice as commanding as possible.

"Why should I?" the Satyr's deep voice growled.

My eyes narrowed. Electricity arced across my body.

Chass' eyes widened as he began shaking his head. Blood trickled down from beneath the claws digging into his face. Before I had time to focus my rage I threw my hand up, and a blast of electricity shot out from my palm and impacted the Satyr on its exposed shoulder, barely missing Chass. The creature howled in pain and fell to the ground. Its claws left deep, jagged cuts in Chass' cheek.

I advanced forward as Chass scurried out of the way, holding his cheek.

Don't hold back! The voice in my head screamed. I couldn't ignore the voice this time. I didn't want to. *Blast it again!* It told me. I did. I heard the creature crying out for me to stop. I saw the fur on its arm smoldering under the heat of each new ball of electricity. I smelled the burning flesh.

"Arianna! Stop!" the creature screamed. Everything froze.

"How do you know my name?" I demanded.

"Your father was right. You have the spirit of the storm in you."

Electricity flared around my body.

"What do you know of my father?"

"He came to us for help."

I threw another bolt of electricity at the Satyr. The electric charge slammed the creature back to the ground.

"Liar! My father would never trust the likes of you!" I could remember every story, every tale of the Satyr I'd ever been told. How they stole children from cradles and drained their blood and ate their bones. Here I was, face to face with a demon claiming it knew my father.

"I was there, Arianna!" He -- it -- said. "That night in the woods, when you were a child. We were meant to start our journey that night, to find the missing relics. But the Mayor and his men refused to believe your father." The memory of that night had played in my dreams so many times over the years I was beginning to think it had never actually happened. That giant, gentle face that had examined me with genuine curiosity.

"That was you?"

The innocent child's eyes I had been looking through then were not the same eyes with which I saw him now. These eyes were wiser. These eyes knew better. The Satyr raised himself to his feet, peering into my eyes with some unnamed question.

"Tell me, why did Carine send you?"

"He didn't. My father is dead."

The Satyr dropped to its knees. "No! It can't be!"

Electricity arced over my body again.

"Don't act so surprised! It was you Satyrs that killed him!"

"No!" He jumped to his feet and stepped toward me. I raised my hand and he stopped in his tracks. "We Fauns do not kill! We live in harmony with all living things."

"That's hard to believe coming from the creature that just ripped my best friend's face open." The charge of electricity was building in my hands. I was forming two small balls of light. I wasn't going to let this creature out of my sight. They would all pay for what they had done to my father.

"We only attack and rob elves because you have refused our cries for help! All we want is to return to our solitude."

"Give me one good reason why I shouldn't blast you beyond the veil right now," I seethed. I was ready to be done with this creature.

"Please trust me," he begged. "My name is Egris. I traveled with your father for many years. Please let me help you finish his mission."

"Why do I need your help?"

"I can offer you protection. No Faun will attack if they see me with you." I stared at the creature for several moments. I didn't trust him, but that didn't mean he couldn't be useful.

I let the energy continue to burn in my palm as I turned my hand toward Chass and marched in his direction.

"Arianna, what are you doing?" Chass backed away from me until he hit a tree and couldn't go any further. I could see Egris shifting uncomfortably in the corner of my eye. Once I got close enough, a spark jumped from my hand and danced up the gashes on Chass' cheek, healing his wounds until nothing but dried blood remained.

"Egris… Lead the way."

·11·
ARIANNA

We still had several more hours of night left as we entered the woods with Egris as our guide. Chass and I agreed to each keep watch over him, still uncertain if the creature could be trusted. As we picked our way through the darkness we heard the sound of something coming from the forest.

"More of your friends?" I asked, turning toward Egris.

"I came alone, that is something else. Prepare yourself," Egris said, poising himself for an attack.

A starving giant boar emerged growling from the forest into the light of our camp. It had short black fur covered in dried blood. One giant tusk and one half tusk, broken from battle. It wasn't just blood that covered its fur, but mud and tar.

"It must have recently fallen into a pit and dug itself out," said Egris.

"A pit? You mean a trap?" Chass asked.

"Yes, we have set several around our village as a way to keep animals and elves away," Egris explained.

"That's great, so what would have happened if we fell into one of your traps?" Chass stood ready to fight the boar with his sword.

"The tar is not deep, our traps are meant to capture not kill. You would have been found by our scouts and we would have freed you once we realized you weren't a threat," Egris answered.

Chass seemed satisfied with his answer at first, then, "Wait, what do you mean, 'not a threat'?"

The boar growled and lunged toward us. Egris jumped in front of it just before it got close enough to take a bite at my leg.

"Stand back!" he yelled. He was baring his teeth and growling back at the boar.

"What are you doing?" I whispered. "Shouldn't we be fighting?"

"The boar is not an enemy, it is only starving," said Egris.

"Tell it to eat someone else," Chass interjected.

"What do you think I am doing!" Egris said quickly before growling again. It worked. A few minutes of back and forth banter and the boar turned in the other direction. It was only after the animal was gone that I realized how short my breath had become. Had Egris actually just saved our lives? I grunted.

"You know, if you hadn't been here I would have just blasted the stupid thing and Chass and I could have had bacon for breakfast."

It took us half the rest of the night to hike to the Faun village.

Egris held up his hand, telling us to stop.

"We can't go any further this way, we must stop and wait," he said.

"Why, what is it?" Chass asked.

"A shrike," Egris said.

"A shrike?" I asked. "What does that mean?"

"Isn't that a type of bird?" Chass added.

"Yes, a territorial one, an omen… if we move forward now we will find ourselves in pain, we must wait," answered Egris.

"I can't see anything," I said.

Egris pointed, "There." I formed a small ball of lightning in between two of my fingers and threw it as hard as I could. It landed against a large thorn bush covered in dozens of small shrikes that scattered. The boar, almost dead, was laying in the thorns.

"I see…" said Egris, moving toward the boar.

"What are you doing now?" I asked.

"The shrike have gone, it is safe to pass now." Along the boar's body were claw marks from the shrike. Egris walked toward it.

"Please, will you help me?" he asked.

"Help you with what?"

Egris began tearing the thorns away from the boar, loosening their grip on the beast and allowing it to crawl forward.

"I have seen what you can do, the magic that runs inside of you."

"You want me to heal that thing?"

"It is a part of nature and I can feel it is not the right time for it to die."

I held my hands out and the boar began to growl as small arcs of light formed between my fingertips.

The wounds on the boar began to close.

I could feel the energy moving between the boar and myself. The connection between my power and nature.

As soon as the boar's wounds closed it jumped up, freeing itself from the rest of the vines and thorns that had claimed it and ran away from us.

CHASS

We emerged from the woods into a bustling village of Fauns. It was unlike anything I had ever seen. Their village spread up the large trees and down into holes in the ground. There were dwellings made of large leaves and sticks, pasted together with clay. Paintings of bright abstract images filled with color and dyes spread across dozens of homes. Egris led us deeper in, past several buildings. Other Fauns stuck their heads out to watch as we passed by.

These were not at all like the creatures in the painting that hung in our home. I had spent years staring in horror at their sharp teeth; their matted, blood-stained fur. The faces that looked out curiously as we passed were soft; gentle even.

"Don't get very many visitors?" I asked.

"You are the first to have visited us in a long time, besides Carine," Egris answered

"My father came here?" Arianna asked.

"Yes. Many times."

A female Faun who was sewing a lush tapestry stopped what she was doing and stared at us. A crowd had gathered and was following close behind.

"This really is starting to feel like a trap," Arianna whispered to me. I couldn't deny that she had a point, but their intentions didn't seem malicious.

A regal Faun exited a large tent and approached us cautiously.

"Egris, greetings," it said in a grave voice, bowing slightly.

"Brau-Na, greetings," Egris replied in similar fashion.

"Is she the one?" Brau-Na asked.

"She is the one."

"The one what?" Arianna asked, the tension unmistakable in her voice.

"The one that will break the curse!" Brau-Na shouted loudly.

"She is the one!" Egris echoed.

Excitement washed over the whole assembly.

"Light the fire! Bring the wine!" Brau-Na said before going back inside his tent. Several other Fauns grabbed torches from the sides of buildings and threw them onto a large pile of old, dried out logs in the center of the village, igniting a large bonfire.

"What's going on?" I exclaimed.

"We haven't had a reason to celebrate in many years," Egris said. "You have brought hope to us all!"

Music filled the still night air. It was strange, percussive music played with instruments I'd never heard before.

A group of revelers danced in a circle around the fire. Brau-Na emerged from his tent with three wine-skins, which he handed to Arianna, Egris, and myself.

"The best for our heroes!" he said, and walked toward the dancing. The music was so loud I imagined our village could hear it miles and miles away. Egris joined the others in dancing around the fire.

Arianna sniffed her wine suspiciously. I took a small sip of mine.

"Do you really think we can trust them?" she asked.

"I know it doesn't make any sense, but if your father trusted them --"

"They claim he trusted them," she cut in.

"How else could they have known his name?" I pointed out. "Or your name? Or about the curse? About any of it?"

"There must be a reason my father never told me about them."

"Maybe he just thought you wouldn't understand?" I suggested. "My father was constantly trying to make me afraid of the Satyrs. Honestly I think I'm ready to believe the exact opposite of everything he's ever told me.

"Come! Drink! Dance!" Egris shouted, waving his arms to beckon us toward the bonfire.

I took several steps toward the revelry, then turned back to Arianna with a shrug.

"Come on, what's the worst that could happen?" I asked.

"For one thing, we could be murdered and eaten alive by Satyrs in the middle of the forest."

I took a heavy swig of my wine and ran to the bonfire. I did my best to mimic the Faun's dancing, no doubt making a complete fool of myself. I bumped into a young Faun girl, and had to hold onto her to keep my balance as we both stumbled out of the circle.

The fur that ran down the backs of her arms was soft, and the skin underneath was dark and flawless. I looked up to her face and realized she was blushing. I quickly let go of her arm, embarrassed.

She smiled and held out her hand. I took it, and bowed courteously. Her sheepish grin was replaced by a mischievous smirk, and she quickly pulled me back into the circle and we joined the others dancing.

It all felt so surreal. The woods, the boar, the colors that surrounded us in the village. This was the complete opposite of our home.

The Fauns were suffering. They were just as low on food as we all were. The colorful tapestries, the wine, the dancing. It had all been saved for this moment. For moments like this… of happiness. Egris wasn't lying when he said we had brought them hope.

I couldn't help but smile.

The night was just beginning.

·12·
ARIANNA

The night went on. The music continued to play. A Faun child came up to me and offered me a tunic with runes embroidered all over it. She smiled when I took it from her and ran towards her mother, who waved and smiled back.

"That belonged to her father, Melos. A brave Faun," said one of the Fauns standing near me. "The runes cast a warming spell on the wearer."

"Why did she give it to me?"

"He died on a journey to the Cyndarin mountains. Your father inspired many of us to action. His mission, his legacy, belongs to us as much as it does to you. It was all she had of her father and a true gift. Keep it close."

"I feel bad taking something like that."

"All of these gifts are for the journey that awaits you. It is with great honor that we are able to bestow them upon you."

"Thank you. What is your name?"

"I am Isoka. I am a scout for the tribe. Your father was a great man, kind to many of us."

"You knew my father?" I was ready to cry, holding the tunic in my hands, looking at all of the Fauns dancing around in circles, singing. I couldn't understand the language but that didn't matter. It was the way their voices resonated together that sent chills down the back of my spine and across my arms.

"We will speak of him one day but for now there is someone else here that wants to meet with you," Isoka said, standing up and whistling. A creature the size of a horse slowly crept out from the shadows of a tent. It looked like a giant cat with several wolf-like features.

"Emery!" I said, tears rolling down my eyes. The giant ran towards me, coming right up to me and licking me across the cheeks. She was smiling and panting heavily. I wrapped my arms around her.

"How... when?" I cried, running my hand down Emery's side. She had grown... a lot. From the size of a small cat to as large as a dire wolf. Still, she had the same eyes, the same colors. She moved her face around in the same way, pressing it against me.

"Your father brought Emery to us many years ago," Egris said, falling to the ground beside me. "Pardon me, I haven't danced like that in forever. My daughter, Chrysalis, has been taking good care of Emery."

Chass and the young Faun girl he had been dancing with were just walking up to our circle, holding hands. That didn't take long.

"I'm glad to see she still remembers you," the young Faun girl was saying. Her voice was calm, soothing, friendly. Emery walked over to her and licked her face, just as she had mine. So this must be Chrysalis. "Uncle Carine told me so many stories about you over the years I almost feel like we're long lost sisters!"

Sisters. I've always wondered what it would be like to have a sister. Someone to explore the woods with me, to share clothes and toys with, to fight over silly things. But I never had any of that. She had called him 'Uncle'. How was it that my father could have had this whole life, this whole other family, and never told me about it?

The pet he took from you he gave to her.

My father had given so much for these people. So many years of his life. He had filled them with hope. And in the end the creatures betrayed him. No, I didn't want to think about that right now.

But it's the truth and you know it.

It didn't matter if I could trust the Fauns or not, for the time being I had no choice but to put my life, my mission in their hands. It was what my father would have wanted. I just wished he had prepared me for this reality.

"I'm sure he told you plenty about me, as well." Chrysalis' comment snapped me out of my thoughts. I scanned the faces of the Fauns around me, all filled with expectation. Chass' face was the worst. It almost looked like he felt sorry for me.

"I'm sorry... I just..." I stammered, "I think I need to lie down." I turned away from the group. I had no idea where I was going, I just needed to get away. To breathe.

"Wait!" Egris said before I had time to leave. "Here, we have one more tradition that is important to us." I turned to see Egris coming toward me with a small brown bowl filled with a crushed herb that had been brewed into a tea. "This will help you feel better." I poked it with my finger. It had a strange thick texture to it like some kind of syrup had been added to boiled water. It smelled like soil.

"What is this?" I asked just as Emery licked the top of the

bowl.

"Drink and you will see," Egris said, handing another bowl to Chass.

"Not the strangest thing I've done tonight." Chass drank.

"Okay," I started to drink and the next moment I felt like I was floating. Any pain I felt in my body withered away and the Fauns began throwing a red compound across the ground, drawing large circles and runes with long walking sticks. The younger Fauns were wearing masks that looked like strange animals. They seemed to glow as the pale morning light began to shine through the clouds. The red powder seemed to rise and sink with the sound of the drums.

"Now, just like your father, you are one of us."

I woke up the next morning buried in a pile of gifts and feeling like I had slept for a week. Emery had stayed by my side all night, curled up next to my feet near the entrance to my tent. My hand still clutched an empty wine-skin. I checked my clothes and my dagger and adjusted myself. Emery stood up before me, letting me use her to balance myself.

As I rubbed my head I realized that the sun was already high in the sky. I began to dig myself out from the tangle of clothes and tapestries. Some of them were beyond what I could have imagined, full of colorful depictions of Faun life and abstract colors while others showed scenes of heroes fighting against monsters and of course spirits and Faun gods, runes of protection, and words of thanks.

"I don't think we can trust it." I overheard Egris just outside my tent.

I emerged to find Chass, Egris, and Brau-Na conversing near a small fire pit just outside. Chass was holding Cypress' talisman. They all turned towards me as I stumbled into the daylight. Chass wanted to laugh at my clumsiness but was too kind to do that in front of the others.

"Look who decided to join the land of the living," he said just as I shielded the bright sun from my eyes and sat down beside the rest of them. Egris handed me a plate of berries.

"What is it you say we can't trust?" I asked, shoving a handful of red berries into my mouth.

"The talisman," Chass answered. "The Fauns say they've never heard of Cypress before. They've traveled that area many times and never seen any sign of a cottage."

"And why is that a reason not to trust it?"

"It just seems a little too convenient doesn't it?" Chass grinned.

"Maybe it's a sign that we're on the right track. The deep magic is working to…"

"Your father spoke of the deep magic often," Egris interrupted. "But I don't think that's how it works. It guides our destinies from a distance. It doesn't interfere. Not like this…"

Brau-Na was studying the talisman closely. How could they possibly doubt the deep magic? Doubt my father, after everything he had done for them?

"My father believed the deep magic would find a way to end the curse, one way or another. Even if he couldn't find a way to break it, someone else would. What if he was right?" I couldn't believe I was having to defend my actions, my father's actions again.

"It's possible," Brau-Na said, slowly, still deep in thought. "But why would this hermit just give you the talisman? It doesn't smell right, if you ask me." I snatched the talisman from his hand.

"I know that my father has joined with the deep magic, and I know that he is using it to help me break the curse. I can feel it." I looked between the two Fauns. It wasn't fair. I felt like I was pleading. "Why can't you trust me?" Their eyes dropped to the ground. After everything.

"Chass?" I said, looking up towards him.

"Fine, I trust you. But we still need to be wary. Someone went to a lot of trouble to start this drought, and they won't like the idea of us ending it."

"Then the sooner we find the relics, the better. When do we leave?" I turned my gaze back toward Egris. The celebration was over.

"We will travel at night. It will be safer that way, when no elves dare traverse the forests," Egris answered.

"When we started our journey our plan was the exact opposite," I said, hoping my true meaning didn't go unnoticed.

"Our situation has changed, Arianna," Chass said in a taught voice, indicating he knew exactly what I meant. "Our allies have changed. The Satyr… excuse me, the Faun, are not what we thought they were," Chass said, with a meaningful glance towards Chrysalis, who was standing behind the rest of us.

It would take us the entire day to sort through everything and pack anyway. "Fine. We will wait until dark. Where is breakfast? I'm starving," I said, stuffing another handful of berries in my mouth.

"Breakfast?" said Brau-Na, furrowing his brow. "We've nearly finished preparing the evening meal. You will be leaving much sooner than you think, child."

·13·
ARGENTIS

We found their campsite just a few hours after dark, following the silhouette of smoke in the moon-lit sky. We also found the horse they had let loose. Or maybe it had escaped. Those two kids didn't have a clue what they were getting themselves into.

I wrote a quick message updating the mayor on our progress and tucked it into the horse's satchel, then sent it on its way back to the village. With our torches lit we followed the tracks back to their camp. I pressed my foot down on the ashes and smothered what was left of the flame. It was a miracle this forest never burned down. A pity. While the plants were still thriving the animals inside were fighting for survival. The green leaves were more brown, yellow even in the summer months.

They weren't far away. Not now. Eldrad knelt down and surveyed the footprints in the dirt. There had clearly been a fight. In the chaos amongst the dirt there were two distinct pairs of elf footprints, and one pair of hoof-prints. Like a goat's.

"They must have been attacked by Satyrs during the night," Eldrad said.

"We'd better find their bodies to be sure."

"Vultures probably carried them off, especially if they were ripped apart."

"We'll still find traces of blood, remains, bones, anything we can bring back to prove we did our job."

Arianna, Chass. Talze sent me to track them down. Kill the girl and if Chass refused to come back with us he was mine to do as I wanted.

We managed to track one of their horses to a nearby village of Esther but found no trace of them. Chass must have realized they would be followed at some point and sent it in the opposite direction. It was an inconvenient diversion, but only a temporary one.

The two of us had been rivals for several years. It wasn't bad at first but the better the kid got, the more I wanted to win. He was a natural with a sword. I had had to train for years, being tortured by some of the worst tutors in the kingdom. I wanted to face him in a true one on one battle. A fight to the death.

While he spent all his time goofing off with that little brat, I had to train twice as hard as everyone else just to keep up with him. I've always had to work harder than everyone else to be afforded the same opportunities.

My mother was a slave. A bit taboo in the 'civilized' Kingdom of Idril, but not in the Southern Wilds were tribal villages still traded furs, bodies, drink. Bought and freed by my father, a squire who soon became a knight. When she was finally free the two of them ventured back to the tribe and murdered them all and once that was done, my mother killed my father.

It was there in the wilds I was born. At ten years old we ventured back to Idril and I learned of my inheritance. My mother took her place in the King's court while I trained. In the wilds my mother had taught me how to hunt, to survive, to kill. I maimed the first master I had and spent three weeks in a dungeon for my crime. The second that tried to teach me I learned to let win. I was a prodigy. At least I thought I was.

A wild boar jumped from the forest and knocked me back to reality. I pulled out my sword just in time to skewer the beast on my blade as it made a second attack. It still hit with enough force to drop me to my back. Its tusk managed to hook itself under my armor and I screamed in anguish as I heard more than felt a rib crack with the force of the impact.

I dug my sword into the side of a boar. Biting my lip. I could feel the creature squirming in pain, trying to work itself free but digging further into my side instead. Sweat dripped down my back. Another three minutes and it would have been over. I only barely managed to get my sword back outside the beast with enough time to swing again.

"Eldrad, a little help!" I shouted, the weight of the boar threatening to crush me. He rushed over just in time to help me push it off to the side. Eldrad offered me a hand, but I ignored it. I pulled myself up to my knees. That was as far as I could get.

"Look at these markings, these scars, all healed," I said, pointing.

"What about them?"

"Talze said the girl was magic right?"

"I believe so."

"So you think she healed the boar? Maybe she teamed up with the Satyrs, too."

Eldrad was starting to chuckle. Every time he did I was tempted to hit him in the gut but it wouldn't do any good. He probably would have laughed more. "I haven't killed a Satyr in what a few weeks, this could be interesting."

Unlike most of the soldiers and scouts in the village, I was always running into the woods to test my skills. Talze liked to call it my wild hunt, the animal inside of me that had to be cured once every full moon. Like the others in the courts, he thought of me as an animal, an outcast born in the wild to a slave. I had inherited the sword only because there was no one capable of putting me down. All of that was what made me strong.

My first day in the village. Chass walked out with Arianna by his side and sword in hand. I had to yell at him to put his gear on. His father might have been forcing him to train but it was my job to make sure that we had results all the same. After half an hour of warm-ups, the two of us backed up to our sides of the court. I can remember the stare in his eyes. It was like everything about him changed. From prey to predator and in an instant I was on the defensive.

Chass was always abrasive. Quick to attack. Like most, he believed in striking first. Before I could even think of striking he whipped around like a Satyr, swinging his blade through the air over my head one moment and back down at my neck a second later. All the while Arianna was cheering for him behind us.

I knew he was fast but I was faster. I dodged his next attack, slamming my fist into his stomach and bringing my weapon down with as much force as I could, banging the hilt against his back. Our third match was just as rough. I rolled to the side to defend against his attack, rearing back to find my footing. I found my opening. Pushing my front leg forward and outstretching my arms.

And there it was. Chass ducked and kicked and before I could stop myself I was on the ground.

It was the first and last time I had let my guard down and embarrassed myself.

"Maggot," I called him.

"Strike first with steady hands," he answered. I wanted to kill him there on the spot but that wasn't what I was there for. The King himself had sent orders for me to station myself at the village to watch over Talze, his family, and the mine. It was all profits, politics. I didn't really care. As long as I had my sword in my hand I was immortal, and yet somehow this kid had beaten me. Each and every match after, no matter how I won, it was never enough, none of it would be. The animal inside me demanded vengeance.

"Argentis? Argentis? Are you okay?" asked Eldrad. I had forgotten myself for a moment.

"Fine, what is it?"

"That sound, do you hear it?"

I listened closely. In the night air in the far distance drums could be heard along with a low roar. Close by there was the sound of Satyr singing.

"Let's move."

·14·
ARIANNA

"And that's when I said, 'Look, Arianna, I've already stretched the truth for you once today, I can't lie to my father about the cat, too!'" Chass said. He was surrounded by young, female Fauns. Chrysalis was hanging on his arm. All of the girls were giggling as he told stories from our childhood. All I could do was roll my eyes and shake my head. At least one of us had to focus on the mission.

The entire village sat at torch-lit tables in an open area. The scraps of the night before had been all that was left to eat. The last few crumb-covered plates were still strewn around us.

I sat with Egris and several others in front of a large map. The map was old, ancient almost, but still, many of the landmarks were the same as they were now. "So we're just guessing that the relic is here because the mountains make a lot of noise?" I asked, staring dumbfounded at Egris.

"Your father believed the rumbling in the mountains was the Spirit of Thunder trapped inside the relic. We have spent years helping him track the source of the sounds, and they all seem to originate in this area." I sighed. It wasn't much, but if this was all we had to go on then it was all we had to go on.

"If my father believed it, that's good enough for me. So what's the plan?"

Egris pointed to a spot on the map.

"There is a Faun village here, at the base of the mountains. It does not put us very close to the relic, but we will be much better off going in restocked and well-rested." Egris gave a small smile.

"Very well. When can we leave?"

"As soon as Chass is finished regaling the maidens with tales of his epic deeds." Egris nodded toward Chass who was acting out some sword battle he had had with Argentis. I almost laughed, but seeing all the girls gasp I decided it was best not to steal his spotlight. I had no idea what waited for us ahead and seeing him and the others all smiling and laughing was a nice sight to behold.

Chass fell silent as Brau-Na stepped into the light around the table. I was continuing to study the map with Egris, drawing over it with charcoal the direction we would take and planning out just how long we would have to rest. It would take us several days to reach the Faun village and a few more to reach the inside of the mountains where the relic was believed to have been hidden.

"Come. It is time," said Brau-Na.

Chass and I followed him to the edge of the forest where a dozen more Fauns waited for us with lit torches and rough, leather armor. I raised my hands as several of them helped me assemble the leather armor around myself. It was tougher than most of the hides back in the village. I hadn't seen a material like it since years ago when my father had gone and sold his. Made from the backs of Snags, the armor was more durable and would adhere to our bodies after we broke it in after a few miles.

Emery came up to me.

"I'm sorry girl, it's going to be too dangerous. This is something I have to do alone," I was nearly in tears. I wanted her to come but I couldn't risk anyone else. Emery sank her nose into my chest. Her eyes looked like they were glowing before she lifted her head back up and licked my face.

"No matter how far," Chrysalis said, placing her hand on mine as I gripped Emery's fur, "If you call to her she will know, she will journey to the ends of the world to find you. You are her kin, her family, just as I, just as many of us here. She is a guardian of the wood and never far behind."

Chrysalis stepped over to Chass and tightened his breastplate into place.

"Will I ever see you again?" she asked.

"I will return after we have found the relics and broken the curse," Chass said, taking her hand.

Brau-Na walked over towards them. He had been listening to their conversation closely.

"Come, Chrysalis, we must let them go. If they succeed in their journey, we Fauns will be able to return to our solitude, and never interact with the elves again." Brau-Na was stern, placing his hand on Chrysalis' shoulder. She looked back at Chass, tears in her eyes. Brau-Na continued with a slight smile, "Though, friends of the Faun will always be welcome guests in our village."

Chrysalis rushed back to Chass, embracing him in her arms. They separated and she stepped to the side with Brau-Na and the others. Armed and ready to venture forward, Chass, Egris, and I began our march into the forest.

Chass paused and looked back, "Chrysalis," he whispered

under his breath, just loud enough I could hear the sadness in his voice.

We spend our whole lives looking for people who we call a part of our tribe. Sometimes they are totally different from what we imagine. For my father it was finding my mother, for Chass it was finding the Faun village.

Maybe in another life I could have had a tribe of my own. A place I could call home. But I knew that was not what my future held. Any hope I had of having a family had been taken away from me on the day I was born. The day my mother died and my father started on a journey that would keep him away from me more often than we were together. His home was never the village. He belonged on the road. And now that fate had been passed along to me.

I couldn't afford to build attachments. I knew it would only lead to heartbreak. I knew how my journey would end. I just hoped that after everything was done, Chass and Chrysalis would find a way to be truly happy.

"Follow the light," said Egris. He was holding a lantern filled with fireflies while Chass and I walked close behind him in the dark. Several dozen of the fireflies were set free to guide our path. The Faun, with an affinity for nature, had trained them so that you could follow their path in the dark without getting lost. Still, it wasn't something Egris needed. Fauns could see far better than elves and that was all there was to it. If we got lost or separated the fireflies would be our only guides.

Along our path, we saw many strange creatures. A giant toad jumped in front of our path attracted by the sight of the light. Egris let out a strange howl and it jumped away just as quick as it came. By the time the first morning light came, we had already moved ten miles away from the Faun village and it hit me just how far from home I was.

"Do you miss the village?" I asked Chass as we set up our tents.

"I don't," Chass said.

"What about your father?"

"My father disowned me the moment I left, I'm sure of it. All he ever wanted was for me to follow in his footsteps. Every time I tried to do something for myself he frowned. Every time I went to visit you he shook his head. I don't miss it at all, living in his shadow. If I wasn't his blood he would have had me working in the mines day and night.

"I used to sneak in. I worked as hard as everyone else and when he found out he sent Argentis after me. I had never seen him so mad, swearing up and down, ashamed someone of his blood worked in such filth. I had never been so mad at him. I managed to sneak in a few more times. I'm sure he knew. I used to sneak food to some of them as well."

"I had no idea."

"The only thing I hate about being gone is now there is no one left to help them. I snuck out rations and water every week. If we can't end this curse I'm not sure how long some of the elders are going to last."

"We have to make it to the mountain," I said, sitting down and picking some figs from a satchel the Fauns had given me. We had enough rations to make it to the Faun village by the mountain but that was it. We couldn't afford to take a ton of supplies, the more weight the slower we were and we had to be quick. It felt like time was against us, if we didn't succeed soon something terrible would happen. I had felt that way since my father died.

"What about you? Do you miss the village?" Chass asked, half-joking. I'm sure he assumed I didn't. I wasn't very close to many people there.

"I miss Maria, I hope that she is doing alright."

"She's probably doing great, after all, she's not having to keep watch over you. I bet she's keeping all those stolen rations to herself now." Chass started to smile again. I know he was trying his best to cheer me up. Despite being the Mayor's son Chass was always looking to make others happy.

Egris approached us, "I will keep watch."

"We should take turns," I said.

"It's daylight, what do we have to worry about?" Chass asked.

"Not creatures, but elves," Egris said.

"Do you really think they will hurt us?"

"Without a doubt. You are traveling with a Faun, they will not see you as one of them." Egris jumped up into a tree. Blending in through the brown and yellow leaves almost invisible to us even from right below. "We will leave before the sun goes down. Sleep well saviors."

Inside the satchel the Fauns had prepared for me I found more of the red compound. I mixed it with some water boiled over a small fire and drank it. It was strange magic. I felt it cover me like a blanket. This time it wasn't all haze and colors as I felt myself drift away.

I saw eyes as black as night staring at me from every direction, like I was trapped in some kind of funnel. The eyes blinked and stared at me from above and below, following my every move. I was holding a greatsword and felt like a giant walking over the land.

When I looked down at my feet I could see the mountain AND the relic. I bent down to lift it up, holding the thunder relic in my hands. I felt it against my palm, vibrating, purring like a kitten against my skin. A moment later it disappeared and Chass stood before me dressed in black armor. Behind him stood Argentis and Eldrad wearing similar garb. Their armor was covered in old Casar runes. They began running towards me as I screamed, turning and running away. I found my path blocked by a large wall. As hard as I tried I couldn't escape. The three were coming to kill me, to steal away the relics.

·15·
EGRIS

Before the curse, before the woods became brown and yellow and when the trees turned bright green and the water flowed freely through rivers and streams, when the wilds were wild and full of life and the air was clean, I traveled among the valleys, the plains, the mountains, the sky. I was one of many that lived in the world, following the path laid out before me by the spirits of the earth, the spirits of the stars. From the southern wilds to the Northern Mountains where I found flowers that sparked visions, that brought me closer to the spirits than I had ever been before.

It all felt like a lifetime ago. There were so many of us at that time, living as one with nature. Guardians of the Great Mother, seekers of peace and tranquility. We maintained the balance of life, and ushered beings into death when their time came. That was before the curse. Before the spirits abandoned us.

"Egris! Quickly, we don't have much time!" Carine shouted out to me. He had just saved my life and now I and many other Fauns owed him a debt. He pulled me to my feet.

We were being chased by a giant. It had been ten years since the curse. Ten years since my people had been hunted and blamed by the elves. In that time we had learned to run, to hide, to be afraid. That all changed the day Carine arrived. He had inspired us, brought us hope. He was energizing, mesmerizing in his single-minded determination to break the curse, and the lengths to which he was willing to go in the name of his mission. He was terrifying.

"The curse has taken more than the land," he said wheezing. We had just barely made it out of the giant's grasp. Together the two of us had gone with a party of five. Three of us survived. Stealing food from the giant horde to feed my village. Giants were a rare sight. This one stood nine feet tall with two heads and a club. It walked nearly naked with skins of wolves and a club made from the dead stump of a tree. The giant itself was rotting. Instead of skin, it was bark, falling apart in decay.

For the moment, I felt I couldn't breathe. Fear. Anxiety. Relief, only as the giant gave up the search. We had stamina.

"Are you alright?" Carine asked.

"Fine, thank you," I said, looking at my other Faun companion, Miev.

"Miev?" Carine asked. Miev was younger than the two of us and this was her first journey outside the village. We were searching for truths. As always. That was our way in life now. Searching for answers to questions we never thought we would have to ask.

"Fine," Miev said.

"Good, we need to get moving," I said. "It will not take the giant long to catch its breath, and we need to be gone when it remembers what it was doing out here."

"I agree. We managed to get food for the village," Carine said.

He was carrying a large bag full of meats and rice.

"Food but still not relics," Miev said.

"It doesn't matter, we haven't searched everywhere. I've heard rumors of a buried artifact near the edge of the Meer," said Carine.

"The Meer is on our way back to the village," I said. I was almost smiling. Carine was always planning. Always one step ahead of the rest of us. He had known the giant had food and promised to help us gather it, should we accompany him in search of answers, his journey to find the relics that held the spirits of the storm. Trapped and imprisoned by some means known only to legend. Half-truths. He knew the giant had no answers, but knew once we had succeeded in our one mission the dominoes would fall to another. We Fauns could commune with the creatures of the Meer and he couldn't.

"Carine, dare I ask. Did you plan this?" Miev asked.

"Not exactly, just luck," he answered, always so modest. Elves. Devious creatures.

"The Meer does not welcome elves," I said.

"That is why I'm counting on the two of you to protect me."

"Very well, we will search for your artifact."

Three hours later we found ourselves treading through swampy waters. We had entered the Meer. Less than half a day from the village, it was a place few Faun went anymore. The water which had once been full of life had turned into a toxic sludge, only the strongest had managed to survive in the dredge. For a long time, we had thought of trying to reclaim the area but found it impossible without the rains of the sky above. The ground was saturated with poison, the rotting dead of all the forest eventually came to rest in this place. For Fauns it was sacred. For elves and other races, it was a graveyard of decay.

"Try not to inhale too deep," I said handing Carine a rag to place over his mouth. I wet it with my own saliva.

"You want me to put that on my face?" he asked.

"Our spit is cleaner than the water you drink, it will help purify and cover the smell," I said calmly and slightly offended.

"Thanks." Carine wrapped it around his face. Following behind me with Miev in the back he had his sword drawn, ready for anything. Carine instructed me that once we reached the Meer we were to head towards an old shrine. A shrine the Faun believed to have been built by goblins. Goblins of course were small creatures that came from the moon. Not good, not truly evil, they were always trouble and lived in large numbers. I knew of the place Carine had believed the artifact to be and as we approached I froze.

Two giant Faun statues rose from above the muck. They were waist-deep, buried like the rest of the shrine in the toxic swamp just as everything in the Meer had always been.

"Stay alert," I said, noticing something in the water.

"What is it?" Miev asked, moving closer.

"Alligator?" Carine asked.

"No, something much worse. A Maw."

A Maw was a type of large snapping turtle the size of a wagon. It had several dozen rows of large teeth and a tail twice the size of a man. It was a violent, deadly creature that even giants struggled to hunt.

"We should leave," said Miev.

"I can't turn back, not without answers," said Carine.

"The path ahead is too dangerous," I argued.

"Every path leads to the same place. Eventually." And with

that Carine stepped forward, sword drawn as he moved towards the statues. I wondered how a man with so much to lose could risk himself so easily.

The Maw attacked. Rising above the water, jaws open as Carine took out a small bag of magic powder and threw it in the air. The powder ignited and sparks flew up around the Maw as it turned the air to fire.

"What magic?" Miev gasped.

"Not magic, Casar fire," I answered. I had seen it used before. Shot into the sky from heavy metal stumps, it was rare. Even rarer to see it found in our part of the world. A hatred for what I saw boiled below my skin. This wasn't right. "STOP!" I shouted.

Both Carine and the Maw turned towards me. I began to speak in the turtle's tongue but found my words fell on deaf ears. The Maw for years had found itself driven by one thing: survival, hunger. Having lost its use for words it digressed into a monster.

I lifted my gaze just as it ended. The Maw floating upside down, Carine moving forward. Diving below the surface of the muck. A few minutes later he emerged from the depths holding a compass.

"The artifact?" I asked.

"Yes," he said, his face turned down. Tears running down his eyes.

"Does it help?"

"No," he said, his voice full of sadness as he walked over towards the Maw. Several eggs floated to the surface. Miev moved to pick them up.

"Leave them," Carine said.

"They will die without someone to raise them," I said. More tears fell down from his eyes and I felt it erase everything I was.

Everything I'd fought my whole life to become. In that moment I was like the rest of the world; hungry, alone, fighting for the survival of my people.

"Come, we have to get back to the village before dark. We will be able to plan another journey once we have filled our stomachs," I said, keeping my voice light as possible. Miev had already collected the eggs.

The next day Carine journeyed back to his village and to that daughter of his which he couldn't stop talking about. He left the compass with us to trade to the Casar for more food. It was worthless in our land but an artifact that would be of great value to their kingdom should we decide to make the journey. Eventually, we did. It gave us enough food for six months.

Carine became a hero to us. Saving countless lives with his sacrifice and yet no matter how many times we journeyed together, he always carried with him the guilt of what had happened. Perhaps the Maw reminded him of who he was, what he had become since the curse. The truths we sought were not always found written in caves or scrolls, nor found hidden in relics.

·16·
ARIANNA

I could just make out the shapes of the two moons behind the clouds as we continued our trek the following night. My body dripped with sweat as we walked the forest path, fireflies lighting our way.

We reached a tall rock that rose high off the ground near a clearing.

"What is that?" Chass asked.

"It is the cave of the shadow spirit, a shrine once existed here before the curse but it has been a long time since my people have made the journey," Egris answered. "We should stop and rest."

As we sat down by the rocks and began to eat Egris kept looking at me with sorrow in his eyes.

"So… your father never talked about us at all?" he asked.

"I never even knew he was working with Fauns," I answered.

"It's just strange. Spending so much time with a person, only to find out his family doesn't even know you exist."

"You have to remember we elves don't think too highly of you guys," Chass reminded him. "We even call you 'Satyrs'. Sounds much more intimidating."

"It's all lies. No Faun looks like those monstrosities in your paintings," Egris said angrily. It was true. The Fauns weren't that much different than elves. Many, like Chrysalis or Isoka, could probably even blend in with many of the elven communities without too much trouble. Egris, on the other hand, had grown his horns out and would have issues. The same could be said for Brau-Na, whose face had more beastly features than most. There were many differences between our two kinds but we were also more the same. Both elves and Fauns were capable of good and evil.

"There must be some truth to it," I said. "Otherwise, where did the stories come from? Just because your village is peaceful doesn't mean they all are."

"You would be surprised how far a little deception can spread," Egris said with disgust in his voice. Both Chass and I could tell my words had hurt him deeply.

"But what's the point?" Chass asked. "What's the purpose of lying to us about this? And who's doing the deceiving, anyway? Everyone's parents tell them stories of disobedient children being eaten by Satyrs in the woods. Surely they're not all in on it?" I stepped away from the group. This conversation was making me very uncomfortable.

I could see a break in the trees a few feet away, so I moved towards it, curious.

"Making your children obey by telling them scary bedtime stories, keeping your citizens in line by giving them a common enemy. It's all about power and control," Egris argued.

"But why do we have to be en…"

I passed out of earshot before Chass finished his sentence. I didn't care to know what they were saying, anyway. I emerged from the tree-line into what could only be described as a barren waste-land. What once, years ago, must have been a fertile farmland, was now nothing but death and decay as far as the eye could see. In the distance I could make out a small village settled right in the center of the tundra. There was a great pillar of black smoke rising from the buildings.

The village was on fire!

Chass, Egris, and I ran across the open plain as fast we could, barely stopping to take a breath. "We have to evacuate the survivors!" I yelled.

When we finally reached the village, we weren't prepared for what greeted us. The dusty streets were totally abandoned. The dilapidated houses showed no signs of life. When we got closer we realized the buildings on the edge of the village were burnt out husks, already destroyed by fire. The odd thing was, the flames that burned now were on the complete opposite side of town.

Egris knocked a half-gone door off its hinges and a cloud of black dust kicked up around it. "This ash is cold," he said. "These buildings burned down years ago."

"Maybe this village is just really prone to fires?" Chass said, questioning.

Over the roar of the nearby flames, I heard a voice shouting, "Now bring us some more food before we burn the whole village down!"

"Argentis," I said to the others, seething. I would recognize the malice in that voice anywhere. "This way."

As we neared the source of the flames I could hear what I assumed was a village elder pleading, "We have given you all that we can spare! We barely have enough for ourselves. I beg of you! Leave us in peace!"

We came around one final corner and saw Argentis and Eldrad standing over a small crowd of fifteen or twenty villagers. They must have been all that was left of a once-thriving community. The blazing building was a great hall at the center of the village. I imagined in the days before the curse it had been the pride of people; home to great feasts, weddings for young lovers, funerals for respected elders.

When the roof suddenly caved in I could hear the cries of the people as they watched helplessly. I couldn't begin to imagine their pain, seeing all of that history burn to the ground.

As I continued to scan the scene I realized their cries were about more than just lost memories. Eldrad stood in front of the building next to the burning hall. A large beam was blocking the door.

There were people trapped inside!

"Stop this!" I yelled. "Can't you see these people are suffering?"

Argentis turned to me with a disgusting grin. "Well if it isn't our little friend. And here I was thinking I was going to have to track you to the ends of the earth."

"You can take me back to Manse Village! You can do whatever you want, just leave these people alone!"

"I don't think you're in much of a position to bargain, little lady," he said, raising his sword and stepping toward the village elder who was on his knees begging.

A glint of something caught my eye, and I looked toward the far corner of the barricaded building. There I saw a girl, no older than myself, peering around the edge. She held two curved daggers in her hands, backward so that the blades ran down the length of her forearms. She saw me watching her, and put a finger up to her lips. I tried to hide my reaction, but Argentis must have seen something in my face anyway.

He turned toward the girl, but she vanished from sight in an instant. She was good.

"Planning a little surprise attack, are we?" Argentis asked. He turned toward Eldrad and nodded in the direction of the spot where the girl had been. Eldrad left his post to check it out, and Argentis continued his menacing march toward the pleading elder.

I squared off toward Argentis and closed my eyes. I focused the spark inside of me and let lightning arc across my body.

You can do this. Feel the power. Use it.

"I hope you know what you're doing," I could hear Chass mumble behind me.

I opened my eyes and yelled. A bolt of lightning shot out from my hand toward Argentis. It missed.

It shot inches in front of him as he stumbled backward, but it didn't stop there. The blast continued on and struck a support pillar in front of the barricaded building. The pillar cracked under the force of the explosion and a portion of the roof caved in. I could hear the deafening screams of the villagers who watched in horror as the pillar erupted into flames which spread quickly to the roof of the building.

I gasped and clasped my hands over my mouth. What had I done? "*What did you make me do?*" I asked the voice in my head that had provoked me to action.

The voice didn't respond. It never stuck around to face the consequences of its outbursts.

"Stop Arianna!" Egris yelled as he ran past me toward the burning building. "You're only making it worse!" Just as he got to the front of the building a flaming beam fell from the roof and blocked his path.

A glint once again caught the corner of my eye, this time from the far back corner of the building. I looked and saw the girl ushering several villagers into the cover of nearby buildings. They had escaped! She must have found a way to pull them out of the back of the building. Once they had all gotten to safety the girl turned and shot me a look that even from this distance I could tell was sharper than the blades she was carrying. I knew I deserved it. She had had a plan, and I had not only ruined it, but very nearly gotten a lot of her friends killed.

"You really are making this too easy," Argentis said, once again approaching the defenseless villagers with his sword poised to strike. I could see Eldrad standing back, chuckling.

I should have known better. All my life I had tried to suppress my powers, and anytime they got the better of me something bad happened. I should have known this wouldn't be any different. I had tried to save the day, and instead had become a laughing stock.

Chass and Egris both stepped between Argentis and the villagers, their swords drawn. I wanted to help, but what more could I do? My father had taught me how to defend myself, sure, but I was no match for someone like Argentis or Eldrad. And I certainly couldn't risk using my powers again.

Argentis, Chass, and Egris seemed to be at a standoff. "Do you need a hand there, brother?" Eldrad called out.

"Not a chance," Argentis replied, "I can handle these maggots on my own."

Chass and Egris both raised their swords to attack but stopped suddenly when the young girl jumped out from behind the burning building and ran, screaming, full-sprint toward Argentis. Argentis turned toward her, his sword dropping slightly. He must have been as confused as the rest of us.

While she was still several feet away she leapt into the air and did a full front flip, coming out parallel to the ground just as her foot slammed square into Argentis' jaw. His head snapped in the other direction and he stumbled back several steps as the girl fluidly landed and rolled out of her flip, twisting somehow so that she came up to her feet facing Argentis.

"What the!?" Argentis yelled. He adjusted his helmet, which had been knocked crooked and was blocking his vision. He barely had time to recover as the girl charged at him, yelling, "Leave us alone!" Her voice was slightly deeper than I had expected from someone so small, and it had a rough, almost smoky quality to it.

She slashed at him with her backward daggers, then spun and slashed again. Argentis was barely getting his sword into position to parry attack after attack as he retreated under the ferocity of her advance. He finally managed to regain his footing and was able to knock her blades to the sides, giving himself an opening to kick her solidly in the chest. I had seen him pull that move on Chass many times, and it always put Chass flat on his back.

The kick knocked the girl back several feet, but she quickly regained her stance and brought her swords into a defensive position. If I looked anything like Chass and Egris, whose jaws were hanging in astonishment, I must have looked like an idiot.

Argentis swiped at the girl's head, but she deftly ducked and rolled between his legs. She came up into a crouch and spun back toward him, taking a swipe at the back of his knee. Her aim must have been impeccable. Argentis howled in pain and fell onto his left knee. If there was a gap in the back of his armor, it couldn't have been more than a few millimeters thick, but the girl had somehow managed to find it.

A moment later, and I could see the blood trickling out onto his scuffed, dented armor. The man had clearly been taking a beating over the last several days.

The girl was standing over him, ready to strike. Her shoulders were moving up and down in a rhythmic pattern as she took slow, controlled breaths. I was exhausted just from watching her.

Argentis was staying down. This fight was over.

Eldrad walked toward the group. Chass and Egris brought their swords back up to the ready. Eldrad sheathed his own sword, ignoring the others as he stepped up to Argentis' side. "I think it's time we were leaving," he said.

He grabbed Argentis' arm, but Argentis shrugged him off. Argentis pulled himself to his feet and limped along for several steps before his knee gave out and he stumbled again. He braced himself against his sword to keep from falling. He regained his composure and continued on, leaning on his sword like a crutch.

Eldrad was following slowly behind him. He stopped as he passed me and whispered under his breath, "This isn't over."

A few moments later and they passed around a corner out of sight. I looked back to the pair of burning buildings, and I knew we weren't safe yet. A section of wall collapsed outward, and the flames gushed out in every direction, catching several nearby buildings on fire. This place was so dried out from years of drought it was like pure kindling.

"We have to get everyone out of the village!" I yelled.

A few hours later we had settled safely away from the village. We would all be sleeping under the stars that night. Those that were able to sleep. All of the villagers stood with their eyes glued to the towering fire in the distance. Even this far away we could still hear the roar of the flames as they consumed what few possessions these people had left.

I noticed the girl from the village sitting by herself several feet away from the group. Her knives were sheathed in an 'X' across her back. I walked over and sat down next to her.

"That was pretty amazing, what you did back there," I said.

"Anyone can learn to fight," she shrugged. "Not everyone is born an elemental."

I turned to look at her. She turned and met my gaze. "That's rare magic," she said.

I averted my eyes and picked at the sparse grass. It had felt like she was peering into my soul.

"I wish I didn't have it," I replied. "It's only ever done more harm than good." That wasn't the only reason I didn't want it. The truth was there were a lot of reasons I wished I didn't have this power.

It was true that throughout history there had been a handful of mages born with such an innate connection to nature that they had the ability to manipulate the elements. But I knew that wasn't the source of my power. My power came from the Lightning Spirit itself. It was the reason my father had been absent my entire life. It was the reason he had died. And it was the reason I was going to die, too.

"Don't be too hard on yourself," the girl was saying. "That fire would have spread eventually anyway. This became inevitable the moment those thugs entered our village."

"I'm afraid that's my fault, too," I said. "They were looking for me." I could feel her gaze piercing the side of my head.

"You must be very important," she said. "Did you run away from the Royal Academy or something?"

"No, nothing like that," I said. I brought my eyes back up to meet hers. "I found a way to end the drought." I held her gaze. I needed her to know I was serious. I needed her to trust me.

After an intense silence, she finally said, "I'm Scyenna, by the way."

"Arianna."

She went back to watching the fire and neither of us spoke for several minutes. There was so much I still wanted to know about this girl, I just didn't know how to ask. Eventually, I gathered the courage to say, "Anyone can learn to fight, but not everyone does. So why did you?"

"When I was a child," she said after a pause, "my father left the village to find out why we had stopped receiving rations. Others said that if the Kingdom wasn't going to help us willingly, then we would take what we needed by force. But my father always believed we could find a peaceful solution.

"Before he left my mother gave him a locket that had pictures of me and her that the village historian had drawn for us. The day our village burned down the first time, a group of travelers saw the flames and came to help evacuate us. I remember standing in the street screaming as people were running all around me. I couldn't find my mother, I couldn't find anyone. Then one of the travelers picked me up and carried me out of the village."

She paused for a moment and swallowed hard.

"When he found my mother… he must have recognized us from the pictures, because he pulled out my father's locket and handed it back to me."

"How did he get it?" I asked before I could stop myself.

"All he said was that my father had been a brave man. That he had died with honor." Her face had become strained, her voice constricted. "All he ever wanted was peace, and they killed him for it. He just wanted to provide for his family and they made him fight for it.

"That was the day I learned that if I was going to survive I would have to learn to take care of myself. If I wanted anything I would have to take it." I could see her knuckles turning white as she pulled her knees into her chest.

"Where is your mother?" I asked.

"Heartbreak, is what the village elders told me. But I think I know what that really means."

"I'm so sorry," I said. It was all I could say.

"What about your parents?" She asked. "They okay with you being chased around the kingdom by a couple of rogue knights?"

"My mother died giving birth to me. My father was killed just a few weeks ago."

"So we both know how wonderful this world can be," she replied.

"That's why I have to finish my father's mission. Why I have to break the curse. We have to build a better world for those who come after us. It's what my father fought for. Both our fathers."

"Is that why they killed him? Because he was trying to end the curse?"

"No, that would actually make sense. He was mauled by satyrs on his way home from a trip. Nothing but senseless violence."

Scyenna looked over to Egris, who was using herbs from his pack to treat minor burn wounds on several villagers. "And yet you travel with a satyr."

I followed her gaze. "They aren't like we were taught, the Fauns. At least not all of them. They believe in living in unity with nature. They only rob elves because they have to to survive, no different than the rest of us."

"If I knew it was a satyr that murdered my dad," she said, "I would kill every single one I could get my hands on."

The malice in her voice caught me off guard, but honestly I understood what she was feeling. It was normal to feel anger at the injustices we had both suffered. Healthy, even. I felt like I had made peace with my anger. I had to focus on the mission, not on seeking vengeance. But still, there was that nagging feeling in the pit of my stomach. That voice in my head that would be happy to join Scyenna on a quest for vengeance.

I wanted to believe that it wasn't a Faun who had killed my father, or at least that it had been an accident. But I knew it wasn't true. His death was no accident. The cuts on his body were too precise, the runes carved into his skin too deliberate.

We sat in silence for several more moments. Meanwhile Chass meandered over and sat down next to me.

"So what happens next?" Scyenna eventually asked.

"Egris says we're close to the next Faun village," Chass replied. "He says they might be willing to take the elves in as refugees."

Scyenna huffed. "Elves living at the mercy of satyrs, that'll be the day." After that, she stood up and walked away.

Chass watched her go. "What's her problem?

By the next morning the flames had subsided to smoldering embers, and we watched as the villagers picked through the rubble, salvaging what they could of the lives they had lost. We had spoken with the village elders and convinced them to come with us to the Faun village. Egris told us all that this village had been built as a home for refugees.

"They call themselves the Lost Tribe," he had said. "They all lost their homes, so they built a new one, together." In fact, he told me later, it was my father who helped them find a place to settle, and he had a hand in building the village as well.

The villagers were hesitant at first, but it was Egris' kindness that persuaded them to trust him. Scyenna made sure to let everyone know she wasn't happy about it, but honestly I didn't think she would be happy about anything. The curse had taken more from her than most.

I tried to imagine what she would have been like under different circumstances. If her parents had never been taken away from her. She was clearly very headstrong and determined, but what if she had been able to direct those energies to something other than fighting? She could have been an artist, a blacksmith, whatever she had wanted. Whatever she had dreamed about being as a child.

She represented both the best the world had to offer, and the worst the curse had destroyed. I hoped that once the drought had finally ended, she would be able to lay her daggers down and find a new life for herself. A life of peace. That thought gave me the strength to continue on my mission.

My father loved to tell me of the amazing things our people had accomplished in the days of prosperity before the curse. Before the days of poverty and desperation. I knew those days could be restored, the days where everyone was free to pursue their passions without worrying about where their next meal would come from. That would be my legacy. It's how I knew I would find the courage to make the inevitable sacrifice at the end of my journey.

As Chass, Egris, and I ambled through the desolate streets we could feel the somber atmosphere of the village bearing down on us like a heavy blanket. The people were in mourning. Weeping for the home and the history which would now only be remembered in stories.

I could see Scyenna sifting through the rubble of what must have once been her home. She pulled a small jewelry box from the ashes and dusted it off. From the box she pulled a small locket on a silver chain; her father's locket. As she placed the locket around her neck, her face was blank, unreadable. Her posture was stiff, betraying no emotion, but even from this distance I could see a single tear gently rolling down her cheek.

Somewhere in the ruins, a violin began to play. Long, slow, melancholy notes filled the air. I looked around for the source of the music, and saw several other elves pulling instruments from the wreckage of their homes. They must have been their most prized possessions. Many were damaged beyond repair, but some had survived the carnage.

From another part of the village a flute joined in the song. As I closed my eyes and listened, several other instruments chimed in, creating a hauntingly beautiful melody that cut straight to the deepest parts of my soul. The music came from every direction;

an entire village giving a final goodbye before leaving their home forever.

In times past this village must have been home to the most beautiful music ever played. Pilgrims must have ventured from all over the world just to hear the gentle melodies that echoed off the walls of the great hall which was now no more than a pile of ash.

A female voice rang out in the crisp morning air. It echoed through the streets, mingling together with the sounds of the instruments to weave a tapestry of pure, raw emotion. The voice sang in an ancient elvish tongue I couldn't understand, but I could feel the sadness in the words just the same.

Music had never been very important in Manse Village growing up. Sure, you would hear the occasional drinking song come from the taverns at night, and there were a few bards who told stories through song, but I had never heard anything like this before. As the voice grew nearer I opened my eyes to see where it was coming from. I almost couldn't believe what I saw. It was Scyenna! She continued to move toward me, singing, and the rest of the town gathered around as well. They carried the last of their worldly possessions with them.

The song came to an end and Scyenna let out a long, heavy sigh.

"It's time," she said. "Let's go."

Thirty-seven is not a large number when talking about the entire population of a village, but it is a large number to make a multi-day trek through dense forests with barely any provisions. Even as the sun hung high in the sky on the afternoon of the second day, we still had not reached the edge of the forest. The mountains loomed on the horizon; a daunting reminder of how far we still had to travel. Our food was nearly depleted, and our water was running dangerously low, as well. It didn't help that all we could see in any direction was barren desert.

As we marched into the evening we came to the edge of a massive canyon. According to some of the village elders, there was once a bridge over the canyon, though whether it still stood no one could be sure. Either way, it would be several hours of walking along the edge of the canyon before we reached it.

I heard a deep rumbling coming from the bottom of the canyon, and I peered over the edge just in time to see a stampede of antelope charging around a corner. Egris and several of the elves immediately pulled out bows and arrows, and I suddenly realized how hungry I was. Just the thought of meat roasting over a fire made my mouth water.

As the archers took aim we suddenly saw what had caused the stampede: Praeg. The horse-sized reptiles charged after the antelope on two legs, snapping at them with their alligator-like jaws. One managed to catch an antelope's hind leg, and several other praeg pounced on it, ripping it to shreds with the three clawed fingers on their stubby forearms.

I had never seen a praeg in person, but I recognized them from my father's journals. He told me once that the praeg's ancient ancestors had been as tall as buildings. He said there was a shrine in Vaeger with a completely reconstructed skeleton of one of the massive dinosaurs, and the Casar worshiped it as a god of war.

After the dust settled Chass, Egris, and a few others hiked down into the canyon to scavenge what meat had been left behind by the praeg. They managed to bring back enough for a satisfying meal for the whole caravan, but there wasn't a scrap left over.

By the time the morning light rose into the sky on the third day we were standing at the front of the Faun village, and we were totally famished. Two guards stood in front of large wooden gates. It wasn't anything like the village Egris had come from. The air was damp and cold as it came down from the mountains and I could see my breath. The temperature had dropped twenty degrees since we neared their camp.

The guards gazed down at me. They were taller than most Fauns I had met. Their bodies covered in wooden armor and scars from animals that had attacked their camp. They held giant spears with serrated edges.

I grasped Chass' hand as we approached. I wanted to scream, the spark in my body straining to be let free. With each second that passed, I could feel the situation intensify. In this moment I was a little girl again, helpless as I was the moment I wandered into the woods. I could feel the guard's anger. He moved to a power stance, holding his spear out even as Egris waved his hands. The other soldier was still for the moment before smiling and holding the other back.

"Relax, that's Egris," he said. The second guard was older. Wiser. His face more a beast than even Brau-Na.

"Thanks, Baga," said Egris.

"I see you have brought guests," Baga's smile became stern. We were clearly asking a lot of these Fauns to share what little they had with strangers, enemies even.

"Their home was burned to the ground," Egris said. "They have nowhere else to go. These two and I," he said, pointing at Chass and me, "are on a mission to retrieve the Thunder Relic from the mountains.

The first guard's face changed form, like a candle melting under a fire, from anger to a smile, "These two are saviors?" he said, laughter wrinkling his face.

"This is the daughter of Carine, show some respect!" Egris demanded.

"I'm sorry, I wasn't aware," said the guard, falling to his knees in front of me. I was completely taken aback, no one had ever done that before. I could hear a scoff somewhere behind me, and I was sure it came from Scyenna.

"You're not aware of much these days, are you?" asked Baga. "Come in, all of you. We will take your case before Miev, she will know what to do. And she will be very happy to meet the daughter of Carine."

As we walked inside I asked Egris who Miev was and he answered, "Thanks to your father, Miev is the leader of this village."

·17·
ARIANNA

We could hear the sound of thunder.

Constant…

… just like the cold that surrounded us the moment we left the forest.

As soon as we entered the village the refugees were escorted into a meeting hall at the center of the town and provided with blankets and a warm soup. I was surprised not only at the hospitality these Fauns showed, but how quickly they had pulled everything together. The great hall itself looked like a large boat that had been banded together and turned upside down. Nearly as massive as Mayor Talze's mansion, the entire village had a layout that felt similar to our own village.

After Chass, Egris, and I had made sure everyone was settling in comfortably, we left to find Miev. As we were being escorted to her private chamber, I heard a voice call out, "Egris?"

We turned to see another Faun walking toward us. "Egris! Greetings! I thank the spirits for bringing us together!"

"Arctis, cousin, greetings!" The two Fauns embraced as

long-separated relatives.

"Did you receive my message?" Arctis asked. "I sent it only two days ago."

"I'm afraid not," Egris replied. "I have been traveling for many days. What news do you have for me?"

"My brother, Ethyos, has been missing for three days. We believe the elves have taken him to their capital. I can't help but fear the worst."

"You think they killed him?" I asked, making myself a part of the conversation. Both Arctis and Egris looked toward me, their heads tilted downward.

"Death… is not the worst," Egris said.

"We are going to the capital to speak to the King," added Chass. "Maybe we will find him there and we can negotiate his release."

"You must promise, if you find him there, you will help him escape." Arctis' voice sounded far away. I could feel the intensity of the situation. I couldn't imagine the depths of hell I would go to if something happened to Chass.

"We promise," I said, exchanging a glance with Chass.

We continued on toward Miev's quarters and I tried to gather as much information about her as I could from Egris. She was young. Not too much older than Chass. Yet because of an adventure with my father she had earned the right to become leader of this village. Not an easy task. According to Egris, dozens of Fauns including Miev and Arctis were being hunted throughout the woods until my father came and helped them establish this settlement near the edge of the mountain. Many of the Fauns here had left Egris' village, while others had come from the North, hoping to find a new home in which they could all flourish.

Miev was one that had left Egris' village. Believing that the Faun would only survive if they found a new home. She knew my father from a mission they had gone on with Egris. She ran into him again when he was searching a temple ruin near the mountains for a scroll on the deep magic. One by one my father helped her gather the essential supplies and taught the Faun how to build the walls, forge weapons, and grow crops from the soil near the edge of the mountain. Even after all these years, there was still a steady stream being fed by melting snow from the mountains.

My father traded knowledge for more knowledge of magic and many of the scrolls that came to decorate our home.

Egris told me of many Faun villages hidden throughout the forests but this one was special. It was a home for Fauns that lost their home. Though it was safe from elven hunters, living near the mountains was a no easy life for a Faun; but it was important to them that they had found a place to call their own. Many considered it destiny. That they had come here to protect and watch over 'the path'.

"What is the path?" I asked.

"The path is a passage into the mountain that is said to lead to the ancient home of the spirits," Egris explained.

"The home of the spirits?"

"The ancient home of the spirits, not where they reside now but where they had come from, birthed from the seeds of the world, from the roots of the tree of life, the path is an ancient temple from before the ages," Egris explained.

"Can I see it?" I asked, curious.

"In many ways you already have. The scrolls your father collected, the artifacts and trinkets he traded. Many came from the path inside the mountain. It is a temple, a library, and a maze. Unfortunately, our journey takes us west. Perhaps one day, once this is over, we will venture into the path together," Egris said.

All throughout the village I had felt my father's presence. As if he was walking alongside me. He had a hand in building every part of this village and yet I had no idea. I wasn't sure whether to feel betrayed or happy that my father had been a hero to so many.

And yet they betrayed him.

I couldn't smile. Thinking of the cuts on his body, the cuts I healed. I should have looked closer. Maybe if I had memorized what they looked like I could match them to the claws of his killer. Egris and my father had been friends, Miev and my father had been friends. All of them saw my father as a hero, but what if they were all lying?

A truth that would be buried with the dead.

The tour of the village was short. We saw the entrance to the path, the meager but flourishing gardens, my father's fingerprints on every building. We walked towards the residence across from the stables and armory, from which Miev awaited our arrival.

A guard greeted us at the door. He told us Miev had requested to speak to me alone. I entered and saw the mysterious leader sitting in a meditative position on a pillow at the center of the room, surrounded by candles and incense. She looked older than I imagined, despite her age. Covered in red robes and a cloak with silver runes. The runes were elven.

There were two cups of kava on the floor, one in front of her and another in front of a pillow directly across from her. I sat and picked up the cup. She had yet to open her eyes. The silence was unnerving.

"Poison?" I said before taking a sip.

She laughed. She finally opened her eyes and looked at me with a gentle, understanding smile.

"In the beginning our world was sand. There were Maji who controlled the water, the fire. Enslaving the spirits. They commanded the sky and heavens above. It was one among them who betrayed the others, and fell upon the sand as a great storm. Winds that stirred, giving rise to the ground and stealing water from the sky that became the lakes. The Maji cried out only to be struck by the lightning and as they fell they became the mountains. The Maji that were left shed tears for them and sank to become the ocean, their bodies giving birth to life. The last two Maji, The Great Mother and Father, freed the spirits who guided life into this world until they fled and became the moons in the sky, watching over their creation in the dark of the night, guiding us when the light fades." Miev spoke in a quiet voice. It was a strange story, one I had heard my father tell me before…

"And every day the Maji disappear back into the great ocean to be with their lost family," I added.

"Yes, that is correct," Miev said. "Each one of us is born with the Great Mother's touch, some use their gifts for selfish deeds, others to create a better world. However, some of us are born with the divine energy of the Maji within ourselves. Able to harness the powers of the deep magic. They became the first kings and queens of our world, the leaders of Fauns, the leaders of elves, Firya, even Casar. The magic that flows through your blood now, dangerous to those in power. Those without the power of the Maji. They will fear you. They will hate you."

"Then they will hate me," I said.

The candles that lit the room flickered.

"Years ago the power of the Maji was used to place a curse on the world, only the gods know why or how, but it happened."

I knew the truth, it was in the deep magic, in my father's journals, in my hands every time I felt the lightning arc around me.

"We seek your help in finding the Thunder Relic," I said.

"I understand. Carine is a part of the deep magic now, and you seek to finish your father's mission."

"Yes. And I do."

"Your father was a great man that helped me build this village from the ground up. The refugees shall be welcomed in his name. He would have wanted our doors to be open to all who suffered at the hands of the curse. Those that wish to stay shall be treated as one of us.

"Your father chose this location knowing one day either he or you would make the journey up the mountain. I am honored to meet the daughter he spoke so much about. The 'path' was always an excuse, a large temple with artifacts and nothing more. We always knew the real answers lay above the mountain path. I will do everything I can to help you on your journey."

"Thank you."

·18·
ARIANNA

We stood at the base of an immense mountain range. I was wearing the warming tunic gifted me by the young girl in Egris' village. It seemed so long ago now.

Arctis and the others outfitted us with dark, heavy coats and climbing gear. Ropes, picks, and small gauntlets with claws on the tips we could dig into the side of the ice to climb our way up. Miev also had our weapons looked at and sharpened, infusing our swords with the same red compound we had been ingesting in our tea.

While the garments Chass was given seemed ill-fitted and patched together from Faun's clothing, mine were a perfect fit. My father really had prepared everything for my journey.

"I'm not sure about this," Chass said, staring up at a large slope and back down to the village below.

"The path lies over the mountain wall," I said. It was a short-cut. Rather than journey another three days to the west to hike up the side of the mountain we were climbing up the slopes, up and over to the path towards the sound of roaring thunder.

The three of us walked up a steep, icy slope. I had never been so cold in my life. I lost my footing and tumbled down the side of the slope. Chass dug his boots into the ice and grabbed my hand as I slid past him.

"Thanks," I said.

"You know if you die this is all for nothing," he said.

As we approached the edge of the cliff we tethered ourselves together with Egris in the lead.

"This is much too cold for a Faun," Egris complained.

"This is too cold for anyone," Chass added.

Hours later it felt as though we had hardly made any progress at all. We had traveled a good distance, all things considered, but our destination still felt impossibly far away.

I tripped again. This time my foot got stuck between two pieces of ice.

"Guys, we have a problem!" I said, pulling on the rope between us. Egris turned back towards me.

"What did you do?" Chass glanced down at my foot.

"My foot is stuck, a small fissure opened up," I answered.

"Looks like we're going to have to amputate," he said.

"Quiet," said Egris, alarmed, sword in hand.

"What is it?" I whispered.

"We are being hunted," Egris answered.

Chass drew his sword as I pulled out my dagger.

"Maybe I can melt the ice," I said, starting to power up.

"NO!" Egris grabbed hold of my arm. "You will melt more than just the ice surrounding your foot, if that happens we will have nothing to stand on."

He was right. I still didn't have control but I couldn't see any other way out. The shadow of something flew over our heads.

"What was that?" Chass asked.

"Ice wraith," Egris answered.

"What is that?"

"A creature of old, a guardian that became lost in the winter and now hunts the skies of the mountain for fresh souls."

"So, not going to give us a ride to the top," Chass said, sarcastic.

"No, Chass, prepare yourself for battle, we must defend Arianna until we can melt the ice around her foot ourselves."

This wasn't going to work. I couldn't risk both of them. I concentrated the energy in my hand. All I had to do was heat the ice a little and I could free myself.

"Stand back!" I demanded placing my hand against the ground. The shards of ice that surrounded my foot started to melt away.

"NOOOO!" Egris shouted.

The mountain began to crack.

Egris jumped forward pulling both of us along with him. At the same time, the ice wraith appeared. Like a wyvern made of ice, it flew down and grabbed the ground where I had been stranded. I nearly lost it but Chass jumped forward pulling both Egris and me along for the ride, sliding down the side of the mountain. Egris grabbed hold of an outcropping as Chass' sword hit the creature's wing.

"Nice swing!" I shouted.

"Pull!" Chass screamed as the Wraith began crawling along the snow towards us. Egris heaved himself onto the ledge, pulling us along through the powdered snow.

"Arianna! Use your power now!" he shouted.

I unleashed an arc of electricity on the ground behind me that caused the snow to turn to steam and ice to shatter. The Wraith found itself barrel rolling down the side of the mountain breaking apart like glass.

"That was close," Chass said.

"We still have a ways to go," Egris said, turning towards the sound of thunder. He drove a spike into the cliff every few feet, reaching up and checking our rope so that if one of us fell we could hang on together. The mountain slope became harder and harder to climb.

I looked up and saw Egris pull the spike out from the ice wall. He pulled himself up a few feet and started tapping the ice, trying to find a new place to drive the stake. I looked down and saw Chass pushing himself up onto a narrow ledge. Just then, the ledge crumbled underneath him and he began free-falling down the side of the mountain.

"Egris!" I yelled. Egris still hadn't driven the spike into the ice. The moment Chass ran out of slack he would pull us all off the side of the mountain! Egris pulled his arm back and drove the spike as hard as he could. An instant later Chass hit the end of the rope. I could see the spike strain against the sudden weight, but it held true.

I heard Chass' body slam against the cliff below me. I looked down to see him hanging, motionless.

"Chass! Are you alright?" I yelled.

After several agonizing moments, he finally struggled to push himself upright and away from the cliff and look up towards us.

"Yup! Still alive! Just…catching…my breath," Chass said, holding his arms, shivering. Using the claws on the gauntlets Miev had given us he pierced the mountain wall and we continued to climb.

After we reached the top of the slope we found ourselves near a stack of stones. Seven in all, stacked on top of one another with a red flag tied around the top two. We trudged forward, neck-deep through snow. Egris took the lead, jumping across narrow stone outcroppings until he disappeared over the ledge far above.

"Egris!" I shouted with my hands against my face.

"Careful, don't want to cause an avalanche," Chass said, grabbing my hands and pulling me forward.

"Hurry! Come see!" Egris yelled from above.

Together Chass and I pulled ourselves up over the edge to join Egris, and across one last valley, we saw a small temple nestled between two peaks.

"This is amazing!" I said.

"Wait, what is that below?" Chass asked, pointing towards the valley below the temple.

Smoke rose from a giant boiler. There were dozens of wooden structures: shelters, storage containers, elevators. The valley was not made from erosion or any of the elements of the world.

The thunder roared around us, above us, below. Sections of rock were being blasted apart and several behemoths, the evolutionary descendants of dinosaurs, were pulling carts loaded with tonnes of material. Some of the creatures I recognized from my father's sketches; the bi-pedal small armed Praeg, the spike-tailed quadrupedal Kamulatitan, a Lythronax whose wings had been chained, and a Rugopos Raptor whose face had been muzzled and feathers cut off. My jaw dropped when I saw hundreds of small lizard-like creatures being forced to work a mine. All toiling away digging up the mountain around them.

"We can't leave them," I cried out.

"What choice do we have?" Chass argued.

"They are slaves! We have to do something."

"They are slaves to elves, look!" said Egris.

The three of us had moved closer to the valley below. Egris was right. Dozens of armored Elves occupied the mine, riding horses and holding whips. I saw one or two who looked like they were mages from the Royal Academy of Magic; their robes matched the sketches in my father's journal.

The Linwir were reptile-like creatures that walked on two legs and had many of the same body types as Fauns and elves. They were one of the lost races, believed to live deep inside the world's core. A few of them looked like they had been starving. Dozens more had wings on the back of their grayish bodies that had been cut or split apart. The larger ones in chains resembled dragons.

"Why would elves do this?"

"They needed workers for their mines, this was too near the temple, too dangerous for their own kind," Egris answered.

"It isn't right," I said. I was in disbelief. Nothing had prepared me to see this. An elder Linwir fell to the ground. Immediately a guard walked over and started abusing him.

"Arianna, calm down, you are starting to catch fire," said Chass pointing at the sparks of light running across my clothes. I couldn't help it. I wanted to scream. I hated them. All of them.

Blast them! Bury them!

I felt the anger rising inside me.

You are the savior of this world! Use your power! Set them free!

"Arianna! Arianna, listen to me," Chass was shaking me.

"What?" I shouted.

"I have a plan to get them out and steal the relic."

·19·
ARIANNA

My father's journals spoke of several cults and societies that had committed evil crimes across our kingdom. My father himself had been enslaved by the Lahari. After it set in what I was looking at I wasn't so surprised. People were born with the ability for both good and evil, and this... was the worst of what we had become.

"Okay, everyone understand the plan?" Chass asked. He had just gone over our plan to free the Linwir twice. I had a good idea of what he wanted from me but there was only a slight chance any of it would work. We all had a part to play. If one of us failed there was a good chance we would all go down or be captured and made slaves just like the Linwir.

"Yes," I said, still unsure his idea would even work.

The sun was beginning to set. The sound of thunder could be heard throughout the mountain. At times it was loud enough to make me cover my ears. I wandered up to the guard, leaving my fur coat and my gear behind. Hopefully they had some heart and wouldn't turn away a young woman who was in distress.

Using charcoal I darkened the area around my eyes, it wasn't that hard to blend. We had been traveling for days and the journey had taken its toll. Since our journey began I had never walked so much in a day. Now my feet were calloused, my legs and back bruised. Even my soft skin had been peeling away, cut by sharp rocks and tree bark.

The guards here didn't look like the ones that came to our village from the capital. Well funded, well armored, but most of them looked like mercenaries. I cursed and jutted forward, letting tears fall from my eyes. Feeling them freeze against my cheek. I would have little time for escape if this went wrong. It was time to find out if they were men or monsters.

"Who goes?" said one of the guards in a deep voice. He was wearing battle armor with Linwir bones crafted to the shoulder plates and helmet. He had a necklace made of their teeth across his neck. It was hard to even tell he was elven.

As I approached I saw the Linwir up close. They looked like small dragons.

"I said who goes!" The guard shouted, loudly this time, and I saw they were beginning to surround me. I moved closer without saying a word. I had to wait for the right moment.

Ten feet away I began walking like I had a limp. The guard had a crossbow and pulled it up. Two others in similar armor pulled out their swords. I was already lucky they hadn't killed me on the spot. Either they weren't used to visitors or they had been expecting company from time to time. Maybe I could show them the talisman and say I was sent by the hermit. No. It was too much of a risk, not to mention deviating from Chass' plan would put us all at risk.

"I am a traveler, I've come to pray to the spirit of the mountain,"

I tried to speak as frail as I could even as I felt my blood boiling beneath my skin.

"She's a wandering fool, that's all," said one of the guards, laughing.

"Spirit of the mountain," laughed another.

"My family is poor, sick. I have traveled far from the east to seek the guidance, the help of the spirits," I said, standing my ground as the guards moved closer to me. The one with the cross-bow lowered his guard.

"We could make a slave out of her," said one of them.

"Been too long since we've had anything fresh," said another.

"Let me kill her! It's been ages since I've spilled any red blood! Killing lizards just isn't the same."

"Put a pretty dress on her, we can make her up real nice."

"Enough," a last voice shouted. The mercenaries were closer now but the voice that shouted 'enough' was farther away. I could only make out the silhouette of a mage.

"Can you not see how far this citizen of our beloved kingdom has traveled? What would the king say of us if we turned her away in such a time of need," the mage stepped closer. The others almost seemed to bow their heads. It was a woman. Older, athletic, with gray hair just below her shoulders. She was wearing a robe with the sigil of the Royal Academy of Magic.

"This must be such a surprise to you," she said, smiling.

"I came to seek the spirit of the mountain, whose roar can be heard across the forest valley. I have heard rumors of great magic," I answered, bowing my head. The mage studied me for a moment before closing her eyes.

"Arianna," she said. I felt my whole world shudder as my heart started to beat in a panic. "My name is Zanna, I am a teacher from the Royal Academy of Magic, you must pardon the words of these fools. They know nothing of spiritual matters. The drought. I am sure it has been hard for you and many families."

I did my best to play it cool. Some kind of magic. That was the only way she could have known my name.

"I am amazed that you know my name, this is truly a blessed place." I looked up and saw Zanna was still smiling, studying me. Around me I could see three more guards approaching us. That was almost all of them now. I could clearly see the makeshift fort they had set up alongside the stables and slave chambers that had been dug into the side of the mine for the Linwir. Dozens of Linwir were continuing to work around us, pulling blocks of iron from the earth with ropes. I could see blood-covered snow around us. Still fresh.

"You must be very curious to come this far on your own."

I refrained from saying more.

"I'm sorry, didn't mean to pry, perhaps we should eat something and drink some tea before you continue on your way. Our mine is located just below the temple. I'm sure you have been trying to find it. Unfortunately, there is little there but ruins anymore," Zanna's smile turned to a straight face.

"I would like to see for myself," I said looking towards the temple and back around at the guards, counting them and the number of Linwir in my head. Thirty guards at most and hundreds of Linwir. The mage must have been powerful if they had yet to rebel against their captors.

"These lizardmen, I'm sure you've never seen anything like them," Zanna said, holding out her hand. "Uglier than Satyr, stronger too, yet dumb as dogs."

"When I left on my journey I knew I would encounter many strange things, our kingdom is a large and majestic place," I answered, trying again not to look alarmed.

"And yet you must wonder… why slaves."

"Our kingdom is full of life, and many willing to work."

"The answer is right in front of you. We came here to do a job by any means necessary. When we found the lizards crawling through the rocks like vermin, hunting, cannibalizing one another to survive… taming them seemed the right thing to do. We are their saviors."

"I understand," I said, lying through my teeth. It was easy to look around and see that the Linwir were suffering far more at the hands of the mercenaries than they would be dealing with the drought.

"And how did you discover the whereabouts of our temple?"

"I followed the sound of thunder."

"From the valley of the Satyr? I'm surprised you survived. You must be stronger than you look."

One of the guards, as if on cue, walked over to a Linwir and stabbed it in the back, pulling back his sword and flinging the blood back down on the snow. I wanted to cry again, to look horrified but I knew it had been a test.

"Interesting," said Zanna.

I looked up at her without saying a word. I was right, it had been a test and, judging from Zanna's reaction, I had just failed.

"A test? Trying to see how I would react to the death of such a weak creature?" I said, lifting myself up. The game had changed. I had hoped I could act weak and feeble and gather their attention but now I had to show them. I had to show them it was I alone that came and survived all the way to the top of the mountain.

"Yes, it was a test. To see where your loyalties lie, we've no reason to trust outsiders even if they are looking as fragile as you."

"You spoke of food and drink?"

"It will take some time for the lizard to cook," Zanna was smiling again.

I looked again towards the Linwir that had been stabbed. It was still alive, struggling, paralyzed on the ground. The blade had broken its back. With no supplies coming in from the kingdom that was how they had been surviving. In the thick, frosty air I could make out dozens of large storage containers. Stockpiling iron ore and other minerals for what looked like a war to come. It was becoming harder and harder to hide how I really felt.

"You passed," Zanna said with delight turning and motioning for me to follow behind her.

You can't let this go.

Zanna stopped.

Her magic isn't real. Cheap illusions.

The voice in my head was louder and it was right. Zanna might have been a powerful mage but I could feel what little magic she had.

"Such an addict for pain, I can see it in your face even if your body does just as you command. You are gifted. There is a spark in your eyes. If you had not come to this place perhaps you could have become a great mage."

"I don't need someone like you to tell me what I can or can't be," I stood higher now. Lightning arcing across my fingers.

It was a simple plan. A good plan. Chass and Egris set the

Linwir free while I attacked the mage and scattered the guards.

I was slightly embarrassed. Of course, a mage from the academy of magic should have more knowledge than I had, but I had my father's notes, the knowledge he had given me as my inheritance. I knew more about the world than the dozens sitting behind desks learning parlor tricks could imagine. I knew ancient legends, stories of cults, temples. I had read about my father facing down the walking dead and fighting ogres.

I had followed along with Chass' plan because it was the right thing. The Linwir could not be kept as slaves, not here, not now, not ever.

"There are two more!" Zanna shouted, turning to witness an explosion from one of the giant storage containers. One of the larger Linwir had broken loose and began tearing through the rafters around the outer rim of the mine. It was all moving forward according to plan.

A few of the guards moved away from us towards a dozen Linwir wielding swords. Chass and Egris had been working fast. Already they had managed to free half of them and unlocked the armory as well. What we lacked in numbers we made up for in stealth and now that our cover had been blown we had a horde of angry Linwir on our side.

Two of the guards rushed me and I jumped back, rolling through the snow and ducking back behind a barrel. Straight down the path from me stood a giant Praeg, broken loose from the chains and free from its slave driver. The Praeg moved closer to me, I could almost feel its breath as I stared out at its long face and sharp teeth, each one the size of the palm of my hand. It had two short arms with three claws on each hand. Each claw looked capable of tearing flesh.

I whistled towards it, hoping to grab its attention. Something told me it knew the difference between who I was and the guards. It turned towards me. I could feel it looking me in the eyes. The other guard's attention focused on the Praeg as one held up its sword only to be snatched by the behemoth's jaws. It swung him in the air the same way Emery used to play with a chew toy. Still famished after its first meal, the Praeg continued to prey on the second guard.

For the moment I was in the clear so I made my way towards the boiler, watching as the Praeg took off with the other Linwir. As far as I knew the Linwir were the only race capable of taming such creatures. Maybe that was something to do with their ancestry.

According to Egris the Linwir were a proud race that dwelled inside caves and mountains. They were deadly at creating traps and great hunters, tamers of large beasts. Born from eggs, a new Linwir could hatch in forty-five days and be full-grown within six months. They required little food and were strong workers. All of that made them perfect slaves to the mercenaries and the mage.

Many set free now probably never knew their tribe, and it would be up to the elder Linwir to see that they made it home safe. They believed themselves to be descended from dragons. This was their chance to prove once again they were mighty.

The boiler was the only warm spot in the mine. I could feel the heat pouring out of it, warming my skin. I didn't have time to relax. My joints were frozen, the pain running through my hands and legs. I could barely feel my feet, and my toes beneath my boots were starting to turn blue as the soles broke. I had a repair kit with my gear but it wouldn't do me any good now. Three more guards came down the hillside towards me. Another explosion rocked the mine. I could feel the ground shaking below me.

Several more of the behemoths had broken free and were causing havoc. I could feel the iron dust in the air. The perfect conductor for electricity, all around me. I studied the wind and let out a spark.

"Three guards down," I said, moving away from the boiler and sending another ball of light towards it. The iron dust had started to collect around the heat. Settling around the boiler. Enough that a simple spark could cause a chain reaction and bury it all in the ground.

"Clever girl, too bad you were nothing but a puppet," Zanna said, turning towards me. She took a totem from one pocket, a small wand from another, and began reciting some kind of curse over and over.

I held up my hand as a guard charged towards me. He was immediately taken back as a bolt of lightning hit his chest and tossed him backward. Zanna stopped speaking, her eyes turned red, she held out her hand with the wand and pointed it towards me and an ice wraith appeared. At least I thought an ice wraith had appeared. It was little more than an illusion. Easily disposed of by a spark of electricity. Another soon appeared, followed by another.

They continued to form, rising from the ground one after another until even the guards that had been following her started running away. None of the specters were real. By the time I stood in front of Zanna, I could see Chass and Egris coming back towards me. Our raid had been a success. In all of fifteen minutes the Linwir had been set free, the guards scattered and running down the mountain, and the mage....

…I snapped her wand in half and told her to run away.

· 20 ·
ARIANNA

"We did it!" Chass shouted.

"And good thing too," Egris said. "The Linwir here had been separated from the rest of their tribe for months, now they have the chance to find them and move forward. They are, it seems, the last of their kind."

"I was shocked at first too, but Egris is able to speak their language," Chass added. I felt relief. I knew what we had done was the right thing.

"We should camp here for the night, we can set out for the temple tomorrow during the day, it should only take us a few hours to reach the relic," Egris said. There was a happiness in his voice I hadn't heard before.

"Do you think the mage or the guards will attack us?" I asked.

"They wouldn't stand a chance!" Chass shouted.

"They will be too busy dealing with the Linwir and trying to figure out how to explain what happened here. I'm certain the mage had never seen true magic such as yours before," Egris answered.

"But she was from the Royal Academy of Magic?"

"The academy teaches tricks, illusions. Only a few are able to actually tap into the stream of energy that surrounds us, the deep magic. Those like her are able to create illusions through the use of sensitive artifacts like that wand you broke, others call upon magic from the elements. Your magic comes from inside you. Carine would be very proud of you right now." Egris put his hand on my shoulder and smiled. It was the first time I had ever acknowledged my own magic as a gift, and it was the first time I had used my magic for something so great.

That night before we went to bed Egris took out a pile of bones from his satchel and threw them down by the small fire we had made inside what used to be Zanna's hut.

"What are you doing?" Chass asked.

"Consulting the gods," he answered.

"And what do the gods say of our victory?" Chass asked, taking a bite of some of Zanna's rations that had been left behind. I tried not to imagine it was Linwir and decided better to believe it was fish. When he offered me a bite I politely declined. Somehow it seemed better that they didn't know.

"Our journey has been full of peril, monsters, mayhem. Our actions tonight may have unforeseen consequences and for that I am worried."

"Worried about what?" I asked.

"War. I don't know who was behind the mining operation here, but to have a mage from the academy in charge of it they must be someone very powerful."

"Someone from the capital?" I asked.

"Possibly a traitor among the King's inner circle. If Zanna reaches the capital before us, I shudder to think what may happen."

"I wouldn't worry about that," said Chass, his mouth full again.

"And why is that?" Egris asked.

"I saw a group of Linwir tracking her before she dropped out of sight. One of them was riding a Praeg. I doubt she's going to make it down the mountain," Chass said, swallowing his food. I was both relieved and disgusted. I didn't want anyone to die; not because of my actions. We had begun this journey to prevent things like this from happening. Chass was also the last person I thought would show no remorse for someone, even someone as evil as Zanna, being sentenced to death.

"I see. Arianna, are you okay?" Egris asked. He must have been able to sense it; it was like the air in the room changed. I felt the collar on my shirt tighten around my chest.

"Zanna wasn't good, but… I hope that if the Linwir do catch her they don't kill her, but I am no judge."

Egris smiled at me again and continued to consort with the bones. I thought about asking what they said but I was tired and ready to turn in. The first part of our journey was coming to an end.

ARGENTIS

Eldrad and I approached a narrow pass that led into the mountains. This leg of our quest was going to be far colder than any elf would ever want to endure, but the sooner we got it over with the sooner we could return home. We had good intel that the maggots would be heading toward a shrine deep in the mountains to re-trieve some sort of relic. "Just follow the sound of thunder, you can't miss it," the hooded figure had said. I couldn't make out his face, but I was sure he was a rogue mage. If not the one that start-ed the curse, then certainly one of his lackeys.

This whole 'relic' thing was starting to get the better of my cu-riosity. Of course, the powers-that-be insisted no such relics exist-ed, that the curse was just an old myth with no truth to it whatso-ever. Even so, they were spending a lot of resources to keep these little brats from finding the relics. Or at least, they were making Eldrad and I expend a lot of energy to that end.

Maybe that was the real truth behind all of this. No matter how hard I had worked, no matter how many times I had proven my-self year after year, I was still disposable. An expendable resource good for nothing but brushing a minor inconvenience under the rug. The king had pawned me off on some backwater mayor, and that mayor treated me no better than a dog in his hunting party.

The sound of crunching snow came from the entrance to the pass, and Eldrad pulled his sword as a gray-haired woman in mage's robes stumbled out from between the rocks. She looked like she had been in a fight.

Eldrad had been chomping at the bit since we left the village, hungry for a good kill. He stepped toward the woman, but I held a hand up to stop him. She might have been able to give us some useful information first.

I could tell she was one of the academy hacks that couldn't do any real magic. It was always easy to tell because they were the ones who tried the hardest to make themselves look like mages.

"Oh good, I'm glad I found you," the woman was saying as

she trudged toward us through the thick snow. "We need to send a message to the king."

"A message to the king, you say?" I responded. "Did he send you out here to see if there were any children needing a magician for their birthday party?" My humor seemed to be totally lost on her, as she pulled a small pouch from her belt and flung the contents in the air: a powdery substance that seemed to sparkle with a thousand tiny explosions. I didn't even flinch as the dust settled to the ground and the sparks fizzled out at my feet.

"I will have you know I am a mage in the order of Mazzenrach, and I have been entrusted with a great and terrible task direct from the king himself."

"Then you'd better get back to your post before the king finds out you've abandoned it," I heard Eldrad quip behind me.

"That's why we have to send a message to the king, you ignorant buffoon. Some rogue mage has partnered with a satyr and managed to take down the entire mine!"

"A secret mine hidden in the mountains?" I asked. "Very interesting. That sounds like our girl, though. Come, Eldrad, we're getting close."

I moved past the old woman toward the entrance to the mountain pass.

"Where are you going?" She yelled at my back. "As an emissary of the king, I order you two witless warthogs to escort me to Fennox Castle!"

"That was a very poor choice of last words," I said without slowing my stride. I heard Eldrad's sword pierce the woman, and a moment later her body crumpled to the ground.

I continued into the mountain pass without looking back.

·21·
CARINE

"This is suicide," I said, tightening my sheath around my chest. I was holding my sword in my hand; I had just finished sharpening it. I was looking toward Egris, who had just consulted his bones.

"Suicide and giving your life for a cause are not the same. Luckily for you, we are not going to do either. This will work," Egris said, picking up the bones and placing them back inside a small bag.

"Not the first time your gods have led us into a dead-end, are you sure this place will have something useful?"

"It is not for us to question the will of the gods. This is the beginning of a descent, a journey that will take us far and wide."

"That wasn't the answer I was hoping for. Can't you just ask one of your seers where the relics are hidden so we can go after them? All this chase is bad for morale."

"Our seers cannot see what is not there, they only see that there is a path. My people have accepted our fate, we know the elves blame us for the famine, they bleed our villages, hunt us, and your king has spread lies."

"They just don't understand." I looked at Egris and back at three other Fauns that were following us. A small party, on the edge of the southern border of the kingdom. "I can't keep leaving my daughter like this, I've been away from her too long, too many times."

"She is strong, our gods have foreseen she has a bright future ahead of her. She will rise, she will fall. You must have faith that you are doing the right thing. This is what Solph would have wanted."

"You have no idea what my wife would have wanted." I sheathed my sword. I was more irritated than I wanted to be but we had been moving south for three weeks and we were low on rations after being attacked by a group of bounty hunters that wanted the Faun dead. And that was before we stole a ship from a fishing village just south of Fennox Castle.

Egris had been one of the first beings to aid me on my quest. I had seen the suffering the curse had caused his people, and convinced him that working together was the only way we could end the drought. He was determined to help me no matter the risks as I told him my story. The story of my wife's death, my daughter's birth. I told him of the adventures I had in the north and together the two of us began to search for answers in the south.

That brought us here. The border of the Southern Wilds, a land of mystery, monsters, and mayhem. Not even the bravest of the king's knights came to this part of the world. Those that did came as nomads, treasure hunters, or death seekers looking for release. Bards sang songs of unbelievable wonders in the south. Praising it as the original home of the Satyr and Elves. Songs told of spirits, gods, dragons, giants, and more that still wandered. The bones led us here.

We had stolen a ship out of dock to sail around the mountains. Small, but large enough for five of us to traverse the great ocean without worry. Two weeks on the water, eating nothing but bottom dwellers. The sun had gone down and the air was cold as winter. I thought I would find a giant desert as we approached the shore but instead, the south was littered in giant trees. One in particular stood above all the rest. Larger than the king's castle, it was home to a variety of life.

"Is there even a curse here?" I asked.

"There is, it's just not visible to the naked eye. Everything here is poisoned, dying, killing one another to survive. The chain is broken. The roots of the world tree are dying and in a hundred years all this will wither and rot away," Egris answered.

"I'm sorry," I said, staring up at the great tree as the other Fauns rowed our ship onto the shore.

"It is not your fault, the curse is a shadow on all the land."

"Get down!" one of the Fauns shouted just as a giant owl appeared above us. It was swooping down fast. I could barely see it at first until it missed us and flew in front of the light of the moons. It was as large as our ship and if I had to guess it had mistaken us for a beached whale or giant lizard.

"This is not good, it's going to come back for another pass," shouted Egris.

"The bones didn't warn you about this!" I yelled, diving down and grabbing a spear from the boat's small armory. As the owl dived once more I threw it through the air.

"Miss!" Egris said.

"No, look the owl grabbed it!" shouted one of the Fauns. The owl snapped the spear in two pieces with its talons.

There was a scream as the owl came back down and picked up one of the Fauns, carrying him off.

"We have to go after him!" I shouted.

"We must carry on with our mission," argued one of the other Fauns.

"I don't think we have a choice," said Egris pointing at the owl. It was making another pass back towards us. It had dropped the Faun somewhere in the jungle. We could hear the roar of another creature as it flew closer and closer. I moved to my left and grabbed another spear. I was determined not to miss this time. I didn't.

The owl fell into the water so hard we could feel the splash and waves rock us back and forth. As it struggled to take flight once more a massive pair of jaws emerged from the depths and the giant owl was pulled beneath the surface.

"Lucky that wasn't us," said Egris.

"Was that a dragon?" one of the Fauns asked.

"Crocodile. Was probably sizing us up, waiting for the right moment to attack after we steadied ourselves on the shore," I explained. I had done my research. I had access to a library inside Fennox Castle for a while and there I had read as much myth and legend as I had scientific journals. It seemed now I couldn't tell the two apart.

"Finn may still be alive, we should leave the shore before the gator digests the bird," Egris said. I shook my head and the four of us tied up the boat as quickly as we could, jumping into the shallows with our weapons in one hand and rope in the other. After the boat was secure and the rope tied to a tree I picked up a small blue shield and wore it on my left arm. I kept a small dagger on my belt and sword in hand. Anything could go wrong and we still weren't quite sure what we were looking for. The bones had told Egris of a ruin, a temple of some kind that would point us towards truth. I had grown desperate.

Several hours in the wild we found Finn. His body lay on the ground among a pit of dead animals. The owl hadn't been hunting the boat; it was smarter than we gave it credit. It had been hunting us.

"A nest. Do you think there could be more of them?" I looked toward Egris, expecting an answer but the truth was he had no idea. Some of the bodies had been torn apart, half-eaten, while others looked like they had been burned by some kind of acid.

"We need to keep moving," Egris ordered. No matter what other monstrosities lay in wait, the sooner we got out of there the better.

We continued trudging through the dense forest, jumping at every sound. There was an oppressive sense of deep foreboding weighing down on us, we all felt it. The stronger it got, the more we knew we were moving in the right direction.

After several of the longest hours of my life we finally came to an ancient temple, totally covered over in vines.

"Carine and I will go in," Egris said. "The rest of you stand guard."

"No," I said, holding up a hand to stop him. I had a nagging feeling deep in my gut. I couldn't quite place it, but I knew it was telling me to go alone. "There is something I'm meant to find in here. I have to do this on my own."

"If you feel the deep magic speaking to you, I dare not

interfere," Egris said. "We will ensure no evil finds its way in after you."

"I'm afraid the evil is already inside."

I made my way into the mouth of the temple and found myself consumed by darkness. Nothing but pure black surrounded me, but I found myself compelled to continue forward. A light shone several feet in front of me, as if a stray beam of sunlight had burst through the dense vegetation above. In the pool of light I saw a table with a small bowl of blue liquid. I took the bowl and drank.

After a moment the table vanished, and darkness prevailed once again. As I stood there, aware only of the beads of sweat dripping down my face, I heard a child's laugh. It was as sweet and soft as a songbird. My precious Aria. The light returned and I saw the child there on the floor, playing with a doll Maria had made for her. There, crouching next to her, was a young woman.

"Solph?" I called out. Could it be? It had been years since I had seen my love's gentle frame, her cascading hair, but I recognized it immediately. It had to be her. The woman stood and turned toward me, and I realized it was not my Solph at all. It was you, Arianna, though much older than you are now. You looked just like your mother. So full of peace, love, and compassion.

As I watched, two pedestals appeared on either side of you, and on each of them a relic. You reached out with both arms and took hold of the relics. In an instant the chamber reverberated with a crack of thunder, water gushed out of the Rain Relic, and streaks of lightning burst out from your body in every direction.

I remember once, when you were playing with Chass in the other room while I worked, you slipped and hit your head on the table. The absolute panic I felt as I heard you scream in pain, and rushed in to sweep you up in my arms. That was nothing compared to the soul-piercing noise you were making now. I fell to my knees.

"Arianna! No!" You were suffering, you were dying, and there was nothing I could do about it. I had always suspected the Spirit of Lightning dwelled within you, but this was confirmation of the terrible fate that had been forced upon our family. Confirmation of my worst fears.

As quickly as the vision had begun, it vanished. I heard a voice call out behind me, "Carine, is everything alright in there?" It was Egris. I wondered if they had been able to hear the entire vision, or only my own cries. I walked out of the temple and past the others. It was time to leave.

"What did you see in there?" Egris asked. I stopped. Somewhere in the distance I could hear a frail blue-bird singing its gentle song. There were no words to describe what I had just experienced, so I said the only thing that came close:

"Inevitability."

ARIANNA

I read my father's journal and cried. I blinked tears from my eyes and held my breath against the pain I felt in my chest. It moved through me like a storm. A hurricane of rage, a flood of wailing pain. I felt a fever as blood pounded in my ears. Nervous, clenching my teeth, but that was all the noise, all the emotion I could allow myself.

Egris and Chass slept while I kept reading. I thought there was no mention of Egris in my father's journal but that wasn't true. I just hadn't read far enough. How many more stories had I missed? How many more secrets did my father have? I wasn't sure if I loved him or hated him more.

He had tried so hard to protect me from a future he knew was coming. Why hadn't he told me? He could have done so much more to prepare me for this journey. He could have trained me to use my powers to fight. We could have done this together, side by side. Deep down I knew the truth. I was his baby. His only reminder of the woman he loved. He wanted to protect me. To shield me from the harsh realities of the world.

He wanted to preserve the true me, the peaceful me, the gentle me. The me that made mud pies and took in helpless animals from the forest. Not the me that was tainted by the spirit living inside me. The me that lashed out in anger at the slightest provocation. The me that lost control and hurt those I loved. Maybe, once all this was over, and I was finally separated from that poisonous spirit, then I, the true 'I', would be reunited with my parents in the deep magic, and together we could travel beyond the veil, for eternity.

Egris emerged from his tent and relieved me of lookout duty. I only had a few hours to sleep before we journeyed up the rest of the mountain. We could see the temple, less than a few hours' climb.

The next morning a fog hung over the mountains, diffusing the light of the sun. Chass and I pulled ourselves up over the edge of a cliff-side to join Egris. It was the last part of the valley we had to cross. The temple sat between two giant peaks, though we couldn't see it through the fog.

"The Linwir refused to venture here," Egris said, motioning at a small blue flag with a rune that signified this place was dangerous. "They believed it was holy ground, for them to step here was to disregard the gods. Even the mages and mercenaries stayed clear of this place."

The temple itself was minuscule compared to the mine below. We followed a rocky outcropping to reveal a narrow path clear of debris. A sheer cliff to one side and a drop off on the other.

"What are we looking for?" Chass asked.

"A relic, we'll know it when we see it," I answered, half smiling. For the moment I thought everything was going to be alright. That compared to everything we had done to get here, this part would be easy. We rounded one last corner onto the path that led to the temple, and stopped in our tracks.

"Fancy seeing you here," Argentis said. He and Eldrad were standing there, waiting.

"Little mage last night had a lot to say about the two of you," Eldrad grinned, cleaning a dagger on his blood-stained shirt. "Least until we cut out her tongue. Seems you've been causing a lot of trouble here and there."

"How did you know to find this place?" I shouted.

"Followed the breadcrumbs, or perhaps a little bird told us," Argentis smirked, running his hand across his burly beard. Eldrad winked towards Chass whose eyes widened at the gesture.

"Huh?" I heard Chass behind me, lost at the remark.

"You should know by now you can't stop me from getting what I want," I proclaimed, stepping forward and forcing electricity to arc around my body.

"Arianna, wait! I don't think using your powers is the wisest decision at the moment," Egris shouted, moving in front of me unsheathing a small sword he had been hiding just underneath his satchel of supplies.

"I mean, unless you want to bring the entire mountain down on top of us," Chass stepped up beside Egris, drawing his sword, and I stood down.

"Fine, you two fight, I'll grab the relic," I nodded as the three of us glanced at one another.

"Not if we get it first!" shouted Eldrad turning and bolting towards the temple. Chass took off after him, but Argentis blocked his way with his sword. Their two blades collided and I could see the sparks fly off their cold steel. Chass stepped back, holding his sword by his side, down but ready to block at a moment's notice. Spacing his feet apart as he steadied himself. Argentis held his sword, longer and more curved than Chass' above his shoulder with two hands. He flipped it around so the curved edge pointed upward before thrusting forward. Chass blocked it but the impact sent him tripping over the rocks on the ground. Argentis didn't let up. He meant to kill him.

Meanwhile, Egris had scaled the cliff wall beside Chass and hopped along narrow ledges along the sheer cliff wall until he caught up with Eldrad. Egris dropped down and caught him off guard, pushing him back against a wall.

"Satyrs, full of dirty stinking tricks," Eldrad shouted.

I noticed a narrow path on the drop off side and lowered myself down, clinging to the cliff walls and scooting forward as I did my best to listen and avoid being caught in the middle of the fight. I heard Egris scream and there was a burst of smoke from above me. I moved further away, further from my friends and towards where I felt the relic calling out to me.

I pulled myself up over the ledge and realized I had overshot the temple. I rushed back toward it and in through a back door, and saw Eldrad was already there!

Outside, Egris had doubled back to help Chass, who was slowly losing his fight against Argentis.

At last brother, we've found you.

Was the lighting spirit talking to the relic? As if in response, a deep rumbling sound echoed through the mountain. If I didn't know any better, I would say it sounded like the word, 'Sister'.

"Looking for something, doll?" Eldrad was already reaching for the relic. The relic itself was shaped like a leaf. Resting on top of the leaf was a large spider. The entire thing seemed to have been formed out of a single orange gemstone, carved with intricate runes that I assumed represented 'thunder' in an ancient Casar language.

As I stared at it I felt it calling out to me, a voice in my head demanding I take it, smash it against the ground, set free the power sealed inside. I felt the electricity wave over my body, sending chills down my arm and legs. And as I screamed "No," Eldrad snatched it up and the low rumbling from deep within the mountain immediately erupted into a deafening roar.

You can't let them have it! You can't let them win!

My eyes widened, I could feel my tears freezing in the wind. The roar continued to echo around us as Eldrad's brow furrowed. Both of us ran outside, stumbling as the ground shook beneath our feet.

A crack of thunder split the air and the relic leapt from Eldrad's hands, but he continued to run.

"RUN! Run for your lives!" he shouted as he ran toward the others.

Argentis still had the upper hand against Chass and Egris. Blood poured down from Egris' side where he had been cut. It was a flesh wound but enough to slow the Faun down. If we made it out alive I needed to remind myself to heal him.

Chass was holding up better than before. Egris had given him an edge and while Argentis was a powerful opponent, he had no choice but to take a defensive position. There was a hate in his eyes, in his face, his armor was covered in marks where Chass had swung and managed to make contact.

As Eldrad approached them they stood, frozen. Argentis

looked up the mountain and quickly realized what was happening. He pushed past Chass and Egris and joined Eldrad as they turned the corner out of sight.

I reach for the relic sitting nestled in the snow. A spark of electricity arced from the tip of my fingers to the relic, and the low rumble shook the mountain even more. I recoiled. Questioning whether this was the right path, whether I might accidentally unleash whatever power lay in wait.

Brother, come to me!

This was the moment. I exhaled deeply and reached for the relic again and snatched it out of the snow. The rumble stopped. There was now nothing but a cold silence. I stood in quiet reverence for several moments, my eyes glued to the relic. How much power did I really have?

I snapped out of my reverie as a loud crack rang out from far above us. We looked up the mountain. Several chunks of ice and snow broke off and started to tumble down towards us. I tossed the relic into my pack and ran toward Chass and Egris. Another crack and a massive sheet of ice slid down the side of the mountain. Argentis and Eldrad had been right to run. Both saw the signs in front of them and reacted the way any sane person would have, should have, but it was too late for all of us.

"AVALANCHE!" I shouted.

We all ran. A boulder flew past inches in front of us and destroyed the path. We managed to stop just short of falling off the edge. I looked around and noticed a large, flat rock perched above us.

"I've got an idea. Stand back!"

I pushed Chass and Egris behind me and bore down. I let the

electricity arc around my body. They had warned me I would bring the mountain down, and they had been right.

"Arianna! What are you doing!" Chass shouted.

"Just trust me!"

A blast of lightning shot from my hand at the rock and knocked it loose. It slid down the mountain, just ahead of the oncoming snow.

"Jump!" I shouted.

"What?" Chass shouted back, confused, so I turned and grabbed both him and Egris and pulled them forward.

"Jump!"

We landed on the rock just as it flew past the ledge.

Chass tumbled backwards, unable to stand his ground and flew off the back. Egris caught his arm and held on as Chass' feet dragged behind us through the snow. For a moment I was afraid I was going to lose both of them. Worried I made the wrong decision. But Egris pulled him back up just in time.

"That was close," Egris said, digging his hoofed feet into the rock.

"Thanks," Chass panted, still holding onto Egris' arm.

In the distance, but approaching fast, I could see a giant, jagged rock sticking straight in the air ahead of our path.

"Arianna!" Egris called out.

"I see it!"

"Well what are you going to do about it?" Chass shouted.

"What do you mean what am I going to do about it?"

"I don't know, blast it or something!"

I set my jaw and narrowed my eyes, thinking. I was beginning to have an idea, and it might just work...

"Lean left!" I shouted!

"What?" Egris looked confused.

"Lean!"

I threw all my weight left and both Egris and Chass followed suit. The rock tilted up with us and curved away, just in time to barely nick the edge of the outcropping as we passed it by.

"Now we just have to steer this thing all the way down the mountain. No big deal," Chass grinned. I knew in my heart he was just happy we had survived this far.

A faint cry echoed in the distance. I looked for the source of the sound and found it. On a ledge to our right, Argentis and Eldrad were jumping up and down, waving their arms in the air. I could hear them calling for help and I pointed in their direction, shifting my weight to the right. Chass and Egris moved left, countering me.

"What are you doing?" Chass shouted.

"We have to save them!"

"No, we don't! They literally just tried to kill us!"

"Everyone deserves a chance to live, no matter who they are! Isn't that what you said, Egris? A Faun would never kill a living creature?"

"I said we live in harmony with nature. Sometimes that means letting things die when their time has come!"

I growled and pushed myself into Chass. If they weren't going to listen to reason I would have to make them. In spite of everything those two thugs had done, I couldn't stand by and watch them die knowing I could have done something about it.

The rock turned right as Egris lost his balance and tumbled into us.

"Get ready!"

"You're gonna regret this," I heard Chass mumble under his breath.

Our rock slid in front of the ledge and the two thugs jumped. Chass and Egris caught them, exchanging understanding and disturbed glances at one another. They all four reached for their swords.

"Put those away and focus!" I yelled.

We all looked ahead. The tree line was approaching. Things would have been much simpler if we had slid into the mine but we were on the opposite side of the valley now. Billowing snow tumbled behind us, hot on our heels even as we continued to pick up speed.

"Right!" We all leaned right and narrowly missed a tree as we entered a wooded area. We continued to bob and weave as we descended the mountain.

A small branch smacked Chass in the face.

"Hey! Watch where you're going!"

"I am watching!" I would apologize for it later. Right then I was in charge, leading the five of us down a cliff in the middle of an avalanche. Not how I thought I would be spending my afternoon.

We broke free of the wooded area and immediately hit a ramp of snow that launched us into the air. We all flew off in different directions and landed in the snow below.

The last remnants of the avalanche blew over us.

Even as electricity wrapped around me like a cocoon I could feel the cold seep in and numb me.

All this power and you are going to die here? Like this? A spark of light frozen in time.

ARIANNA

Darkness surrounded me. It was like I was waking up in a strange place, not remembering where I was, as had happened so many times on this journey. Only this time I wasn't waking up to a place at all, but to a void. I tried to think, to remember what had happened.

The avalanche. I was buried in snow. I couldn't tell which way was up. I tried to squirm my way free, but the icy powder was tight around my limbs.

Get up. This is not where our story ends.

The voice echoed in the darkness of my mind.

"Who are you?" I asked.

I am you. We are us.

"What do you want with me?" I yelled. A spark of lightning filled my vision, and the spark formed itself into the shape of a person, fluctuating and buzzing with electricity. She looked just like me.

I want you to stop resisting me. All your life you have pushed me into the deep recesses of your mind, only letting me out when it served your purposes. If we are going to win this fight, I need you to surrender.

"When I let you out, innocent people get hurt. We burned down an entire village, don't you remember?"

WE did nothing of the sort. That was all you, dear. You will never be able to control my power on your own. As her anger intensified I could feel the electricity surging across my body, melting the snow around me. *You will never be good enough. This is my fight, you are only a vessel. Now let me free!*

"No, if we win this fight it will be on my terms." I worked my arm free and thrust it as high as I could. I could feel the cold air as it broke free of the snow. I could hear muffled voices calling my name in the distance. Chass and Egris were looking for me. "And if we lose then we will have fought with dignity and honor. If you wanted a fighter you should have chosen someone else."

I felt a gloved hand take hold of mine, and an instant later I was pulled free from the snow. Bright light flooded my vision, and I took a deep gasping breath. Our journey was far from over.

"Well, that was an adventure," Chass said, holding me in his arms. I felt his warmth against my body. We had just barely survived.

I heard a rustling noise nearby. The three of us, still in shock that we were alive, turned towards the sound. Argentis and Eldrad were pulling themselves up from the snow. I pulled the thunder relic from my pack and held it out towards them.

"You still want it?" I demanded.

They both recoiled.

"Go home. Tell everyone what just happened. We have the first relic. Only two more to go. And nothing is going to stop us."

The two thugs turned without a word and walked away as I

collapsed and tried to catch my breath.

"We need to get out of here, somewhere warm, I'm freezing."

"If my bearings are correct," Egris started, "We are about a day's journey from the edge of the mountains, due east. There is an Inn nearby, a small tavern that welcomes both elf and Faun alike, the owner is an old friend of Carine's and will put us up for the night." I couldn't have been happier to be heading back into the woods.

I pulled myself up to my feet, but stumbled and grabbed a large trunk from an old fallen tree and leaned against it.

"Arianna? Are you okay?" Chass asked, concerned.

"I may have twisted my ankle on the way down, no big deal, I'll manage. Just try and keep up," I said. As my heart rate slowed down and the adrenaline dissipated, I could feel every pain and injury. I closed my eyes and focused hard, tapping into the pain to control the spirit within me, forcing it to heal my wounds.

We walked for the rest of the day before finally approaching the inn well after dark. Egris went in first before motioning for us to follow inside.

"Arianna, Chass, this is Talos, an old friend," he said.

"The daughter of the great Carine!" Talos said, lifting his muscular arm into the air and stroking a long braided gray beard. He was a Casar, a dwarf, dressed in a leather shirt and pants with an apron hanging down from his shoulders. "And the son of Talze. I am honored to make the acquaintance of the both of you. Pardon my mess, I was just cooking some Vulta. Caught 'em in the mess after the mountain came down trying to eat some giblets. Good protein, some of the best bird in all of the kingdom of Idril." Talos had a strange accent. It was obvious he wasn't from around here, but what had brought him from Vaeger was a mystery. Perhaps, I thought, he might have been one of the Casar that fought with my father years ago.

"We seek shelter, food, clothes," I could hear the fatigue in Egris' voice as he spoke. He looked at Talos the way he looked at his own people.

"What is mine is yours, I do have one room available. And of course, for the little lady, the basement is ready, just as Carine left it. Though I'm assuming by the fact he is not with you, that he will not be making use of it again."

"No," Egris answered, "Carine has fulfilled his part of the mission and moved on to commune with the spirits."

"Aye," Talos responded in a somber tone, "May his name ever be blessed by those who speak it."

It was a simple platitude, but meaningful. In spite of everything my father had done in the name of his mission, in spite of the person the curse had forced him to become, he was always a good man at heart. Even to the very end.

"My father came here often?" I asked cautiously. "Do you happen to know if he left behind any journals?"

"Journals? Didn't think Carine much of a scholar. Afraid not. Mostly bows, arrows, a few of his swords and some coin I let him bank in case of emergencies," Talos answered, much to my dismay. It was another new discovery. How much had he been hiding?

Egris looked over towards me, "Your father and I had many safe houses in and around Idril. Don't be upset with him."

"Carine was a smart man, a warrior, leader, and he spoke very highly of his daughter. Everything he did was because he was passionate about you. Protecting you and ensuring that you grew up in a world that wasn't besieged by horrors from long ago," Talos poured a warm milk into a cup for us to drink. "Drink up. There are clothes downstairs."

It was the first warm drink I had in days and it was now that I realized how truly dehydrated and malnourished I was becoming. Standing in front of a mirror in the basement surrounded by my father's weapons, pieces of chain mail and strips of leather armor, wristbands made of fur I felt like a skeleton. I felt like I was starting to look like a draugr.

As I scavenged through my father's things I found a large chest marked, 'Arianna'. My father really had prepared for everything. Inside the chest were various pieces of armor, weapons, and a few potions and mystical artifacts I recognized from his sketches. As I dug through the chest I found a small box wrapped in a white ribbon. I opened it, and inside was a blue dress, alongside a few small pieces of jewelry. A necklace carved in the shape of a bird, a bracelet with beads carved with protective runes.

"Food will be ready in ten minutes," a voice called down. I think it might have been Egris or Chass but it was too far away and I was too enthralled to take note. I pulled off my wet, snow-covered clothes and wrapped the laces of the dress around me. It fit perfectly. Like it had been waiting for me. I spun around and for the first time in a long time I smiled, imagining that this had been a gift from my father. I wrapped my arms around myself in a tight embrace. Warm tears fell from my eyes. It was so nice to be out of the cold.

Talos cooked the Vulta over a giant fire in the middle of the tavern. When I came up everyone had changed clothes and was already eating in a circle. It reminded me of the celebration at the

Faun village, minus the smiles and dancing.

"You look beautiful," said Egris.

I said thanks and took a bow, showing off the dress.

"Not bad, kiddo," Chass agreed.

Talos had risen to his feet the moment I entered the room. "You look as beautiful as your mother." The words shook me to my core.

"I never knew my mother," I said.

"It was in my tavern back in Vaeger that they first met. Solph came down the stairs in that very dress, and turned every head in the place. I don't know what it was about your father that caught her eye, but I remember watching them dance the night away, oblivious to the rest of the world. The tavern could have been raided by marauders and burned to the ground and they would have never stopped dancing."

"If you had a tavern in Vaeger," Chass asked, "How did you end up out here?"

"Business wasn't too good after the curse," he replied. "And the Casar can be a violent lot when they get hungry. It was Carine's idea to set up here, as a safe haven for those few creatures still brave enough to venture into the wide world. He helped me build it with his own two hands. His blood, sweat, and tears are in every wall of this place."

Talos continued to talk about my father and how he would drop in from time to time. Sometimes he would be accompanied by others, sometimes alone. At times my father came here after a long adventure and stayed in the basement room, taking a breath and healing before he would return home. Talos' tavern had more than just drinks on hand. A shelf below the bar was littered with herbs and jars of mystical origins that could help mend wounds and heal the sick. He spoke of an acacia berry in our drinks that would help with our appetites and fatigue.

After dinner we continued to sit by the warm fire.

"This is the quietest it's been in a long time," said Talos.

"What do you mean?" Chass asked.

"The mountain only recently stopped roaring. Usually the thunder's echoes can be heard into the middle of the night like a wounded animal that never stops crying."

"Wouldn't know anything about that," Chass said, looking up at me.

"No, you wouldn't, would you," Talos winked. "I'll let the three of you continue to talk, my old bones need to retire. If you need anything, help yourselves."

Talos stood up and left us in the great hall. The fire continued to burn though not quite as bright as before.

"What's next?" Chass asked. "It's so weird to think that we actually have one of the relics. After everything we've been through, this is the first time it's started to actually feel real."

"I know what you mean," I responded. "Our next step is to speak to the king. Between the relic and Cypress' talisman, he's bound to give us all the help we need."

"The castle is over two weeks away and that's on horseback. If we go by foot it will take us months. Not to mention we have enemies now. Argentis and Eldrad are going to come back. I know it."

Egris stayed quiet.

"You're thinking about your cousin, aren't you?" I asked.

"Yes. I feel bad. Eating. Warm. Knowing that my blood is being tortured and that there is nothing I can do."

"My father used to say that the only way we can make a difference is to hold onto hope. To press forward as the best version of ourselves. If you refused to eat and stay warm, if you let yourself be weak you wouldn't be doing your cousin any favors. The best thing you can do is continue to press forward," I said, taking another sip of the acacia milk. Despite the fact that it was mystical I was glad I wasn't hallucinating as I had when I drank the kava with the Fauns. At the moment the last thing I wanted was another voice whispering in my head.

The next morning we awoke to the sound of horns.

I felt like I had slept for three days. We changed into our leather gear now dried from sitting beside the embers of the fading fire of the night before. I took my mother's necklace and tied it around my neck and sheathed my father's tempered sword. It was a longer blade than I had before, made of Vaeger steel. Talos was nowhere in sight as we looked for him to say our goodbyes. In fact the entire tavern looked as if it had been abandoned for years. Strange that this was the first time I noticed. Outside, standing on the edge of the road was a large crowd. I looked down from the rocks just above and saw the rolling fields and abandoned farms of the valley. The whole area had once been some of Idril's richest farmlands and estates. Massive abandoned mansions had now fallen to ruin. We were two weeks' ride from the castle, two months if we attempted to walk. The sun was warm overhead but I still shivered in my armor as I looked out over the horizon.

We moved closer to the crowd. Egris hid himself behind a hood and scarf dug from my father's old wardrobe. Unless someone looked too close he looked like a dreg, a poor beggar, or maybe they would stay their ground and think he was a leper. Hundreds of refugees were fleeing the fallout from the avalanche. Most were elves, though I spotted a few Casar and Fauns among them, as well. Some rode on horseback while others rode on large carts pulled by praeg. The ferocious reptiles almost looked comical wearing bright red and blue harnesses.

"Out of the way!" shouted a soldier. "Watch yourself!" I quickly stepped to the side and ducked my head, hoping not to be recognized. I hadn't noticed the soldiers before, but now as I scanned the crowd I realized there were a dozen or so patrolling the edges of the caravan.

I quickened my steps, moving back through the crowd. Looking around for a face I could trust. I could feel the soft breeze on my back. The cold wind still blew down from the mountain even as the snow a mile away was beginning to melt. Dozens of the carts were carrying sheets of ice. It must have been a hassle to haul, but in a world without rain it was a gift from the gods.

"They are using alchemy to keep it from melting," said Egris.

"Alchemy?" Chass asked.

"Mixing elements from two or more materials to create another," Egris answered. I knew this practice from my father's journals. It was fake magic but no less useful.

Somewhere in the crowd someone was singing. I immediately recognized the voice, and my heart sank. My eyes darted through the crowd, searching. I finally found them, Scyenna, Miev, and several others I recognized from the village. Unlike the other refugees who roamed free, they were all shackled and chained to a cart. I imagined they must have put up a fight.

I pushed my way through the crowd, careful not to attract the attention of the guards, and fell in step beside Scyenna. "What happened?" I asked.

"You did, apparently." She responded. The resentment in her voice hit me like a punch in the gut.

"What? How?" I asked, dumbfounded. "The Thunder Temple was miles away from the village."

"Whatever you did triggered a chain reaction through the entire mountain range. We were lucky to get out before the whole village was buried in snow."

"After we fled the village," Miev said over her shoulder, "We were captured by these knights making their way to the capital. We're all going to be taken in as slaves."

"The elves, too?" I asked. "The king would never allow…"

"The king himself decreed it!" Scyenna spat. "Anyone caught fraternizing with a satyr is guilty of treason. I knew listening to the girl who burned down our village was a bad idea."

"This isn't Arianna's fault," Miev said. "We have to work together if we're going to figure a way out of this."

Let me, the voice in my head said. *I can handle this.*

I knew that I couldn't let her have control. I also knew I didn't have a choice.

"We have to fight," I said. Lightning arced over my clenched fists.

"Calm down there, sparky," Scyenna said. "I think you've done enough damage already."

"This isn't the time," Chass said, as he and Egris came up behind me. He knew exactly what I was thinking. I glared at him as everyone in the crowd continued to move around us.

"Egris, How many guards are there?" I asked, my eyes on

Chass.

"Twenty armed with rifles, fifteen with swords, five of those with iron bows," Egris answered.

"Is there any way we can get ahead of them and plan an ambush?"

"They are too spread out. If we attacked we would be putting everyone in danger. I'm afraid Chass is right, there is nothing we can do."

"We freed the Linwir against a mage, fought Argentis and Eldrad in the thunder temple, survived an avalanche…. How can you say there is nothing we can do?"

Because you're too weak. You can't save them now, but I can.

I clenched my eyes shut. This wasn't right. I knew the king was willing to do whatever it took for the good of the kingdom, but had the curse really made him so desperate as to enslave his own people? Did 'the greater good' really justify torturing Fauns? I just had to speak to him, to show him that we really could end the drought. He would listen to reason, he would set the slaves free, and he would help us break the curse. In the meantime…

"There's no going back," I could hear the words coming out of my mouth, but they weren't my own. She had taken control. "If we don't stand up for ourselves now, then even if we break the curse nothing will change." I could feel power surging through my bones like I had never felt before. A ball of blue light was forming in the palm of my hand. "We must fight!"

Everything that happened next was a blur. I threw the ball of light towards the closest cart with a Praeg, breaking loose its chains and setting it free.

Everyone ducked for cover as all hell broke loose. The Praeg went after the soldiers, ignoring the captives. It was a beast but it was smart enough to know the enemy. Egris grabbed one of the riflemen from behind. I think he might have broken his neck as he took his musket and fired at another. I felt myself flying through the crowd, blasting soldier after soldier. One at a time they fell and as their numbers dropped and scattered the refugees began to flee while others fought and celebrated. After twenty minutes it was all over, and my world went black.

When I finally came to, I was told that Miev and the others had decided to stay in the abandoned village and make it their new home. Chass and Egris had prepared three of the fallen soldier's horses, and so we embarked on our two-week ride to the castle.

·24·
ARGENTIS

Morning was a blur. In fact most of the days following the avalanche were a blur. Stealing some horses from a ruined stable and joining up with a group of surveyors, all a blur.

We were waiting our turn to board a skiff to take us straight to the castle. It was that or join the refugees that were traveling by foot. We could have ridden by horseback but that would have taken two weeks time. Traveling across the red river streams was dangerous, but it was the fastest way to report back to the king.

Eldrad had insisted we go back and report to Mayor Talze, but I didn't care if I never saw that fat pig again in my life. The truth was I thought there was something more going on, something way over his head, and the King needed to know. I couldn't be sure if Talze was in cahoots with whoever caused the curse, or if he just wanted to maintain the status quo to keep the cheap labor flowing through his mine. Either way, if Carine's kid really did have a way to stop the drought, King Drevon should have been the first to know.

And that knowledge was my salvation. My ticket out of that

forgotten dump of a village. Arianna had said there were three relics, and she already had one of them. She was carrying it straight for Fennox-Calil, and thanks to me, the King would be ready for her when she got there. He would take the relic and see for himself the power that it held. He would put me in charge of my own expeditionary regiment to retrieve the final two relics. He would break the curse and be a hero to his people, and I would be his champion.

Behind me I could hear Eldrad getting up out of bed. The skiffs were sleds rigged with enormous sails that could skate seamlessly over the ruined valleys and dust-lands. Across the dead red rivers and back towards the roads that led to Fennox Castle.

Animals were too scared of the dead red river but there were still creatures of darkness that could tear the flesh from a living being. Cursed creatures, subjects of madness that lived without living. Shifting through the sands of darkness beneath the dust.

Patiently I stood as Eldrad gathered his gear and joined me on board. The captain of the skiff called out to his crew. Monks dressed in blue sat in pews in rows of two, praying. The captain was a superstitious man and he had been the only one willing to take our bribe.

"In an hour we'll be over the dead red river. I hope you have made peace with your gods," he said before ordering some of his crewmen to unleash a giant sail that caught the wind in front of the ship. The wind propelled us forward. I felt my calves stiffen as I tried to find my footing. The kingdom was dying. The dead red river was once a thriving lake just as the ruins of the village had once been a great estate. As Eldrad and I left I could see the imperial soldiers coming over the horizon. The castle never ran out of bodies. The more villages abandoned the more the walls of the kingdom grew.

"Listen!" the captain shouted. His voice was low, hoarse, full of terror at the realization that we were being hunted. I clutched the steel blade at my side and looked over towards Eldrad who was doing the same. The monks were unarmed but the captain had brought several hired mercenaries along for the ride. My eyes were straining to see anything in the dust that surrounded us. I heard the sound of the musket firing, the explosion of gunpowder. Somewhere, in the darkness, another sound. A shriek of pure horror as it drew closer.

"Be ready," I whispered.

The sound of wings beating the air grew louder. I thought I could feel the wind around me as the hair on my arm beneath my chain-mail rose. We were being circled. I squinted again towards the horizon, another strike of gunpowder rippled through the dust bloom and erupted in flames in the distance against a winged creature.

There are creatures in the dark that cast shadows in corners the sun never touches. Creatures that should have never been awakened. Drawn up from the world below to the dried ground searching for resources just like the rest of us. We picture fear and we think of a shadow in the woods, a creature in the night. If only it were that simple.

The worst appear without warning, primal. A reminder that just because we couldn't see the threat it wasn't already there. The curse that inflicted our kingdom had burned all the way to the roots of the world below. I had failed to best Chass, failed to take the relic, to kill Arianna, and I wasn't about to let some mythic horror rob me of my redemption.

I dove. Ducking down as the winged dragon came for us. It picked up a monk with its claws and tore him apart. The archers let loose their iron arrows but they dissolved in fire. The nightmare surrounded us as people screamed, soldiers locked in place. I saw Eldrad clutching the rail. His mouth agape, terrified eyes, and the winged creature with gray arms standing just in front of us. Its talons wet, red with blood. Eldrad slipped and I leapt after him.

"Hold on!" I cried out.

"Argentis, what is happening?"

His screams faded into the sounds of the wind as the dragon took flight again. Another burst of flame filled the sky as it disappeared.

"The shape of darkness has begun to unfurl around us," I said pulling him back up and falling over to one side.

"Move!" shouted the captain as another, smaller winged creature dove out of the dust. It moved forward, flying through the air followed by a horde of the scaly demons. I held my sword in front of me and swung against the milk-colored eyes of the beasts. Sharp, crooked black teeth cracked as they came into contact with my blade.

An explosion on the side of the skiff sent one of the winged serpents crashing down, crawling its way across the ship. It rushed toward us, claws slashing against the wooden hull, muscled flesh, slimy, covered in dirt. Its talons tore across the Captain's throat. He tried to scream in pain but was mute. His vocal cords severed. I grabbed the beast's broken wing and stabbed my sword through its shoulders. It thrashed as I gripped it, hugging it in my arms. I could feel the talons tear against my flesh. Eldrad held it from the back of the neck and kept its jaws from snapping around my head.

Another shot from a rifle exploded in the air around me. Black blood poured from the creature's mouth. It stopped moving. In the dim light I saw Eldrad move backwards and let the creature go. One of the monks had taken up arms. All around us everyone was fighting for their life, others weeping. The sound of creatures feasting.

This is it… Divine retribution.

"More are coming!" a voice shouted.

Something inside me gave way. Fading. I looked down at my body, my bruises, my wounds, bleeding through my chain-mail. I couldn't feel any of it. The shock and awe of battle.

A talon came down on top of my shoulder and still no pain.

Even as the world went white. I closed my eyes and focused. Not since I was trying to survive in the southern wild had I felt this sense of instinct consume me. Piercing the flood of dust and flesh I hacked and slashed the threshold that formed around me. Several of the winged creatures fell dead to the ground. From somewhere above I heard the dragon roar. I felt the smaller creature loosen its claws. I hadn't even realized it had still been hanging from my back. I could see the dragon's gray arms, claws, and teeth as it dove down towards our skiff. My sword was starting to shatter so I got rid of it and slid towards the rifle and rail. Picking it up I fired. I felt the fire move through me as it hit the dragon's eye.

"You hit it!" shouted Eldrad. I would have been smiling but I was already slipping over the rail.

Out in the wild, in the cold winter woods I no longer felt fit for this world. I gave in to the darkness. I resolved to fight on and kill that which stood in my way. Looking back I was so naive to think I could do all of it on my own. The further I saw into the darkness the more I struggled to see anything at all.

I fell to the ground. The dust of the dead red river threatening to swallow me like quicksand. I untied my armor and let it fall. My bare chest covered in claw marks, blood, and now sand. The skiff was moving away from me as I tried my best to swim for it. I barely moved no matter how far I reached. They weren't going to stop, not for me. I was an animal. If I died it would be my own fault. Still, I crawled to the surface of the sand, straightening myself out and moving as quickly as I could. There in the distance was a rope, an anchor. I moved like a snake against the grain. I grabbed the rope and felt it pull me forward.

"We have him," a voice shouted.

They pulled me back to the skiff and one of the monks started bandaging my bleeding wounds. Across the deck I saw the dragon struggling to move, wings bound in chains.

"You injured it, blinded its right eye and clipped its wing. When it hit the deck the monks used chains to bind it." Eldrad stood next to me. He looked just as worse-for-ware as I did.

As I sat on my knees, heaving, I looked upon the great creature I had brought low. Not only was I delivering to the King a way to break the curse, but I was bringing him a new pet. A live dragon. My reward would be great indeed.

Three days later we arrived. I was fading. Nearly at the end of my journey, but it wasn't over yet. Even in my half-aware, half-dead state, I could hear the surviving crew members singing my praises to anyone who would listen. The Great Argentis, Dragon-Slayer.

We were given a heroes welcome, and those that were injured in the fight were ushered into a great courtyard in the center of the castle filled with healing streams. I was carried in on a mat and lowered into a gently flowing pool. As the water seeped into the cracks in my skin I felt immediate relief.

All of my muscles relaxed and I let out a long, deep sigh. Then, something strange happened. A voice echoed inside my head, but it wasn't my own.

You've seen them, haven't you, son of Alahara? The relics.

I opened my eyes and saw King Drevon standing over me. Had he been the one speaking, and I had just been too dazed to realize it? "Yes," I answered with great effort, as sleep began to overtake me. "The thunder relic. She has it. The girl from Manse."

"The thunder relic, you say?" The King asked.

My brother. The voice echoed. Maybe it wasn't the King after all.

"She destroyed the mine," I answered, barely above a mumble, "and took it from the temple."

"And how did a young girl manage such an incredible feat?" The King asked.

"Her... powers."

"You witnessed these powers? How did they manifest?"

"Lightning. She... controls lightning."

My sister. This voice was really starting to freak me out.

"Interesting," I heard the King reply as darkness flooded my vision. "Very interesting."

A moment later, and I fell into the deepest sleep I had ever experienced.

· 25 ·

ARIANNA

"Well, here it is. The City!" Chass said. The three of us emerged from a forest overlooking a massive city.

"Fennox-Calil. Capital city of the elves, and source of great terror for Fauns," Egris said somberly, looking at the city with an expression of sadness.

"You think your cousin is in there somewhere?"

"I am sure of it. But if I were to go in with you, my fate would be the same as his."

"We can disguise you like before," said Chass.

"Don't be so naive, the guards will know what to look for, a simple hood will not fool an elven knight," Egris snapped. I knew Chass was only trying to be helpful but Egris was right. It was dangerous. Our journey together was coming to an end.

"You don't have to come. We understand," I said, getting down from my horse. I looked at the city. Fennox Castle stood on the side of a mountaintop, it almost looked like it had been carved into the stone itself. Along the right side we could see the ocean, endless over the horizon but lifeless as far as we could see. A handful of ragged boats stood in the harbor. Dozens of towers were also easily visible along with channels for running water.

The city had a water purification area that filtered water and sewage throughout the kingdom. Aqueducts led out from the castle walls, feeding water throughout the entire city and into the farmland beyond the outer walls that protected it. That was at least one benefit of living in the city. The city itself spanned for several miles. Even from the hill on which we stood it would take us a day to walk to the main gates.

"I have other business to attend to. We will meet back here in two days time. You, hopefully, with the locations of the final relics and whatever other help the King is willing to offer, and me with news of your father's killer."

I nodded.

It had been eating me alive. Everything in me wanted to believe it wasn't a Faun who did it, but I couldn't deny the evidence I had seen with my own eyes. There were several villages hidden in the woods, places Fauns had gone to hide. At the very least they knew things. They had seers they could speak to. Bones they could use to guide them. Egris had spoken of a temple near the city which housed a library full of knowledge; past, present, and future.

"Sounds like a plan. What are we waiting for?" Chass said, breaking the wave of thoughts that bounced around in my head. The two of us rode south towards the city and away from Egris.

We passed by several houses on the outskirts of the city. Our eyes widened as we saw how large and extravagant each house was. Some of them put Talze's mansion to shame, while others were just slightly smaller but no less elegant.

Giant stone statues of unknown origin lined some of the

well-tended gardens of lush flowers that grew over white fences. We came around a corner and found ourselves in the middle of a busy market. Fresh food was being cooked and sold from stands. I could smell fresh meat and fish as vendors poured wine from jugs half the size of my body into cups made of bronze and copper.

A blacksmith was working in an open-air shop. He looked nice enough. A short, rugged black beard, like he hadn't shaved in a few days, long gray hair with braids and gold beads. He was hammering against a longsword.

"Excuse me sir? Can you help us?" I asked.

The blacksmith scowled at us.

"Get lost! We don't want any trouble," he grunted.

"Trouble? No, we're just trying to get to the castle!" Chass said.

The blacksmith laughed. Several of the surrounding elves were pointing at us, whispering amongst themselves.

"Nice one kid. The Castle? What business do a couple of tramps have at the castle?" He was still laughing. We had clearly made his day.

"What? We're not…" I stammered, "We've come from the villages to end the curse that plagues our land!"

The gathering crowd of city elves chuckled as they gave one another sideways glances. They were dressed in fine robes. Some colorful, others gray with bold strips of gold. A few looked like they hadn't worked a day in their lives, while others looked like off-duty officers. Several of the women were wearing jewelry that looked like it had been lifted from a dungeon crypt. Silver necklaces and bracelets marked with runes. All of them would have stood out in any of the villages we had been.

"They're loony. Maybe the king has called for more jesters!"

said one of them. I furrowed my brow and looked around at the crowd.

"We need your help to end the drought!" I proclaimed loudly, hoping to appeal to their sense of loyalty. They laughed.

"What drought? What are you talking about?" said two, maybe three of them. Both Chass and I exchanged bewildered glances with one another.

"Have you not noticed we haven't had any water for fifteen years?"

"We get all the water we need from the springs in the castle," said the blacksmith, still laughing at us like we were putting on a show.

"And what about the villages? Where do you think we get water from?" I asked, frustrated by everyone around me. How could they laugh at this?

"We get news from the villages all the time. They're doing fine," said one of the laughing elves from the crowd.

"We've just come from the villages! In Manse…"

"Manse Village! As much as I pay for Manse metals you must be the wealthiest of them all!" the blacksmith laughed, cutting Chass off. Everyone continued to laugh all around us as both of us stared at one another confused. A pair of armored guards approached the gathering crowd.

"What's going on here?" the first armored guard asked.

"Just a couple of dregs trying to stir up trouble," the blacksmith laughed.

"No! We don't want trouble, we just want to speak to the King!" I argued.

"The King, eh?" the armored guard said.

I scrambled to pull the talisman from my pack. It would make things clear. I had to show them just how serious we were.

"Here! See this talisman? It's from the mage Cypress! He sent us to speak to the King," I said, holding the talisman, showing it around for all the crowd to see.

"Oh, Cypress sent you, did he? Well then I guess we'd better take you straight to his Majesty, hadn't we," the guard said as the crowd chuckled. Finally, someone with some sense. I lowered the talisman and stepped toward the two guards.

"Okay. Thank you." Just as I waited for them to start leading us away, Chass grabbed my arm. He was looking around the crowd. They were still laughing, smirking, smiling at us like we were a joke.

"I don't think they're being serious," he whispered.

"What?" I asked.

The two armored guards placed their hands on their swords.

"RUN!" Chass yelled, grabbing me. We bolted through the laughing crowd, knocking several city elves out of our way as we went. I quickly tossed the talisman back into my pack. It should have worked!

We weaved through several buildings and ducked behind an alley and climbed up a long ladder that led to a small rooftop. We jumped down. The guards were staying close behind but we had escaped the crowd. We pushed through another crowded market-place and into a narrow alley. We leaned against a building to catch our breath. There was no sign of the guards following behind us.

"What was that all about?" I said, gasping for air.

"Not the welcome party we hoped for," said Chass.

"They didn't even know about the drought, they called us names, they thought we were joking."

"I know, it's not what I expected either."

A loud crash came from the far side of the alley. Chass and I both snapped our heads in that direction, worried it was the guards coming back for us. There was an indistinct chatter of disgruntled yells. I moved towards the sound.

"Arianna, wait!" Chass yelled out to me.

I turned back towards him, "What if someone needs our help?" Despite what happened, I knew not everyone could be the way the city elves were. Chass rolled his eyes and followed behind me. I poked my head around the corner. Across a busy street, a horse-drawn cart had stalled out. The horse lay on its side, whimpering from a broken leg. A family was getting out of the cart as a crowd gathered. They were dressed less like the rest of the city elves and more like elves from our village. I pushed into the crowd as Chass reached out to grab me but I moved too fast for him.

"Excuse me! Coming through! I can help!" I said.

A succession of city elves turned towards me then backed away in disgust as I pushed past them.

Chass ran up behind me, "Arianna, stop!" he shouted, too late. I emerged from the crowd to where the family stood around the injured horse. A young boy about my age was kneeling beside the horse's head. He was handsome. Short dark hair, brown eyes, wearing a blue leather jacket and brown pants. He had a small satchel on his leg.

He was petting the horse's head, trying his best to comfort it and fight back tears in his eyes. A man in his fifties I assumed to be his father stood over the horse, scratching his head. The man was rugged, with a short gray beard and a receding hairline. He was wearing a weathered blue vest and his brown jacket had seen better days.

"Let me help," I said, standing over the boy and smiling.

The older man spun in my direction, "Get lost, kid!"

"I'm a mage! I can heal your horse!" I proclaimed proudly.

The crowd around us chuckled. The old man was fuming.

"I said get lost!"

"Why not let her try? What's the worst that could happen?" the young boy said, smiling towards me. I smiled back.

"The tramp'll rob us blind is what will happen!" the old man shouted.

I approached the horse while his back was turned towards the boy. He turned and saw me kneel at the broken leg.

"Hey! Stop it! I said we didn't need your help!" he shouted. I didn't listen. He reached for my shoulder as electricity arced over my body. He recoiled, aware of the danger. "What the?"

I reached for the broken leg. A spark of electricity zapped the horse. It pulled back and kicked at me. I jumped back just before the hoof made contact, and turned toward the boy. His eyes widened and he gave me a nod, patting the horse's head, "It's okay girl. She's here to help," he reassured her. I reached back for the leg again. The horse whimpered and shivered. Electricity flowed from my hands and bolted up the horse's leg. The horse squirmed and kicked its leg. Both the young boy and I jumped out of the way as the horse leapt to all four legs and stomped its feet. The crowd and the old man gasped.

"Incredible," the old man said, smiling now.

The boy gave me a sideways glance.

"You're not from the academy are you?" he asked.

"No, I've just sort of always been this way."

The old man stared at the horse, his mouth ajar. I approached him slowly.

"I don't believe it," he said to himself.

"Excuse me sir? I was wondering if I might ask a favor?"

"Of course. Anything!" the old man's demeanor had completely switched. Chass came up behind me. "My friend and I need help getting to the castle, to see the King."

"The King? What?" the old man pondered the question.

"I think we should start with a decent meal and a place to sleep for the night," Chass interjected, smiling.

"Yes! Of course. That we can do. My name is Arnin, and this is my son, Luuk."

ARIANNA

Arnin and Luuk led us through the city walls, vouching for us with the guards at the city gates. We were out of the outskirts and inside the actual city. It took us several hours to actually arrive in the district that they lived. A small house made of stone.

Chass and I sat at one side of a lavishly set table. Luuk and his little sister, Isly, about seven years old, sat opposite of us. I wished the two of us were sitting closer. I felt something in the pit of my stomach every time I looked at him; butterflies? Arnin sat at the head of the table while his wife, Henna, a woman in her fifties, sat at the foot. Everyone but Arnin was laughing.

"Wait, wasn't that the same girl that left you for that squire boy?" Henna said, laughing out loud with a cup of water in her hand.

"Mom!" Luuk said, trying not to be too loud or disrespectful. He was embarrassed. Henna was nice. I liked her. All of us had just met and yet they had welcomed us in with open arms. I covered my mouth to keep from spitting out the food I was chewing.

"Luuk has been trying to get taken on as a squire since he was twelve," Isly said seriously, whispering the information to me like it was some secret.

"I'll get it someday! There just aren't a lot of openings when we aren't at war," Luuk argued.

Arnin wiped his mouth with a napkin, "Peace is something to be thankful for, Luuk, you would be wise to learn that."

A hush fell over the table. Luuk looked down at his plate, "Yes, father."

Henna cleared her throat, "What about you Chass? I'm sure you have plenty of tales of your brave heroics?" Kind of her to change the subject.

"Boy does he!" I said, swallowing my food.

Chass gave me a sideways glance.

"As a matter of fact, I do," he said and looked from Luuk to me.

"Oh, do tell," Henna insisted.

"Yes, brave Sir Chass, do tell," I insisted.

Chass pointed to me, "Well, it all started when this one let her temper get the better of her, again!"

Luuk raised his eyebrows toward me, "Oh, you've got a temper, do you?" he said and I blushed. Isly gave an exasperated sigh.

"Luuk's last girlfriend had a temper, too," she said, whispering it again toward me. Luuk dropped his fork, "Shut up!" he laughed.

A knock on the door made the room fall silent.

Arnin folded his napkin and set it on the table. He went to check. The atmosphere felt completely different. From fun to tense as he walked into the other room.

Muffled voices spoke to one another, "Excuse me sir, we've had reports of a couple of vagrant kids stirring up trouble near here. You haven't seen anything out of the ordinary, have you?"

Everyone at the table avoided eye contact as there was an uncomfortable pause.

"No, I'm sorry. I haven't seen anything," Arnin answered.

Every one of us at the table exhaled.

"Thank you. Let us know if you see anything suspicious."

"Will do."

Arnin returned to the dining room and sat without speaking a word.

None of us said anything for several moments.

"So what is this about you needing to get to the castle?" Arnin asked, taking a bite from his steak.

"You see, sir, Chass and I believe, as did my father, before he died, that a powerful mage has placed a curse over the entire kingdom by trapping the three spirits of the storm into three relics, causing a never-ending drought. We have been traveling with a…"

Chass coughed, thinking I was about to say Faun.

"…We've been traveling with others from our village, but we decided to split up to find the final two relics. That's why we're the only ones here."

I gave the speech like I had been practicing it for hours, giving Chass a confused look and glancing toward Henna.

"Yes," Chass continued. "And we believe the King knows the location of at least one of the relics. We hope that when we show him we've already found one, he will help us in any way he can."

"You've found one already, you say?" Arnin asked, amazed.

"Can we see it?" Luuk asked, astonished.

Chass and I looked at each other and nodded. I pulled the relic from my pack. Luuk reached out to touch it but I pulled it away from him.

"I wouldn't do that if I were you. It can be very unstable," I insisted.

"Hmm. It doesn't look unstable." Arnin remarked.

"It caused an avalanche when we plucked it from the temple in the mountains. But it stopped as soon as Arianna touched it," Chass said.

"Interesting. You must be a very special girl." Arnin noted, straight-faced.

I clutched it in my hand and held it against my chest.

It wasn't whispering anything to me, not anymore. I had control.

"I must be," I said.

Arnin dabbed his mouth with his napkin. No one spoke.

"You'll go right down the main road in front of the house. When you see a tannery, you'll turn left. This will take you to the main square. You'll be able to see the castle from there. The road by the butcher will lead you straight to the gates. Getting past the guards, there I cannot help you."

"Thank you! Thank you so much, sir. You have no idea how much that means to us. And don't worry, we already have a way to see the King," I said as Chass gave a skeptical grimace.

Inside Isly's bedroom that night Luuk sat with his sister in his lap. He was reading her a book. I stood over his shoulder. He read with his best narrator voice, "Once upon a time there was a little girl named Jo-elle who hated cleaning her room." There was a cute picture of a little girl playing with a doll on a cluttered floor filled with toys and clothes as her mother stood over her with her hands on her hips and an exasperated smile. Luuk turned the page.

Now the mother was shaking a finger at the girl who was giving her best pouty face. "One day her mother told Jo-elle, 'Clean your room or you'll go to bed without any dinner!'" I couldn't help but laugh at Luuk's awkward attempt at a motherly voice. The next page showed the little girl packing her things into a small bag, "I don't need her to cook dinner for me," Luuk's voice cracked as he did his best squeaky little girl impersonation, "I can run away to the woods and take care of myself!"

Luuk turned the page to reveal the girl alone in a dark forest. I suddenly realized what was about to happen. I looked up at Chass who was standing in the doorway. He shook his head ever so slightly. This wasn't the right time.

"Little did Jo-elle know," Luuk continued, "deep in the forest there are evil creatures, just waiting to eat little girls who wander into their trap."

Isly didn't react.

I glanced down at the next page. It featured a gruesomely mutilated Faun howling at the frightened child. I covered my mouth. I wanted to throw up. Luuk turned the page. The Faun sat against a tree patting its bloated belly. The girl's clothes and fresh-picked bones sat nearby.

"And that, dear children, is why you do not wander into the woods alone."

I awoke the next morning with a start, feeling the rush of warm air on my skin. I opened my eyes to see what looked like dark clouds of smoke in the sky out my window and the smell of fresh bread. The ovens next door were burning bright as the morning sun. I was on my back, in a bed, in Isly's room. On the floor was Chass, still snoring. I sat up and felt a small pain in my back. It had been a long time since I'd slept on an actual bed; so long my body had grown used to the ground. I ignored it and pushed myself up.

"Wake up, we need to leave," I said, lightly kicking Chass in the side.

"Five more minutes, please," he grogged.

We said goodbye to Henna and Isly. Luuk and Arnin had already left for the day to pick up rations and sell their goods at the market. Luuk had left a blue flower by the door for me along with a note. Thanking me for using my magic and hoping the two of us would see one another again.

I sniffed the flower and smiled. Perhaps it was better he wasn't here to say goodbye in person. I had my mission to focus on, I couldn't afford to be distracted. And there was no use letting myself get attached, anyway. It would only end in heartbreak.

Outside we passed several groups of soldiers. More than the day before but none of them seemed to notice us. Luuk had left us clothes to wear that made us look like we belonged in the city. Green and blue robes that we could wear over our armor and cover our swords. We followed Arnin's directions, stopping once to get some fresh bread from a baker. We used some of the gold I had taken from Talos' tavern. My father's gold. As we walked alongside an aqueduct channel flowing with water, the wooden frames holding it up rose higher and higher, and we knew we were getting close.

We stood before the towering castle gate in awe. The wall was so high it was impossible to see the castle itself. It might have been higher than the wall that surrounded the city itself outside. Two unmoving gatekeepers stood at either side of the large gate.

"Excuse me? We need to be taken to the King, immediately." I said standing tall and confident. There was no response.

"The talisman," Chass said.

"Oh, right!" I began to dig through my pack. "I have a talisman that was given to me by a mage who was friends with the King…" the two gatekeepers briefly glanced sideways at each other. I pulled various items from my bag. None of them were the talisman. As I reached down further into my pack I began to panic. "It was right here! I just had it."

"You didn't lose it, did you?" Chass asked, nervously.

The gatekeepers were starting to look annoyed.

"No, of course not. I just…" I tried to think. I had pulled it out to show the guards the day before, then… oh no! It must have fallen out of my pack as we ran! I threw the bag on the ground. "Listen! A terrible drought has been plaguing our kingdom for years and I have to assemble the three relics holding the spirits of the storm to break the curse and end the suffering of our people!" One of the gatekeepers let out a chuckle, then clasped his hand over his mouth. The other looked at him, wide-eyed before both snapped back to attention.

"Is this a joke to you?" Electricity began to bristle over my body. I was tired of this. Tired of everyone laughing at me. The relics were real. We barely survived getting the first one and I wasn't going to let anything stop me from finishing my mission.

"Arianna, calm down," Chass said nervously.

"The entire kingdom is at stake, and you think this is a laughing matter?"

Sparks of lightning began to course over me.

"Arianna, please."

See, this is what I was talking about. You can't do this without me. Let me loose. I'll take care of these guards for you.

"No! Stop it!" I yelled.

"Arianna, who are you talking to?" I heard Chass ask behind me.

The two gatekeepers were moving toward me now.

Come on, we can take them.

No, they weren't our enemy, they just didn't understand. We had to make them trust us.

"She's using magic!" one of the gatekeepers said.

"Hey! You can't do that! Do you have a permit?" asked the other.

A permit? They want to control us! To use our power for themselves! Blast them!

"No!" I yelled one last time, dropping to my knees as the power dissipated around me.

Half an hour later we were inside the castle. A cell door slamming shut. A lock fastening into place. Chass and I were inside a dark, dingy dungeon.

27

EGRIS

Arianna and Chass left towards the gates of the elvish capital. I dared not venture with them knowing it would be the end of my journey. My eyes wept as I rode away from them. Carine would have been so proud of his daughter and how far she had come, but I worried about the boy. Chass was tempered, sharp like a sword, dangerous. Still, there was a light in him that brightened even the darkest of days and he loved Arianna as much, more even, than I ever could.

I had not expected her to know so little of my kind, my people. I had thought Carine would have told her of our adventures, but I was wrong. It felt strange reliving so much of it… sharing the stories of our past and smiling, laughing even as the words slipped out. I left out so much. Not because I had chosen to lie or because it wasn't written in his journals, but because I knew the truth would do more harm than good. Carine was a good man but he had been addicted to breaking the curse. An addiction he passed down to his daughter.

What would happen to us when this was all over? What

adventures would we have to move forward on? Time would tell. For the moment all I could do was keep my word as I headed into the woods to seek the library and speak to the Oracle of Winter.

Three miles deep into the woods I could feel the deep magic around me. Heightening my senses. The swamps of the moor, the muddy bogs that blew bubbles of poisonous gas. No choice but to leave my horse behind and venture forward on hoof. My horse set free to wander the borders of the edge of the world just beyond the gates of death.

I was no seeker. No amplifier. No mage and yet I pushed forward into this dark place. I could remember hearing stories of the Oracle of Winter, the seer born before the beginning of the world, the keeper of the library of knowledge and wisdom of the flame. I could remember the stories my parents told me of the darklings, demons of the undercity that rose to lay claim to the land.

How the elves, dwarves, Faun, and humans banded together to defeat their lords. How the Oracle had brought them together despite their differences. I can remember hearing how they vowed to secure knowledge. To unite and stand indefinitely. How the years grew dark and the area around the Oracle became ruined as a result. The bog created from the rotting marrow of men. The trees that rooted and grew that fed on the blood of elves and the dwarves whose hearts turned to stone and became the rocks that cut from below.

"Carine, what would you have me do," I asked myself, treading carefully through the waist-deep water of the swamps. I could feel small fish bite at my flesh as I moved slowly over jagged rocks like daggers.

No answer came.

I didn't know why I chose to talk to ghosts when the living were so close.

I missed my people. The songs of the village, the dancing, the wine.

Carine; the old fool may have been dead but he still had me going on quests.

I moved quietly and pulled myself back onto dry land to rest.

Slowly I addressed my wounds. I would have more before I left this place.

The Oracle was close. I could feel it. Never in my life had I felt such a presence. Strange, mystical, full of magic. It sent chills down the back of my spine. Dangerous. Dark. Distorted. The curse hadn't left any of the world untouched but this place had become ruins long before that day.

A shadow crossed the light that broke the canopy above but that is not what startled me. There was something in the muddy water. Something that had been following me all along. Studying me. I was not alone.

A Praeg? A dragon? No. This was a creature who had come to call this place home. I was the trespasser. The land around me was a nest. Massive pale eggs sat grouped together in bundles of three and four scattered several yards apart. Crocodile… no, Sarcosuchus, a Sarcos for short. Larger and meaner than their smaller descendants. The Sarcos could grow to be 40 feet long from head to tail and have teeth as large as the palm of my hand. From where I stood on land I could see the Sarcos slowly begin to rise above the water. Its nose larger than the rest of its long jaw. Thirty-one teeth waited to bite me. Tear me limb from limb. This monster could eat dinosaurs for breakfast. Even dragons would have a hard time escaping its jaws of death.

I reached for my sword. Instinct taking over.

My people. We had lived in harmony with nature. There was balance to all things, but this place was wicked. There was no balance here. The Sarcos was guardian and I was an uninvited guest.

A voice inside my head told me to turn around. To run. To climb. To get away by whatever means possible.

I couldn't. Not for myself. For Arianna.

The answers were here. Hidden in the swamp.

"Come on," I whispered again and again as the Sarcos moved closer. It was slow. Studying me. Strategizing how best to eat me I presumed. I'm sure it recognized the sword as some kind of weapon. Maybe it was afraid. Sarcos' used to be hunted for their leather. No. Wrong. It was watching me. So close to its nest it dared not make the wrong move.

I stepped towards one of the eggs. The Sarcos' head rose out of the water and I heard a deep growl from its gut. It echoed through the trees and caused the water to ripple.

"Not so fast," I said as if the beast understood my language.

I was closer to the egg than before.

"Carine, I'm really in trouble now, I could use some help down here."

Nothing. Not that I expected a ghost to answer.

"Okay, just you and me big buddy. How about you turn around and I start walking away. That way neither of us has to die this day. I'll leave your nest, leave your swamp and you'll never have to worry about another Faun coming here again so long as I live." I chuckled, wishing the creature understood what I was saying.

Its eyes glossed over, large black pupils. Its mouth widened and

I feared for an attack. I shut my eyes. No sword would do me any good and I wasn't going to swing. The Sarcos had called my bluff.

"Strange Faun, what do you want in my swamp?" a voice called out.

My eyes jerked open. The Sarcos hadn't moved. It looked almost as if it was frozen in time.

"Who said that?" I called out.

"I believe your kind have called me the Oracle of Winter, but I have many names. What are you called?"

"Egris. I come here to seek knowledge, truth of events. A dear friend of mine lost his life and my people were wrongly accused of his murder. I am here to clear our name, to bring justice, to bring truth to his daughter."

I felt a hand reach out and grab my wrist.

My sword fell to the ground.

There was a pressure wrapping, warping itself around me. I felt like my body was becoming stiff and I couldn't move.

"The library is not one of books, as you have come to understand, but of pure, unfiltered truth. I will open the door for you but you must know that truth comes at great cost."

"I am prepared to pay the price, whatever it may be," I responded.

"The cost of knowledge," the ominous voice said, "is that it cannot be forgotten."

As the strange voice disappeared I saw a large group of fairies appear, lighting the way towards a ruined doorway leading down. It looked as if the doorway had been there the whole time but I couldn't see it. The fairies flew around, hundreds, like little lightning bugs guiding me down as the Sarcos itself retreated back into the dark water of the moor.

"What is this?" I asked aloud, hoping the voice was still with me.

There was no answer.

Perhaps it was better that way.

Deep in the ruin I quickly found I was inside a tomb, not a temple. Catacombs filled with the skeletons of elves, dwarves, and other creatures from long ago. Soldiers lost in a long-forgotten war. I held onto my sword, worried several would pop up, attack me, but none moved. The stale air was hard to breathe, almost toxic, but the smell was the worst. A part of me wanted to pass out from the fumes but I pushed on. Always the worst part of adventures. The smell of sweat, bodies, rotting meat. Could no one light incense anymore? No matter where Carine led me the smells were always the worst. Still, I pushed on.

The walls were painted. Once vibrant I was sure. Images of elves, dwarves, all fighting together. Even humans with their round ears and bearded faces were depicted. Some of the images showed them fighting shadowy figures while others looked like mutated dragons with wings that filled the sky and hundreds of eyes. Other creatures had multiple heads, arms, legs, even wolves with three eyes. The giant mural showed a woman holding a sword above her head, lightning falling from the sky. I could still make out the blue from the chipped clay that was peeling away. I placed my hand against the image. Below her stood several figures. Fauns, knights, even dinosaurs and dragons.

"Arianna," I said to myself, tears were starting to fall from my eyes.

Was this image a depiction of the past or the future?

A tomb. All that was left of the library. Buried beneath the swamp.

Carine would have loved discovering this place. I could see him now. Using paper and charcoal to trace the wall lit up by the light of a torch. I continued to follow the fairies. Only slightly worried they would disappear and leave me in the dark.

Large corridors led me to a large throne room where an ancient king sat on his throne. The throne itself was giant. Made from the bones of dinosaurs and dragon teeth. The back of the throne was ten feet tall and had once been painted in beautiful colors, now faded.

"Who were you?" I asked. Just as before there was no answer. I studied the dead king. In his hand he held a gem. Amidst the bleak gray of death and decay it shone with an effervescent blue. It must have been a powerful relic. The source of the truth the Oracle had spoken of. The same truth that had once united the kingdoms of the world in peace, and also turned them against each other in a bloody thirst for power.

I took hold of the gem, and the world around me vanished. I stood in complete darkness; not even the smell remained. Slowly, a familiar feeling began to grow around me. The sounds of the woods. The smell of dirt, decaying leaves. I was standing in a forest.

I recognized the path on which I stood. It was not far from Manse village. Why had the Oracle brought me here? The sound of horse hooves came from around the bend. A moment later the creature emerged, though it almost seemed a mist, a shadow, a memory. I looked up to observe the rider, and my heart leapt for joy!

"Carine!" I shouted. "You're alive!" But he didn't seem to hear me. The horse continued on, and before I had time to gather my wits and jump out of the way, the animal plowed right through me and trotted along, unfazed. So I was only an observer. This was the past, and I was about to witness the death of my dearest friend.

A few meters more and he pulled the horse to a stop, scanning the tree line to either side of the path. There was a rustling in the leaves. An uneasy sense of being watched. Carine pulled out one of his journals, scribbled a note with that magical ink of his, and tore the corner of the page from the book. He clenched it in his fist and whispered a spell onto his hand. So that was how he had insured no one would find the message but Arianna.

Carine dismounted his horse and pulled out his sword. Knowing they had been spotted, two knights emerged from the forest edge. So it had been elves, after all. I knew in my heart it could not have been a Faun, but even so I found it hard to imagine any creature capable of such barbarism. I couldn't shake the feeling that there was something different about these two knights; the dark runes on their armor seemed somehow familiar…

"We both knew this day was coming," the first knight spoke. His voice was unmistakable. It was Argentis! How had I not seen it immediately?

"Then let's dispense with the pleasantries and get down to business," Carine replied. He never was one to waste time on words when there was a fight to be had. As the two knights attacked him I wanted to look away, but forced myself to watch. It was the least my dear companion deserved. He had lived with honor, and faced death with bravery and dignity. This was my chance to finally pay my respects.

I had never ceased to be amazed at his agility in combat. Even as he fought with one hand, his other sealed closed by a simple spell, he held his ground against the two thugs.

Tears streamed down my face as I watched him parry, dodge, and strike at every opening that presented itself. He even managed to find a gap in Argentis' armor, just inside his elbow. As he pulled his sword through the narrow opening, he ripped a piece of fabric from Argentis' under-tunic. The cloth blew towards me in the wind, but I ignored it, expecting it to pass through me, as the horse had. Instead, it hit my leg, and stuck. Curious, I bent down and snagged it, observing the runes embroidered into the blood-stained fabric.

It wasn't long before Carine was overpowered, and the knights ran him through. I watched, unblinking, as they mutilated and desecrated his body. I wanted to fall to my knees, to cry out, but I stood, stoic and unflinching, as they carved the sacred runes of my people into his skin.

The vision began to fade, and the smell of rot once again filled my nostrils. I felt reality rushing back into focus around me, and the dry forest was replaced by the hollow eyes of the ancient king on his eternal throne.

As I turned to leave I noticed something soft between my fingers. I looked down. I still held the torn fabric in my hand.

ARIANNA

I woke up with tears in my eyes. My back hurting. Angry. After being nearly knocked unconscious by a guard outside the castle gates we were taken inside by force to the dungeon. Bags put over our heads and all.

There were bones tied with string and ripped cloth hanging down from the bars of my cell. Every time I started to use my magic I could feel it being pulled away. Not that it was gone but that it was being absorbed by the bones. I was certain I could overpower it, but it would be incredibly draining. Not to mention the last thing I wanted was to bring the king's wrath down on us. We were here to save the world, not end it or cause trouble.

A burly guard with armor too small for his body grunted like a pig as he turned away from us. He dropped my pack and Chass' sword on a table about ten feet away from us. The table was filled with other weapons and small torture devices. The guard scratched his stomach and ambled slowly around the corner, leaving the two of us alone in the cell together.

"Now you've got yourselves in a sticky situation," a familiar voice came from a dark corner of the cell, causing Chass and me to spin toward the sound. Cypress! I hadn't seen him there before.

"They got you too?" I asked.

"I can teleport, remember?" Cypress said as he emerged from the shadow. "I've been keeping tabs on the two of you, but I lost track of you for a minute there. So I decided to come check on you." He suddenly disappeared and a moment later his voice came from behind us. "And it's a good thing I did, too!"

We turned back around and he stood just outside the bars, smiling with his crooked teeth, running his hand through his beard. Chass looked at him, puzzled and confused, but I had read about magic like this before. Tapping into the power of the aether, Cypress was moving in and out of our dimensional plane. He could probably do it for a few seconds but no more. Not a mere illusion, but something he must have spent a lifetime working to master.

"You can get us out?" I asked, smiling.

"I can talk to the King for you. I can't make any promises, but there shouldn't be any issues," Cypress replied.

"And what issues might there be?" Chass asked, more suspicious than ever.

"Oh, they take the use of magic without a permit very seriously around here. You're both scheduled to be executed first thing in the morning."

"Both? I! I didn't..." Chass started to yell.

"Along with him," Cypress interrupted Chass and stepped aside. In the far cell, a Faun sat chained in a corner. He was mutilated beyond recognition, more resembling the Satyrs from the stories Luuk was telling his younger sister. Both Chass and I gasped at the sight of the Faun.

"He is accused of murdering an elf. A 'Carine' something or other," Cypress said in a dismissive voice.

I screamed and slammed into the cell door. My knuckles turned white as electricity arced through me and I gripped the bars. Cypress looked at me sideways and narrowed his eyes. I didn't care. Not what he thinks.

"Perhaps you knew him?" Cypress asked.

Lightning sparked over my entire body. From head to toe and burning the ground below me as it flickered back and forth. Chass reached his hand out. A spark hit him and he recoiled backwards. He looked towards Cypress, but he had already disappeared.

"Arianna, I don't trust that man. We can't wait for him to speak to the king. We have to get out on our own." Chass said, trying his best to stay calm.

"We're not waiting for anyone anymore," I said as my eyes turned gray as storm clouds. Lightning ran around me in circles and I extended my hand out towards the lock. No bag of bones was going to stop me. I blasted the lock to our jail cell with a bolt and it shattered. "Let's go." I marched straight to my pack and picked it up. Chass followed right behind me. After he picked up his sword he ran back to the Faun's cell. I moved towards the corridor.

Burn him! This is our chance!

No. Not now. I couldn't let my thirst for vengeance get in the way of the mission.

This is the creature that stole your life from you! Now steal his!

"Arianna, we have to rescue him," Chass called out.

I didn't stop. I couldn't. I knew what I wanted to do to him, and the thought made me sick. The mission was all that mattered.

Breaking the curse. Preserving my father's wishes, his legacy. Not repaying death with death.

There is nothing left but death!

"We promised Egris!" Chass shouted.

I paused. Tears fell from my eyes. The storm still raged inside me.

"That was before we knew the truth," I said as calmly as possible. The King's men had caught the killer that murdered my father. Talze hadn't been telling a lie. Egris probably didn't know, maybe he wouldn't understand but it was clear to me. We were all too different, too far apart. Enemies just like in the storybooks. The Satyr were monsters. And in that moment I knew I was no less a monster.

Chass looked toward the Faun, "I'm sorry. I am so sorry." And without another word he turned and followed me.

We approached an imposing set of wooden doors that led out of the dungeon. A blast of my lightning knocked the doors off their hinges. Several elves jumped out of the way. Others turned to look at the commotion, covering their mouths from the dust that textured the air in the room.

I stepped through the open door frame as Chass stumbled out after. I marched along with my eyes locked straight ahead. Bystanders ducked into the side rooms as I passed. They were afraid of me. Good.

This is power. This is what it takes to win.

A trio of guards rounded the corner with staves and spears in hand.

"There she is! Get her!" one of them shouted.

Without slowing down I raised both hands and blasted two of

them away.

No hesitation. No remorse. I felt the storm continuing to swell inside me, threatening to break out at any moment.

"Take me to the King now!" I demanded, staring down the last guard. My eyes flickered with light and even I felt a twinge of fear at what I was becoming.

"Yes ma'am," the guard said, nearly choking on his words. He dropped his weapons and ran toward another heavy wooden door that led into the throne-room. Two guards stood at attention to either side of the door.

"Halt!" One of the guards shouted. "What is the meaning of this?"

Our escort looked back at me with sweat on his brow, and managed to stumble out, "The prisoners have demanded to see the King."

"What?" the guard replied. "Prisoner's don't make demands! Do you want to go back to being a squire?"

I stepped forward. The lightning still swirled around me, my footsteps burned the ground. If I had been walking on sand it would have turned to glass under my footsteps. "Let. Us. In." I said, spitting out each word.

Not a moment after I had finished speaking, the throne-room door opened from within. There in the doorway stood King Drevon. He was tall, imposing, and looked at his guards with an expression of stern admonishment. His crown was formed from the teeth of praeg, with brilliant, faintly glowing gems fashioned throughout.

"Guards! Stand down at once!" He barked in a voice that made me take a step back from the sheer force of it. The guards all snapped to attention and stared straight forward, unblinking.

The King turned his gaze to Chass and me, and his face immediately melted into a look of compassion and understanding. "Come, children. Let us speak. I am terribly sorry for how you have been treated. All a misunderstanding."

His voice, while still deep and forceful, was now soothing, disarming. Still, something inside me refused to let it's guard down.

It's him! The spirit inside me hissed. *Don't trust him!*

"*What are you talking about?*" I said silently to the Lightning Spirit. "*The King wants to help us!*"

The King reached out to place a gentle hand on my shoulder, but a spark caught his finger and he pulled back. I could hear the Lightning Spirit hissing in anger.

"I'm sorry," I said to the King, embarrassed. "I guess I'm still a little on edge."

"Understandable," the King replied. "Come, we have much to discuss."

As I followed the King I admonished the spirit yelling inside my head, "*Silence! We have to trust the King.*"

No, it replied. *He is the one who enslaved my brothers!*

"*What?*"

Kill him! Burn him now!

"*I can't just kill the King!*" The spirit must have been mistaken. My father had insisted in his journals that the King would help us break the curse. He had been trying for years to get an audience. Surely we hadn't come all this way for nothing...

We were approaching the throne. It sat on a platform raised several steps off the ground. The throne itself was fashioned from the bones of praeg, and had several teeth lining the top which must have worked to accentuate the already intimidating effect of the crown when the King sat in it.

King Drevon stepped to the side and noticed me staring up at the throne. "Come," he said. "Let us speak in my private quarters. You will perhaps be more comfortable there."

He guided us around behind the throne and through an ornate door into what must have been the foyer for his personal living space. A massive desk sat near one wall, and at the center of the room sat a table with a map of the entire kingdom built on top of it. A fireplace was built into the far wall, and the head of a dragon was mounted over the mantle. An intimidating trophy, indeed.

"I've just spoken with Cypress," the King explained as he moved toward the desk. "He explained everything."

"Is Cypress still here?" I asked as I moved toward the map at the center of the room.

"No, I have allowed him to return home," King Drevon replied. "He has finished his mission here, and needs his rest. He is very old, you know."

"You can say that again," Chass chuckled. He had been totally disarmed by the King's demeanor. I wanted to relax as well, to celebrate a clear victory that brought us ever closer to completing our mission, but something was holding me back. What if the spirit was right? What if the King wasn't to be trusted?

"He tells me you managed to retrieve the Thunder Relic. Is that true?"

"Yes," I replied absently. "It's here in my pack." I turned to look at the King. His gaze had shifted to my pack. He took a half step toward me and his fingers fidgeted at his side.

"I'm impressed, honestly I am. I've had my best men searching for the relics for years."

"So you will help us find the others?" Chass asked.

"Of course," the King replied. "We will bring them all back here and—"

"They must be taken to the Ruins of Kakara," I interrupted. The King froze, mouth still ajar. "That is where the curse must be broken. It's all in my father's research."

"Yes, of course," The King responded slowly. "If I had known your father was so close to finding the relics I would have enlisted his help at once."

I looked back to the map. It was covered in small figurines of soldiers, all pointed toward Faun villages. In the corner of my eye I saw the King's shoulders relax. He was regaining his poise.

"What do you see?" He asked.

"War," I replied, the realization weighing down on me. "You mean to attack the f... er, the satyrs."

"The satyrs have been a nuisance for years," He replied. I looked over to Chass. He looked back at me with his brow furrowed in confusion. There was dread behind his eyes.

"We've managed to survive the curse here in the capital thanks to our enchanted springs," King Drevon continued. "But our plans to spread that wealth to the villages were foiled when the satyrs came out of hiding and attacked our caravans."

I found Manse Village on the map. A small, blue flag was stuck into the area over the mines. I noticed several different colored flags scattered throughout the other villages.

"Do the flags represent each village's key resource?"

"Very astute observation," the King replied with a smile. "You see, we couldn't rely on ending the curse through magic. We knew it would be too difficult. We had to evaluate each village's strength, so that once the satyrs were exterminated we could reunite as an economic whole, pooling our resources to meet the needs of the entire Kingdom."

I shuddered at his use of the word 'exterminated'. A lone blue flag in the middle of the Cyndarin Mountains caught my eye. It was placed over the Linwir mines. Had the King been the one behind the mines? Had he known they were so close to the Thunder Relic?

"I've been hearing a lot about your powers, Arianna." I could feel the King staring at me, but I couldn't turn to meet his gaze. "You will be a very valuable asset in our war against the satyr," he continued.

"But what if there's another way?" Chass asked. "What if the satyr aren't what we think?"

"There is no other way," the King replied. "They're not like us. They're animals, pests. Nothing more."

Near the Linwir mines there were several strange figurines I didn't recognize. They almost looked like siege weapons, but larger and more mechanical than anything I had seen before. They seemed to be mounted with massive muskets on top. Did the King intend to use my electricity to power these machines somehow?

I thought back to the Linwir mines. The massive amounts of earth that had been moved. The tonnes of ore that would be required to build these terrible weapons. Surely it would be too much for the Linwir slaves to have done on their own. There could be only one explanation.

"What is the source of your springs?" I asked.

King Drevon paused and cocked his head. "I don't understand," he replied.

"You said there were enchanted springs supplying the entire capital, that they would be enough to feed the whole kingdom."

I turned to meet the King's gaze. His eyes narrowed. "Yes, that's right."

"Even the enchanted wells in Manse must be carefully guarded and rationed lest they run dry. Surely no one spring could provide water to the entire Kingdom."

After a pause, the King said, "They told me you were powerful, temperamental even. I didn't know you would be so cunning, as well. Follow me."

King Drevon led us out of the throne-room and through a series of hallways and staircases. All along the way guards and royal elves stepped out of our way, bowing to the King as he passed, then looking up in time to eye Chass and I with suspicion.

We continued to climb staircase after staircase. We must have been getting close to the top of the mountain the castle was built into. Finally, we reached a set of wooden doors that led into a lush, green, open-air courtyard. I stepped around the King to get a better look, then froze in my tracks.

Chass stopped behind me. The two of us stared in awe, unable to believe what we were seeing. At the center of the courtyard was a fountain spewing water out into a basin which fed several streams that flowed out of the courtyard in various directions. The aqueducts. The spring that provided the entire city with water. This was its source. And atop the fountain, the true origin of all this water, was a brownish gem in the unmistakable shape of a spider on a leaf. The Rain Relic!

Guards stood around the room, their focus trained on me. I could tell there was something different about them compared to the others. They stood tall with large broadswords and triangular shields covered in ancient runes.

"And now you know the truth." The King's voice was softer than it had been before. Calm, collected. He spoke as if he was rationing all of his thoughts, pausing to form sentences. Slowly, as if every word resonated with some kind of mystical power.

I was staring at the rain relic, speechless. My father suspected the King knew its location... but this? The storm raging in my mind was immediately rekindled, rising to the surface.

Here we are, the three of us together at last. Along with the man who enslaved us. Kill him.

It took everything I had to maintain control. All of the pieces were coming together. "The rain to keep the people dependent, the thunder to level mountains for your mines, and the lightning to power your machines of war."

"So this was all just some vain power-grab?" Chass asked through gritted teeth. "You'll never get away with this." Chass drew his sword and the guards surrounding us moved a step forward. The King held up his hand and the guards stopped.

"Oh, you misunderstand. I'm not doing this for myself. No, it's for the greater good. Don't you see it?" The King continued to smile. He walked up the fountain, his feet sloshing through the pool that surrounded it. The bottom of his cape soaked up water as it floated along behind him. He moved his hand into the fountain and watched as the water cascaded around his fingers. Chass and I gave each other a confused glance.

"I could feel my power slipping away from me, that much is true. Democracy. It sounds good on paper, but I could see its inevitable outcome. I knew that each person would only vote for their own self-interest. 'We need more money to bolster the blacksmithing industry.' 'We need to support our farmers.' Where is all that money coming from?

"Some even think they're doing it for altruistic purposes. That is the greatest lie of them all. 'We need to feed the poor.' 'Education for the children.' There are a finite amount of resources in this world. There must be an impartial judge to allocate those resources."

"But why go to war with the Fauns?" Chass asked. "Why not just let them share in your plan, rather than painting them as something they're not?"

"It gave the people a common enemy. Something to focus their anger on. It's not just because they're different from us. It's because they are vile, malicious creatures who desire nothing but to steal, kill, and destroy. Elves will jump at the chance to fight for King and Country. All of our resources will be poured into the effort. We will eradicate the scourge that has plagued us for so long, and in the process become the greatest military power the world has ever seen. Not even the Kingdom of Vaeger will be able to oppose us as the villages are lifted from poverty and our Kingdom expands. One large, united nation. Ruled by elves. And I will be their hero."

"Why are you telling us all this?" I asked. My voice came out much smaller than I had intended.

What are you waiting for? Strike! End this now!

"Because you know as well as I do I can't do this without your help."

We all stood, frozen in time for several moments.

"Arianna, what is he talking about?" Chass whispered behind me. I could feel more than hear the pain in his voice.

"You are right about my intentions for each of the relics. The rain and thunder spirits were easy enough to control."

This is my family he's talking about! We are not slaves to be commanded about. We must free my brothers, now!

"But the lightning relic, that one turned out to be something of a dud." The King produced the third and final relic from his robe. It was shaped just like the others, though formed from a yellow gem. He tossed the relic to the side. "But you know all about that, don't you, Arianna?"

I felt my world go silent.

A door at the other end of the courtyard opened, and two guards came in, hauling the Faun from the dungeon behind them. Ethyos.

"When I learned the truth," The King continued, "I decided to do a little investigating of my own. Turns out I, too, can possess the power of one of the spirits by extracting it from the relic and subsuming it into myself. All I need is a little blood sacrifice."

Realization hit me. Not just about what was going to happen to Ethyos, but that the same thing had happened to my mother all those years ago. *"You killed her, didn't you?"*

It was necessary. The rules of the deep magic cannot be ignored.

"YOU KILLED HER!" I shouted at the spirit living inside me. The spirit that had invaded my life. That had stolen everything from me. I felt the electricity surging across my body. It had been trying to control me my entire life, but I wasn't going to let it. I wasn't going to give in.

It was the beginning of the end of the world.

The King's madness.

The start of a new mission: Regicide.

ARGENTIS

In the wild I had been free.

Now, I was a part of the machine. The war engine.

After everything I had done, everything I had delivered to the King, I was still just an errand-boy to be ordered around. One last mission, he had said. One last delivery, and then I would receive my reward. It was always one more. And what reward?

"The power of the gods," he had told me. Some vague promise of a magical gift to dangle in front of me and make sure I followed commands. But follow his orders I would. I was a soldier; what choice did I have?

Eldrad and I were to return to Manse Village, retrieve Mayor Talze, and escort him to the ancient ruins of Kakara. There the King's grand plan would be revealed. Not just for reversing the drought, but for establishing the Kingdom of Idril as a global super-power like nothing the world had ever seen.

We were instructed to convince Talze to come with us under the pretense that he was to be commemorated for his ingenuity in surviving the curse, for making the Manse mines the most prosperous in the kingdom. In reality, he was to be punished for hoarding all that wealth for himself, suppressing Carine's attempts to break the curse, and for attempting to prevent Arianna from reaching the capital. A week ago I was trying to kill the little brat, now I was on her side. Just following orders.

I surveyed the map laid out before me. It would still be a few days before Arianna and the others would reach Fennox Castle. Assuming the King would set out for the ruins the moment he had her in hand, we would have to keep up a brisk pace to reach Kakara first. Traveling fast with the fat pig would not be easy. It took at least two horses to haul his cart, and it wasn't exactly designed for the narrow, uneven paths of the forest.

I traced the path with my finger, and lingered on the pencil-drawn image of the once-legendary fortress. "Castle Kakara," I muttered under my breath.

"Your people have stories about those ruins, don't you?" Eldrad asked. "You south-dogs."

I snarled at the derogation. It was meant as a slur, an insult, but I had learned to take it as a sign of my grit, my sheer determination to survive under any circumstances.

"It was once the capital of the great kingdom of Alahara," I replied.

"So a fairy tale, then?" Eldrad interrupted. I continued without acknowledging his insult.

"We were a peaceful people, farmers. We had no way of knowing the armies of Idril were going to attack. They sieged our capital, scorched our crops, took all of our riches for themselves, and erased our names from the history books. Many of our people were able to graft themselves into the towns and villages of Idril.

Over the years their descendants rose into positions of power. It's ironic, really, as their influence led the Kingdom of Idril to become more peace-loving, those of us who remained in the southern wilds were forced to become violent to survive. We become something we were not. Something we never wanted to be."

"So what does all this have to do with the curse?"

"I'm not sure," I replied. "Though it is said that our elders were able to commune with the avatars of the gods within the castle. It wasn't just the seat of our government, but a very spiritual place, as well."

"Hmmph," Eldrad said, turning to enter his tent. "Sounds like a bunch of religious nonsense, if you ask me."

"You saw what the thunder relic did," I reminded him.

He responded without turning back to me, "I saw an earthquake cause an avalanche. Hardly the work of gods." He pulled the flap of his tent closed behind him before I had a chance to answer. It didn't matter anyway. If the relics really did possess the power of the spirits, we would have proof enough once we reached Kakara.

I turned my attention back to the map. I had heard stories of our old capital all my life, but had never visited the ruins myself. I wished I could have been making the pilgrimage under different circumstances.

Before I realized what was happening, I felt a curved knife press against my neck, and a furred, clawed hand clasp over my mouth. A satyr. I had let my guard down. I had let him sneak up on me.

"What is happening at Kakara," it whispered into my ear. Quiet enough for Eldrad not to hear. So the creature wasn't just a dumb beast after all.

As soon as it removed its hand from my mouth I answered, loud enough to get Eldrad's attention, "You think I'm scared of death, satyr?" The creature closed its hand over my mouth again.

"And what of Arianna? What are the King's plans for her?"

The brat really had betrayed her people and gone all-in with the satyrs, hadn't she? "She deserves what's coming to her," I said when the beast gave me a chance to speak. I could see movement from within Eldrad's tent. Any second now…

"If anything happens to her," I could feel the creature's foul breath against my neck, "I will personally kill every one of you mindless —"

Before he could finish his sentence, Eldrad burst out of his tent, a crossbow at the ready. Without hesitation he fired a bolt in our direction. I pushed away from the satyr and only just barely managed to dodge the arrow. It skimmed off the side of my armor, deflecting it just enough to pierce the creature's arm, rather than his heart. The satyr dropped its knife as it howled in pain and grasped at the bolt sticking out of its shoulder.

Eldrad had never been one to worry about collateral damage. He saw that killing the satyr required going through me, and he hadn't even blinked. For as much as I was called a ferocious dog, a merciless beast, I knew that Eldrad was the true monster. If he thought for a second that killing me would help him grasp the next rung on the ladder of power, he would do it without thinking twice.

I pulled out my sword and spun around to face the satyr as it yanked the arrow from its arm and unsheathed its own sword. Several more of the creatures emerged from the forest edge nearby.

"Go!" The first satyr yelled at the others. "Find Miev, tell her to go to the ruins of Kakara!"

Eldrad fired another bolt toward the creature's face to shut it up, but it managed to deflect to the arrow with its sword and charge at me. The others all bolted back into the forest.

"I can handle this one!" I yelled at Eldrad as I locked swords with the satyr. "Don't let the others escape!"

Eldrad ran toward the forest edge, and without slowing down he launched another bolt into the trees. A moment later I heard a howl of pain accompanied by the distinctive sound of an arrow piercing flesh and bone. Perhaps Eldrad wouldn't have to kill me to rise to power, after all.

The blood-gushing wound on the satyr's arm didn't seem to slow him down at all. He continued to berate me with barrage after barrage, filled with rage and anguish.

"Slow down, you'll spend all your energy too quickly," I taunted.

"I will never rest until you and all your kind are extinguished from the face of the earth!" This creature meant business.

"What did my kind ever do to you?"

"I am Arctis of the Lost Tribe," the satyr said, standing back and puffing out his chest, "Your people burned down my village, slaughtered my parents in front of me, and even now you have my brother, Ethyos, enslaved behind your castle walls."

"Oh," I said nonchalantly, "You animals have names?"

The creature roared and charged at me, this time not with his sword, but with his horns. I quickly side-stepped and grabbed hold of his horn with one hand, letting his momentum carry him into a flip that landed him square on his back. With my other hand I brought my sword over my head and let it follow him down so that it pierced his chest and pinned him to the ground.

"Rest, dear Arctis," I whispered into his ear, "in the knowledge that your entire species will be joining you shortly."

A few moments later Eldrad returned from the woods. Judging by his face, his hunt had not had an ideal outcome. He tossed his crossbow into the fire as he stomped past it. "Useless piece of Casar garbage," he spat.

"The satyrs will travel faster than we can with the Mayor in tow," I said. "If we hope to beat them to Kakara, we must ride through the night.

30
ARIANNA

My body surged with a storm of electricity. My hair stood on end and I felt like I was floating off the ground.

I let it go.

An explosion, a storm of light and shadow surrounded the courtyard as everything turned bright white for a moment. Several of the guards fell backwards but more were rushing in to take their place.

I threw a ball of lightning straight at the king but one of his men jumped in the way. They flew backward and tumbled across the ground. I wasn't sure if I'd killed them. Everything was spinning, happening fast. I felt the lightning swerve around my fingers, my hands... I felt the charge run up and down my spine. My heart was beating, full of adrenaline.

"So, you've made your choice, then. That's unfortunate," the King muttered, sounding just as calm as before. I hated him more for it.

Guards were starting to converge on us. I could see Chass out of the corner of my eye unsheathing his sword and assuming a defensive stance. His legs no more than two feet apart just as they were when he fought by my side at the Thunder Temple.

The guard carrying Ethyos, shaken from the waves of magic, arrived by the side of the King. The other guard was still laying there. He couldn't be dead… Had I? I still wasn't sure. The King pulled out a short knife, slightly curved like one of Egris' daggers. He was holding it to Ethyos' throat. I could see him laughing, chanting in an ancient language. Two guards came up behind us. Chass swung at one guard, then the other, and dueled both at once. I let out a small blast. Trying my best to control my rage, my fear. I didn't want to kill them, I only wanted the King to stop.

"We have to get to the King! We don't have much time!" Chass yelled out.

I turned back. The King was raising the knife over his head.

I crouched down. Putting my hands together I focused my attack. Remembering to look straight ahead. Deep breaths. I shot a blast of lightning into the ground beneath me. It shot me into the air and I launched over the heads of the guards around me and landed, tumbling and rolling next to where the King stood over the Rain Relic. I shot again and hit the knife.

The King let out a cry of startled pain as it fell away. As I charged up another shot he growled and pulled out his sword. I shot several blasts towards him but he deflected them. A darker magic. He pulled back and swung, dashing several yards my way. I threw up my arms. Arcs of electricity formed a pair of gauntlets over my wrists. That was a new trick.

That's only a taste of my power. Let me fight. Let me free my brothers.

The King's sword crashed into the gauntlets and they absorbed the impact. With a spark, I flew back into the stream of water. The electricity reacted. It surged through me, more powerful than I had ever felt before. Painful. So much so I cried out and rolled onto dry ground. If I didn't want to end up dead, I would have to keep my powers under my control. The King stopped and stood still for a moment. His smug grin seeped into the deepest parts of my soul.

"Careful. Water and lightning don't mix," he grunted, turning his attention back toward Ethyos. He dashed back and thrust his sword into the Faun's stomach.

All I could do was scream as blood poured over the ground. Chass reacted to my cry. Distracted, a guard disarmed him and backed him against a wall on the side of the courtyard. The King rubbed some of the Faun's blood onto his hand, then took hold of the relic. The water stopped flowing. The King let out a guttural cry that morphed into a sinister laugh.

He rose and tossed the relic aside. "Let's see what this spirit can do."

Look what you've let him do. We were not meant to be weapons of war, subject to the fickle will of mortals.

As I looked on, aghast, the King held his hand up in front of him. Water seeped from his pores and formed a bubble in mid-air. I recognized the stance. The style of attack. It was not so different from my balls of lightning, the sparks I used to create when I was young. The same attack I had just been using moments before.

The King continued to mimic me, thrusting his hand in my direction. Water poured out just like my lightning, releasing from his palm. Water and lightning really don't mix. The stream hit me full force and knocked me backwards to the ground.

My pack flew open and the Thunder Relic rolled out.

"Interesting," the King said, turning his hand over, studying it. He put his sword away. Sheathing it back down by his side. With a simple gesture of his hand a stream of water picked up the Thunder Relic and carried it to him.

"Very interesting," he continued. Not only could he summon streams of water, but he could control them. He'd had his powers maybe two minutes and already mastered them more than I had in a lifetime of living with them.

The King turned his attention toward Chass and launched a second volley of water. The two guards who had subdued him leapt out of the way. The water formed a bubble around Chass and lifted him into the air. I could see him suffocating. Drowning. Surrounded by water. I ran toward him.

"Be careful. You wouldn't want to hurt your friend with a stray bolt of lightning, now would you?" the King mocked me. I froze and stared upward. The area around Chass' head gave way and formed a small air pocket. Just enough so he wasn't drowning mid-air. He looked down at me, his body squirming, floating in the water. "Don't worry. I'm not going to kill him yet."

The King relaxed his hand and the water dissipated. Chass fell several feet to the ground and crumpled. A soaking wet mess. He took in a deep breath. I ran towards him and propped him up. His wet clothes weighed the both of us down. "He'll make a perfect sacrifice to pull the Spirit of Lighting out of you. Guards!" the King commanded, turning away from us and toward a door that led back into the castle.

The guards began to converge on us as I searched for a way to escape. I noticed a large wooden trough sitting next to an outlet where the streams flowed out toward the city.

Chass followed my eyes. I could see him shaking his head.

"Get ready to run," I ordered. He looked back at me, still trying to catch his breath. I knew the last thing he wanted was to dive into more water.

"Run!" I jumped up and sent a shock-wave of electricity out in all directions, just over Chass' head. The guards closest to us fell on their backs. Guards farther away were hit by the wave of lighting and stumbled backward. The King turned back to look at us once more just before he reached the door. I could hear him muttering to himself in the confusion as I grabbed Chass' arm and dragged him to the trough. I pushed it into the stream and helped Chass in before jumping in behind him as we passed from the courtyard into a dark aqueduct. The King didn't see that coming.

The last thing I heard was the King's frantic voice shouting, "Find them!"

·31·
ARIANNA

We burst out of the castle walls in our trough, carried away by the aqueduct. From dark tunnels to bright daylight. Like a strobe of light. It felt like we were traveling through waves of time. I could feel the water splashing upwards, forcing me to lean back as the two of us did our best to stay balanced. I felt Chass leaning against me. Protecting me as much as he could. He was probably worried about the same thing I was. What would happen if we hit a gate?

We leaned left and right, passing through several wide slopes that lead us through the lower parts of the castle and out into the city. Just like riding down the mountain ahead of the avalanche. We were practically experts at this.

Several elves pointed and yelled, "Hey! You kids know better! Get down from there!" and all I could do was laugh and wave as we passed them by.

If they knew the King had just tried to kill us; if they knew what was happening inside the castle, what would the people do? A pair of guards took notice of our antics and chased after us. As they yelled for us to stop we hit a flat straightway and slowed down. We'd come too far to get caught here. The last thing I wanted was to end up in another prison cell.

This time I knew the King would be coming for our heads. Chass and I jumped out of the trough on the opposite side of the aqueduct as the two guards. There was no easy way around. One of them tried to climb over the edge, but fell in with a splash.

"Somebody grab those kids!" he shouted, wiping water from his face. Chass and I looked at each other and ran through the crowded street. Several elves jumped out of our way as we passed. We turned several corners before stopping to catch our breath.

"And how do you propose we get out of the city?" Chass asked between exhaling and inhaling.

I pointed behind him, taking notice of where we were, "The tanner!"

"The what?"

"The tanner! We're close to Luuk's house!"

"Oh, right. Luuk." Chass said as I ran off.

A moment later we rushed up to Luuk's home and banged on the door. Henna answered just as Chass came up behind me.

"Arianna? Chass? What's going on?" she asked.

"We need your help," I said, nearly out of breath, soaking wet, tired, hungry, and now more lost and confused than ever. Henna rushed us in. Isly was standing nearby, curious as ever. Henna closed the door behind us as Luuk came running out of his room.

"What's going on?" he asked, noticing the water dripping over the floor. He stared at the two of us with a confused expression across his face.

"We need to get out of the city. The King's guards are after us," I answered as seriously as I could. Arnin emerged from the back room.

"The King's guards?" he asked.

Neither Chass or I had time to explain.

"Will you help us?" Chass begged.

"No, this has gone too far," Arnin's eyes glared at us.

"But, father!" Luuk shouted.

"I stuck my neck out for you once already. I'll not have the King's guards coming down on my house like I'm some kind of criminal," Arnin's eyes looked different. More stern, more serious than ever before.

"Please, sir…" I begged.

"NO! I want you out of my house, and that is final," Arnin demanded.

"I can't believe it!" Luuk shouted toward his father before storming back into his room and slamming the door.

Arnin was right. We couldn't put his family in danger. We had already asked too much. If the King found out anyone was helping us, they would be stripped of their home, exiled, or worse, and I couldn't let that happen to them. I smiled at Isly who was standing in the corner.

I remembered being that young. That innocent. Always looking for the good, for the fun to be had. Unaware of the 'grown-up' problems going on all around her. I hoped she never had to experience that being taken away from her, like I had. The pain of losing a parent. I hoped the curse would end and she would get to live the life of a normal child. Never having some 'greater purpose' thrust upon her. That would be my gift to her, whether she knew it or not.

I bent down to her level. "Everything's going to be alright," I said. "There's just been a misunderstanding, but we're going to fix it now."

"We're leaving," Chass added. Arnin was still glaring at us. He wouldn't risk his family for our sake, but I knew he wouldn't turn us in, either. As we exited their home, Henna closed the door behind us and wished us luck. A part of me wanted to scream, to tell them everything the King was plotting, but there was no point.

"We have to go, we'll find another way," Chass reassured me. He placed his hand on my shoulder.

The two of us wandered down the street and found ourselves crossing a busy intersection of travelers and merchants. Several pigs and goats were causing a ruckus in a broken pen. Several guards were trying to catch them all while shouting at the old farmers who were apologizing again and again. Several of the well-dressed royals were mocking the pigs and laughing.

We strayed behind an open wagon full of linen and grabbed a hood and a scarf to cover our faces. Chass placed the hood over his head and armor while I wrapped the scarf around my neck and face. I took my hair and pulled it back using a small piece of yarn Maria had wrapped around my wrist before our journey began.

"Try to blend in," I whispered to Chass.

"Lucky for us it's too soon for any wanted posters to be put up around the city," Chass was almost smiling. Trying to lighten the mood.

We'd been turned away once now and the only thing we knew for sure was we needed to move away from the castle.

"We could head to one of the poor districts," Chass said.

"Look around," I said. "I doubt the capital has a poor district."

One way or another, to exit the city we would have to go through a gate, and that meant we'd be seen by guards.

Several ravens flew above us in the sky.

We continued walking. The two of us almost hand in hand as we passed from one canopy to the next, waiting for one of us to break the silence. Chass finally did.

"The King was able to manipulate the Rain Relic and control water. Do you think you can do that with your lightning?" he asked.

"I have no idea. I don't think I've ever tried. I can control the direction of strikes and where I throw balls of light, but not much else. Though, during our fight I was able to create gauntlets around my wrist. Maybe I can do more."

"We'll have to ask Egris if he knows anything," Chass added as the two of us continued to walk away from Luuk's home. It blended in with the rest of the city and I felt lost.

"We need to find Cypress," I said.

"Why? He left us in the prison cell before. And he is friends with the King. Why should we trust him knowing what we know now?" Chass fired back.

"He may not know what is really going on."

"That or he's a part of it."

"He knew my father, if anyone should have known the King was evil..."

As Chass and I argued a hand reached out from around the corner and grabbed the side of my arm. I squealed only to find myself staring at Luuk.

"Hey! Over here," he said.

Chass and I ducked down and followed him into an alley between buildings.

"What are you doing here?" I asked.

"Helping. Quick, before my dad realizes I'm gone."

He turned us back toward the castle, then down an empty street that led down another alley.

"Where are we going?" Chass asked.

"There will be guards stationed at all of the main thorough-fares. But I know another way out."

Luuk led us through several twists and turns and down a dozen staircases. It felt like we were lost in a labyrinth. He walked faster. Afraid his father would figure out he was gone. Hoping that after he slammed the door, it was enough that his family would be more than willing to give him some space. He was holding my hand. His fingers were softer than my own. For the first time I felt just how calloused our traveling had left me. It was never this way at home.

"One more flight of stairs," Luuk said, leading me down.

Chass followed behind, still on guard, his hand never far from his side.

When we reached the end of the staircase the city opened up and we were surrounded by a small but beautiful pasture and three stables made of wood. Several stone pillars stood tall with ropes hanging down from them. And a dozen horses wandered freely, eating grass from the field. The pasture was surrounded by a gi-ant wall as big as any of the capital homes. I envied the creatures. Enclosed. Safe. Ignorant. Luuk led us into one of the stalls. The closest one. He started petting one of the horses inside.

"I work here a few days a week. It's a part of my squire train-ing," he said, placing his head closer to the horse and whispering something as he closed his eyes. It was an unfamiliar bond. One I could have had with Emery.

In a way I was glad Emery had Chrysalis. Staying with me would have only ended in heartbreak for the poor creature. I approached one of the horses in a nearby stall and gently reached my hand out. Luuk nodded in reassurance.

"You know," I said, "We could really use a couple of these to get out of the city."

"That's why we're here," Luuk answered.

A stablehand came around the corner and froze.

"Luuk, I wasn't expecting to see you here today," she said.

"Oh, uh, yeah. My friends and I were just wanting to go for a ride." Luuk smiled, his dimples showing.

"Hmm… I haven't seen either of you before. I'm Gris. The head stablehand here. What are you two training for?" Gris asked. Luuk pointed to Chass.

"This is my friend…" he paused, "Uh, Corrillian. He's a…"

"I'm a squire. Luuk here doesn't like admitting that I was chosen before him," Chass smirked and gave Luuk a friendly punch to the shoulder. Gris chuckled.

"You mean he doesn't like admitting that it would take a war breaking out for him to be chosen," she laughed.

Luuk scowled at Chass, "That's not true."

"And who might this be?" Gris asked, looking at me with a sly smirk.

Luuk stepped between us, "This is…" he paused again, "Angel. She's in the Royal Academy of Magic." I blushed. That idiot. His smile was larger than ever.

"Wow! The Academy!" Gris sounded impressed. "They let you wander this far from the Castle?"

"When you're as powerful as I am," I said smugly, "They let

you have…" I paused and snapped my fingers, igniting a small spark of electricity, "…special privileges."

Gris' eyes went wide, "No way!"

Chass butted in, "So did you hear about those two kids trying to escape the city?" Both Luuk and I glanced over at him. What was he doing?

"Yeah, everybody's talking about it," Gris answered. "Wouldn't it be awesome to go on an adventure like that?" She actually sounded kind of jealous. If she only knew.

"Actually, I'm sure it's pretty scary… probably," Luuk added.

Gris shrugged, "Whatever. You kids have fun. Just don't stay out too long. I've got to lock this place up before dark."

"Sure thing," Luuk said, exhaling a breath of relief.

Gris walked out and the three of us, all on horseback, left the stable. Together we galloped along an open field. Luuk led us through a small passage that took us through a small underground tunnel and outside the walls. A dark forest lay in the distance. As we approached Luuk stopped his horse and dismounted.

"Once you get to the forest you'll be safe. No guard will dare go into the woods at night."

I dismounted from my horse and gave Luuk a hug.

"Thank you. We'll never be able to repay you for everything you've done."

Our embrace was only broken when Chass coughed, a not so subtle reminder that we needed to keep moving.

As I walked back to my horse, Luuk called out behind me, "Will I… ever see you again?"

His question sparked a strange feeling in the pit of my stomach. I knew that I was closer to my death now than ever before.

The King had two relics, and I was the third. Either I would find some way to succeed in sacrificing myself and releasing the spirits, or the King would succeed in killing me and stealing the power of the spirit for himself.

I wanted to believe that I could return. To entertain the thought of us having a life together. But I knew it would never come true.

Love isn't meant to last. You're here now. Make the most of the moment.

Without thinking, I turned around and marched back to Luuk. Just as the sun was beginning to set I took his head in my hands and kissed him on the lips. Electricity bristled over my entire body. I felt it arc from my lips to his. Luuk's hair stood up on end until I broke away. I looked him in the eyes, still holding his face in my hands. "That's a promise."

It was a moment I will never forget. I could feel the butterflies in my stomach as my arms shook. I could still feel the electricity running through my skin as I bit down on my bottom lip. Slowly I turned back. My cheeks were bright red. Tears were rolling down from my eyes. I felt like a mess. I moved my hand away from Luuk's and walked slowly back to my horse, mounted it, smiled one more time, and directed the horse to carry me away.

My heart was racing. Luuk was staring at me wide-eyed. He was still in just as much shock as I was. Of all the crazy things I'd done. I wished I could have stayed in that moment forever.

I hoped he would never forget me, but at the same time I hoped he would be able to move on and find happiness with someone else. I knew that I shouldn't have kissed him. Given him hope of a life we could never have. The lightning spirit had come over me in an instant, and disappeared just as quickly. It struck in anger, it struck in passion. I was ready to be done with it. Ready to be reunited with my parents. It was time to end this.

I tried not to look back, but I couldn't help it. Chass gave Luuk a slight nod then turned his horse to follow me.

·32·
ARIANNA

Night fell as we entered the woods. We tied off our horses after we were sure we weren't being followed and stopped to rest on a pair of logs. The air of the night was cold as it blew down from across the mountains. I wrapped the scarf around my body. I was still trying to come to grips with everything that had happened.

Wondering if I had really killed that guard when I attacked the King. Wondering if he hadn't gotten in the way, would I be rotting in a dungeon now? Would I be on trial for treason, or would I have had the strength to break the curse and save my country? How many knew his secrets? How could they stand by and watch as so many starved to death in the villages?

I had more questions than ever and my father's journals were wet, ruined, most of the pages lost. Chass had managed to scavenge a few here and there by grabbing my pack on our escape but the ink seemed to come and go as if a part of the great ocean's shore. I would trade it all for a warm fire but that was too dangerous.

"So let's recap," Chass began. "We started the day with one relic, certain that the King would help us find the other two. Turns out he's a super evil guy who started the whole curse in the first place. Now he's sucked the Spirit of Rain inside himself, stolen the one relic we did have, and oh, by the way, you've actually had the Spirit of Lightning inside you this whole time!" I sighed. It was true. My father had said this was my mission.

"Sounds about right," I sighed again.

"So where do we go from here?"

I didn't have an answer. Not at first. I stared off into the distance.

"We go to the ancient ruins of Kakara. It is there that the ritual to break the curse has to be performed. King Drevon will have no choice but to follow us there."

"What makes you so sure?" Chass asked. It was a fair question.

"He has to. He wouldn't dare wage his war without the power of lightning on his side," I said, knowing I was right. The King was vain, determined. Despite all the power in his possession he wanted more. He wanted me.

"And what if he doesn't even know that's where we are?"

"He will. Everyone always seems to know where we are."

"I know. It's almost like they've been tracking us somehow."

"Or someone has been telling them where we are."

A dark thought entered my mind and I felt my heart sink in my chest. Chass was right. Argentis and Eldrad had been able to follow us with no problem. The King, he knew we were coming... what if?

"Like who? My father's goons? How could they have known where we were?" Chass continued as I looked him in the eyes. Mayor Talze must have been taking orders straight from the King. And if he was part of the conspiracy, that must have meant...

"No, I don't mean them. I mean…"

Just as I was about to confront him our conversation was interrupted by the rustling of leaves and running footsteps. Egris burst out into the clearing near us and ran past us at full speed.

"Run!" he shouted. In the light of the moon I could see several new bruises and bloody cuts on his body. His clothing torn. His weapon in hand. My questions for Chass were going to have to wait. The two of us jumped to our feet.

"What?" we both asked.

Two capital guards ran into the clearing near us. They stopped when they saw us and looked at each other, "There they are! Get them!"

Together the two of us took off behind Egris. The wind brushed against us as we moved through the woods, following as close behind the Faun as we could. Egris came to a sudden stop at the edge of a cliff. I ran into him, pushing him closer to the edge. Chass plowed into both of us and we all launched down the side. After tumbling and rolling through tree branches and mud we landed on a slick incline and slid down to the bottom of a flat clearing. Chass looked back up at the hill and whispered, "Guards!" as we all listened intently for several moments. There was no sign of them.

"Do you have the relics?" Egris asked, glancing back and forth between us. "We must act quickly to break the curse."

"About that," Chass answered as both of us bowed our heads towards Egris.

"The King did not help you?" Egris looked more confused than ever.

"The King is the bad guy, he stole the Thunder Relic from us, he now IS the Rain Relic, and it turns out Arianna has been the

Lightning Relic the whole time," Chass answered, sounding more surprised than before.

"Of course she is. How else could she be throwing bolts of light everywhere?" Egris didn't seem surprised at all.

"Am I the only one who didn't know about this?"

Egris shrugged. I still felt ashamed. Confused. I wasn't surprised Egris figured it out. The Fauns seemed much more in tune with the spirits than we elves were.

"Did you at least find news of Ethyos?" Egris asked, worried. I could hear his voice shake as he asked. He was holding his hands together as if praying for good news. Anything to brighten the mood.

Chass pursed his lips and looked towards me. He couldn't say it. I would have to.

"I'm so sorry, Egris, it was my fault," I started to cry.

"What? What happened?" Egris' voice quaked.

I couldn't find the words to describe what had happened. I searched and searched but all I could think about was the King stabbing the tortured Faun. The blood pouring out to the ground of the courtyard and the rage I felt inside. Rage at myself for letting it happen. For believing the lies.

I started to mutter but Chass put his hand on my shoulder and spoke in a soft voice, "the King used him as a blood sacrifice to transfer the Rain Spirit into himself."

The forest grew silent for what felt like an eternity.

I thought back to the moment we broke out of our cell. The look Chass gave me as I turned my back on the Faun.

How at that moment I had turned my back on Egris.

"I could have saved him, but they told me he was the one who killed my father and...."

"And you believed them?" Egris' voice sounded more disappointed than anything.

"My anger just took over. I don't know what I was thinking. I don't know why I didn't..."

Egris' temper began to rise. "While you two were busy ruining our entire mission, I managed to find out who actually killed your father." He pulled a small piece of fabric from a satchel on his waist. I took it from him and turned it over in my hands. There was something familiar about it, about the runes embroidered onto it...

The memory came flooding back. The day my father's body was brought back to the village. The guard that had held me back. My fingers digging into the cut between his armor. The fabric that tore loose. I remembered now the armor that guard had been wearing. Not normal armor, it was dark and covered in runes. The same dark armor that had threatened me in the mines, that had hounded us all along our journey.

"Argentis?" I whispered, staring at the cloth in stunned bewilderment.

"You saved the lives of the men who killed your father, but when one of my kind was accused of the deed...."

"No!" I shouted in defense. "It's not like that! He was..."

"He was what?"

"He was..." but there was nothing left I could say.

"He was like me?" Egris stood back. Tall as a tree. With the moonlight behind him all I could see was his shadow and horns.

I closed my eyes and balled my fists.

"But if those men work for the Mayor, and the Mayor works

for the King, then…" I turned to Chass. I thought back to the Thunder Temple. The moment I asked them how they had found us…

'Perhaps a little bird told us.' Eldrad had said. The way he had winked at Chass, the way his eyes widened.

"It was you."

"It was me what?"

"You've been reporting on us this whole time, haven't you?"

"Arianna, I have no idea what you're talking about," he pleaded.

"You told your father's men where to find the Thunder Temple." I was pounding my finger against his chest, electricity sparking every time I did.

"Arianna, you're not making any sense," Egris cut in.

"You're the one who started me on this journey in the first place! You were just trying to get me out of your father's hair, weren't you!" I was on fire.

"Arianna, calm down and think about what you're saying," Chass pleaded again. He was holding his hands up in the air in front of himself. His guard was up.

"You knew we were playing into the King's hands the whole time!"

Betrayed, just like your father. Trust no one. It's only you and me now. Burn the rest.

ARIANNA

"Stop this at once!" Egris shouted as he stepped in front of me. Lightning began to pulsate through my fingers. A lethal dose to anyone but me. I could feel it arc through my veins as Egris moved closer. The smell of his fur burning as he pushed me hard against the ground. I felt the electricity course through my body, burning the sticks buried in the dirt. It concentrated itself on my back like a shield.

My hands were scratched, bloody, my body bruised from all the running. I felt like it was never going to end. Our mission to save the Kingdom was a complete failure. And it was all my fault. I looked up at Chass and Egris, standing over me. Pitying me. They had been my loyal companions, by my side through everything, and I had turned my back on both of them.

I knew Egris hadn't meant to push me so hard, but it was the only way to bring me back to my senses.

Egris held out his arms. I could see in his eyes he was still hurting from the pain. The pain I had caused. His cousin, his family. Gone because of choices I had made. My father had told me once in a journal to never leave anyone behind and yet I had chosen not to listen. I had chosen wrong. Now, it was likely the whole world would pay for my sin. The suffering of the storm.

Tears were starting to fall from my eyes. Looking up at Egris towering above me, it was like staring at the eye of a hurricane. The branches of trees seemed to mimic his horns in the light of the moon. I could feel the cold air blow over me. Behind him was the shadow of another figure, familiar and yet so far away. At first I thought it was the King again but my eyes adjusted.

Cypress.

"You've really messed things up now, haven't you?" He said it with a question mark but this was far more of a statement.

"Okay, you have got to stop doing that!" Chass said. Cypress had managed to startle all three of us. I could feel the tears welling in my eyes. He was right. I had messed this up... but it wasn't entirely my fault.

"You lied to me!" I screamed.

"I've been lying to you the whole time. You still don't get it, do you?" he snarked, pulling the lost talisman from his pocket and flipping it through the air. "It was never Chass who was spying on you."

"The talisman," I said, looking towards Chass who was just as surprised as Egris and I. I felt ashamed. Chass had known the whole time. He had tried to warn me, but I had refused to listen.

"Did you really think you were so special that the deep magic itself would take the time to conveniently give you everything you needed to complete your quest?" Cypress was chuckling now. Snarling at me. Mocking me.

"But the lightning chose me," I began.

"It was a coincidence that you happened to be coming into the world just when it needed a fresh vessel to inhabit. There is nothing special about you. I have been manipulating you from the beginning, and it was the easiest thing I've ever done," Cypress grinned again.

"No, it can't be true."

"I made you turn against your best friend, didn't I?" As he spoke I turned toward Chass. His jaw set and eyes sharp as steel daggers. I could see the look of betrayal. "And it was inevitable that you would allow that Satyr to die," Cypress finished, looking toward Egris. Egris was cowering backward, holding his burned hand with a look of pure sadness in his eyes. "In spite of everything your father tried to do to shield you from the propaganda we put out about them, that little seedling of prejudice managed to plant itself deep in your subconscious, and just when it mattered most, it reared its ugly head and turned you into a monster more gruesome than any painting of a Satyr has ever been." Cypress smiled like he had won. Not yet. I couldn't let him.

I screamed, "NO! That's not who I am!" in defiance.

Cypress answered, smiling, "It's not who you are. It's who we made you to be." I lifted myself from the ground and extended my arm out towards Cypress to unleash a devastating bolt of lightning. It struck and destroyed a tree behind him. He was gone. He had only come to gloat. The sick satisfaction of seeing us fail and suffer. Both Chass and Egris were staring at me with pity.

"I am so sorry. This is all my fault," I admitted. I had no more lies to tell myself. Cypress was right. I had played my role just as the King had wanted.

Chass moved closer to me, "No, Arianna, it's not. Cypress

was…"

"No. My actions were my own choice. And now it's time to pay for my mistakes," I said, cutting him off and looking back towards the direction of the woods.

"Where are you going?" Chass cried out.

"To the ruins. It's time to end this once and for all."

The Temple of the Storm Spirits. The one place my father had mentioned in his journals as being the start of all of this. I remembered it on one of his maps. All my life I had been staring at it, displayed in our home for all to see. I helped him pin it to our wall when I was just three years old and he had been adding to it ever since. Searching for answers when they were in front of us the whole time.

Between our village and the castle was a place that had been calling out to me in whispers since I left home, all those weeks ago. I pulled the map out from my satchel. It was still folded. Some of the edges had been torn but it had survived as much of the journey as I had. Slowly I unfolded it. With the map in hand I searched for the ruins. Covered up with a giant X like most of the places my father had gone. It wouldn't take me long to get there.

If I headed west of the constellation of the seventh king I could make it to the temple by mid-day, if I walked through the night. I could sleep for a few hours in the early morning. I still had some berries Chass and I had picked before coming to a stop.

I felt like curling up in a ball. Could I really go through with this? My father had entrusted me. Believed in me. Believed in the power of the storm inside me.

I paused just before passing out of the clearing and back into the dark forest. I looked back and Chass and Egris, who exchanged determined glances.

"To the ruins," was all Egris said. It was all he needed to say.

A small smile crossed my face. Happy that despite everything, we were still together and I wasn't going to do this alone.

CARINE

We left the library in Fennox Castle in the light of the early morning. Five of us total. We were all so full of hope, until we were ambushed by bandits in the woods by the Arbar Springs. The springs had dried up and they had buried themselves in the mud. It was like the bandits had been waiting for us; it was not a well-traveled path. Lervo was the first of our party to fall. Stabbed through the gut by a rapier.

The bandits were well armed. About a dozen in all, though it was difficult to get a count through the cover of the trees. Most wore leather armor while two I believed to be the leaders, possibly brothers, were armed in chain-mail. Half hid in the withered trees with crossbows. They aimed for the horses first.

Milla was one of the best shots in all of the kingdom, lucky for us, too. With a golden longbow she aimed with her hazel eyes, thick brown braid swinging in the air, and took out one of the archers as we found cover behind our crashed wagon. We were all wearing decent leather armor beneath our capes and hoods. We hadn't planned on entering combat, but we had been prepared nonetheless.

"Ambush, think someone knew we were coming?" Milla asked, looking back towards the trees and counting. When she made it to three she turned and lifted herself up and fired a single arrow. I heard one of the raiders grunt and smiled knowing if we waited long enough, Milla could probably kill all of them on her own.

"It's possible. Maybe someone in the market saw we were preparing for a journey," I answered. One of the other soldiers with us, a surveyor named Charik, pointed upwards, "I doubt that; we were pretty good at covering our tracks. I think this was a set-up. Must mean we're looking in the right direction." I smiled and looked towards Milla and Eger, the youngest surveyor with us. His baby face was a stark contrast to Charik, who had a full gray beard, bald head, and eyes as black as the night. Eger was fresh out of the academy and a licensed mage. He was also one of the few I had trusted with our family secret.

All of them knew. All of them a part of the few. The trusted. All of us had become close over the previous few months. After I had learned to trust them, I told Milla first. Followed by Lervo and Charik and lastly Eger. Eger had the most to say. Promising to take you to the academy after he became a master. Promising to keep you safe from those that might try to turn you to evil. He even gave me a few pointers I could teach you to control your powers.

I also learned from him just how rare actual magic was. After I told him my secret he told me his. The Academy was full of frauds. Not that magic wasn't real. It was. It just came at a great cost. Living vessels with magic that could tap into the aether without paying a price, whether by blood or bone, were one in a million. All the more reason, he would say, to keep you secret and safe.

Together the five of us ventured out to find answers as to what caused the curse that now plagued our kingdom. So far most of our adventures had been in libraries and poring through interviews in small villages and interrogating rogue mages.

The five of us all came from the villages. Milla had been an old friend of Solph's, having grown up beside her. She shared with me stories of your mother, my wife, that even I had never heard. She joined our collective when she lost her family in the mines. It was much the same for Lervo and Charik. Each of us had our reason for being there, searching for the truth.

Eger probably had the most to prove. Having gone from poor villager to the magic academy, he was treated with disdain from all of his noble peers. He believed in the deep magic with all of his heart and had volunteered to be a surveyor when none of the others would.

"Five down, six to go," said Milla. She was still taking them down one at a time with her arrows but she was running low. The rest of her arrows were broken or scattered across the ground on the other side of the wagon. We hadn't been ready for the attack even though we should have been ready for anything.

I could hear her cursing. Both she and Solph cursed in Casar tongue. They had learned it as a joke when they were young. I almost laughed the first time I heard the word, 'Leek' being used by an elf. Solph always had a talent for languages. I remember when the two of us planned to travel the entire country, even as north as Firya.

"Eger, cast a light spell and Charik and I will flank them from behind. Right and left," I nodded towards Charik who nodded back at me. We had trained for things like this. Being in it was much different. My hands were shaking as I unsheathed my sword, knowing I would have to kill or maim someone to survive. I sighed and took a deep breath.

"Go!" I shouted as Eger cast a blinding spell. Milla, Charik, and I held up our arms and shielded our eyes from the white light. A moment later Charik and I were running up behind the bandits. I lifted my sword in the air and swung downward, but stopped before making contact.

He was disoriented from the spell and totally unaware that death was hovering over him. I couldn't just murder him without giving him a chance to defend himself. I kicked him in the back so that he tumbled down the side of a hill, away from the rest of the battle and out of the line of fire of any remaining archers.

I ran down after him as he got up and shook his head to recover his vision. "Who put you up to this?" I yelled.

"You think I care who hired me?" He responded. "I was paid to do a job, and that's what I'm doing."

He charged at me with a high swipe, which I parried and returned with a thrust to his gut. He dodged and we continued to spar back and forth.

"Not exactly what I would call an 'honest living'," I retorted between jabs.

"We all gotta make a living somehow," he said. "You should know better than most, I don't remember surveyors carrying swords before the drought."

"Fair point," I replied, parrying another thrust and responding with a slash across his chest. He wasn't able to jump out of the way fast enough, and my blade sliced across his leather armor, giving way to a slight trickle of blood. He stood back, the tip of his sword resting on the ground, his chest heaving.

"It's nothing personal," I said. "I'm just trying to take care of my family."

"Aren't we all?" He responded. He raised his sword as high as he could and charged at me one last time. I could see the anguish on his face as his arms pulled at the wound on his chest. I knocked his sword to the side and lodged my own into the slit in his armor. We both collapsed to our knees.

I could feel the warmth of the bandit's blood as it covered my skin. I wasn't ready for this. Hunting animals was one thing, but I felt like a traitor killing my own people.

I was staring at the dead bandit. His armor torn. Had I just orphaned a child? I couldn't be sure. I searched his body for something. Maybe something to ease my conscience. There was a chain around his neck. A locket. Inside, a professionally drawn portrait of a woman and young girl. The child was no older than you, Aria.

Milla walked over to comfort me. I could feel her hand on my shoulder as tears fell down from my eyes.

"You did what you had to do," Milla said.

Charik and Eger were already digging a grave for Lervo.

"We can repair the wagon, get more horses and bring the bodies back," I said. "We can at least cover them up and give them a proper funeral."

"I'm sorry," Charik said, shovel in hand.

"The mission must come first," Eger said beside him. His eyes were bloodshot and looked like they had been bleeding. There was always a price to pay for using magic.

We piled the dead and burned the bodies with the wagon and the horses. A warrior's funeral.

We continued our journey on foot, hiding our supplies and taking only what we needed to survive.

"Something wasn't right about that attack," said Charik.

"They knew we were coming, they were hiding in wait," Milla agreed.

"Isn't it possible they were just waiting for anyone to pass through, this is a road used by merchants," I said, trying not to be as paranoid as the rest of them. I looked at Eger and waited to see what he had to say.

"They were sent by nobles," he said, sure of himself.

"How do you know that?" I asked.

"I knew it!" Milla yelped out almost smiling. Even in the worst situations she enjoyed being right. Something about it made her feel calmer. I admired that about her. She was always looking towards the future and taking it one step at a time.

"I found a royal emblem sewn to one of the leaders, on his tunic underneath the chain-mail. The emblem of the 'Celestial Sky'. The other bandit in armor I'm sure would have been wearing the same emblem under his but I didn't bother to check. I'm a hundred percent sure that they were brothers of noble birth. They want to stop us," Eger answered.

"Why would the nobles be trying to stop us?" I asked.

"Look at the kingdom. The capital is flourishing while the rest of the country goes to work in the mines and factories," said Charik, making a fist. It was true. Most inside the gates of the capital still had fresh food and water. Business as usual. I doubted half of them even realized that the world was being ravaged just outside their walls.

"All of the noble houses signed off on our mission."

"The nobles are corrupt from the inside out, they wanted to send us out and watch us fail," Charik added. More than any of us he had reason to hate the noble families. His family had been cast out. His grandfather had once been mayor of a small village that had begun to grow. Less than fifty years earlier another family had accused his of colluding with beasts. His noble family crest was taken away and his grandfather cast out.

Charik had found his grandfather once, in the woods. Living with the Faun. Smiling, dancing, drinking kava. He had thought he would find someone broken and alone.

This was before the Faun became known as the Satyr and were blamed for the curse. His grandfather was happy, and the Faun welcomed Charik into their village for a time. I think that was a part of Charik's reason for being here. If he could clear the Satyr of being blamed he could somehow clear his family name. I admired him for it. Like all of us he knew change was possible.

On our way to the ruins of Kakara we crossed a village set on fire. It was the middle of the night and yet the sky was lit up by an orange haze. I could see the ash falling around me like snow. I felt an ember burn against my skin as I covered my mouth and nose with a wet cloth.

Milla was the first of us to rush into the blaze. She wrapped her face with a cape and dropped her gear. The rest of us rushed after her.

"Summon some wind, water, anything!" Charik shouted at Eger.

"I can't, not against a blaze like that!" he answered back.

"We have to evacuate the village, get them as far away from the flames as possible!" I shouted, pointing at villagers trying to navigate through the plumes of smoke. The village had at least a few hundred of our elven brothers.

"Take heed, let light shine through," Eger cast a beacon of light in the sky and I shouted at anyone that would listen to 'head towards the light'.

Running in and out of homes, trying my best to make sure anyone that might have been sleeping or injured was able to get out, I found a little girl crying on the floor of a burning inn. Her mother and father were nowhere to be seen so I picked her up and carried her to safety, covering her eyes as the inn fell apart behind us. When I made it back to Eger I found Milla and Charik were both missing.

A young woman rushed up to me, screaming what I assumed was the child's name. As I handed the child off I looked into the woman's eyes, and felt that I knew her somehow. I looked down to the girl, and remembered. I knelt down to the girl's level, and pulled out the locket I had taken from the dead bandit.

The child's eyes lit up with recognition. "That's my daddy's!" She said. Her mother took in a sharp breath and clasped her hands over her mouth. She knew what this meant.

I held the child's gaze as long as I dared. I could see the question beginning to form behind her eyes. "Your father was a brave man," I said as I handed her the locket. "He died with honor." I turned away from the child and her mother as I choked back tears. There were more survivors. I had to keep moving.

"Eger, I'm going back for Milla and Charik, keep the light on," I shouted, turning towards the raging fire and never looking back.

I moved towards the southern part of the village. The doors to the Mayor's mansion opened, and five bandits came through, heavily armed. One of them was wearing iron armor. He must have been feeling the heat, but somehow I could feel he was being protected. Three of them had muskets while the other two carried crossbows and swords. They were killing villagers. They had probably just gone after the Mayor. I followed them, hiding behind the flames until I saw them break away from one another. I could hear the musket fire as a villager screamed.

I crouched behind one of the less armored thugs and stabbed him from behind. I felt nothing. No remorse. I heard another villager scream. It was bad enough they were burning. I picked up his rifle and aimed. I had taken a few classes inside the castle gates.

Rifles were rare. Almost as rare as magic.

I fired a shot, taking another one of them out.

"I thought I was going to burn for sure," said Milla from behind me.

"That was close," agreed Charik, running up behind her.

"Nice to see you, Carine. I guess you've met our new friends," she said pointing towards the dead bandit.

"What is going on?" I cried out.

"The light, we have to tell Eger to turn off the light," said Charik, panicked.

"What is happening?"

"Moths to a flame, that's what's happening," said Charik, the three of us were already moving back towards the light but we were minutes behind the iron bandit even as we ran through the flames. Charik and Milla had suffered burns on their arms by the time we saw the others.

"Eger, shut off the light!" Charik shouted as loud as he could. His words were lost among the sound of burning homes. In the distance we could see the armored thug moving closer to Eger and the others, swords in hand.

They had run out of arrows and bullets, at least.

I stopped and began loading the rifle with gunpowder and a round piece of shrapnel I pulled from the dead bandit. I was lucky. Had the gunpowder caught on fire I would have been a dead man.

I held the metal sphere in my hand. It was the only shot I had left.

I threw it over to Milla. "Best to make it count."

She crouched to one knee and aimed at the armored thug. Just as he and the other bandits passed under the awning on the side of a burning building, she jerked the gun to the left and fired. The shrapnel plowed through a support beam, and the roof collapsed on top of the bandits, trapping them underneath.

"What have you done," I cried.

Eger's light faded away from the night sky.

"I made the shot count," she said.

Both Charik and I glanced at one another. I felt numb.

I ran towards Eger and found him alive among the rest of the villagers. His hand had been grazed by a bullet and several fingers had gone missing. He was holding his side and coughing up blood. Some organs inside him had started to give away. "The cost of magic," he coughed. Milla ran up behind me smiling, followed by Charik who at one moment looked ready to kill her and the next ready to kiss her.

In the early morning, after only a few hours of sleep, Charik and I hunted a Praeg for the village to eat. They were grateful for everything we had done. It would be enough food to last them a week or more, and with aid from the capital they would be able to rebuild in several months.

That afternoon we made it to the Temple of the Storm Spirits and found it in ruins. The temple itself was at the center of the Castle Kakara, a once-mighty fortress. Unlike the village which was still smoldering, these ruins had been burned years ago. At the center of the temple sat a great stone disc, covered in the evidence of a massive slaughter. Dried blood across the ground as if hundreds, maybe thousands had been brought to the temple and sacrificed all at the same time.

"Someone did this," Milla said, studying the decaying runes. She was using a small piece of charcoal to trace what was left of the story on the wall.

"Who could do something like this?" Charik asked, disgusted.

"A noble, a King?" said Milla.

"Cast shadow of night," said Eger, before screaming.

His eyes began to bleed and he was blind, unable to speak.

"What did you see?" we begged.

Eger held out his hand and Milla handed him a piece of chalk. He used what fingers he had left to write down a rune before coughing up blood.

"We have to get you to a doctor," Milla cried.

Eger shook his head. This was it. He was going to die and he knew it.

"You can't die, you have to teach my daughter. I need you. We need you," I pleaded. Eger smiled. Charik stood back hitting his fist against a wall.

"The cost of magic," tears fell from Milla's face to her hand as she closed Eger's eyes. He had given all he had.

We returned to the castle a few days later. Three out of five of us. There was no party, no nobles welcoming us back. Our small group was told to disband. Our mission was considered a failure.

"We learned one thing. The Temple is where the curse originated and it took a lot of blood sacrifice. Like all magic it had a cost, and that means if it was made by elven hands it can be broken by elven hands," Charik said, taking a gulp of mead. I sat with Milla and Charik drinking in a small tavern for the rest of the night. We translated Eger's last rune. It was the Faun sigil for 'rebirth'.

We spent hours debating what it meant. It couldn't have been a coincidence that he wrote in an ancient Faunic language. Could it be that the Fauns themselves would find 'rebirth'? No longer branded as satyrs and falsely accused of murdering elves. Or perhaps it meant that it was the Fauns who would break the curse, and thus bring a new beginning to the whole kingdom. We couldn't be sure.

I was preparing to head back home when Milla and Charik found me and told me they were reassigned to a group of surveyors heading into the Southern Wilds. Their mission was to explore a new region known for being home to giant lizards and ancient reptiles, Khendalai. If the curse continued our Kingdom would have to expand and with the Firya to the North and Casar to the East, our only option was to re-discover the wild. Our mission was over for now but they promised they would return.

I couldn't accept that. There was no way I could give up on Eger, Lervo, and all those that died and suffered at the hands of this curse. I couldn't give up on you. I promised them what I promise you now. I still haven't seen Milla or Charik but I believe they are still alive.

From beginning to end I will always be by your side. I will break the curse on our kingdom and deliver to you a new world. My Aria. My songbird. My daughter. This story is one of the first in my journey but last in my journal, hidden in ink. One day I hope I can look back and tell you about all of this with a smile on my face. That all of it meant something. Hold you in my arms and smile as we pin pictures on our walls. It doesn't get easier, but that's okay because I have you. Sometimes it's all we have. Your mother taught me that.

·35·
ARIANNA

I pushed back tears from my eyes as I read the last scrap of my father's journal while we took a short rest deep in the night. The child. The locket. It was Scyenna. It had to be. My father had killed her father. In striving to end the drought, had he done more harm than good? But then, could it really be said that it was his fault? The curse had driven everyone to desperation. Forced good men to do terrible things to protect their families.

It was a harsh reminder that in order to win, compromises would have to be made. Innocent people were suffering, and I was the only one who could do something about it. Just like my father, I would have to learn to do what was necessary for the sake of our people.

It broke my heart to think of how the curse had changed my father, warped him. Especially considering he had never let me see it. He always wore a smile when I was around. He wanted me to see the world as it could be, as it should have been. Not as what the curse had turned it into.

I had heard him talk of Eger before. Even his friends Milla

and Charik, whom he told me I would meet one day. He was always happy when he spoke of them. I imagined they had spent a lot more time together than just what my father wrote about. It was probably harder to write the happier memories because of all the bad.

I found one more page before going to bed. A poem to my mother, written over a sketch of her. It was beautiful. I thought about what a renowned bard my father could have been, if it hadn't been for the curse. For all I knew he had written hundreds of poems. A whole other side of him that I never got to see.

I'm sure Maria knew more than she let on. I didn't doubt my father had kept more journals hidden in places other than our home.

For now, my father had said what he had to say and I was more determined than ever to follow my mission and break the curse.

We stopped twice. Once to eat and once to rest. The Temple of the Storm Spirits was close. I could feel it. Lateral lines. Places of power across our world were magic flows strongest. The Leviathan, also called the Churn, that my father wrote about was one. The Thunder Temple and the path made up another. Egris had spoken of a place called 'the Maw', and Fennox Castle was built on the ruins of another. The Temple of the Storm Spirits, no different than the rest of them. My father was right to begin his search there. It was just… he couldn't feel the deep magic like I could.

"Arianna, I do not believe what you did was right," Egris said, sitting down beside me. I could feel his claws as he reached out and put his hand on my shoulder. How could he still trust me? Still travel with me? I must really have been the Faun's only hope.

"I do not believe what you did was right, but I understand,"

Egris continued. "Your father was distrusting of my people at first, as many others have been. The King's curse does not just dry up the rivers or plague the oceans. It does not only wither the trees and starve families. The seeds of the curse had been planted a long time ago by hatred. Hatred without any meaning that has passed from one generation to the next. I believe in time things will get better. I believe you know in your heart." I stood silently for a moment before bursting into tears. Placing my head on Egris' chest, I let it out. Everything. I hadn't cried so much since I saw my father's body brought to Manse village. The hatred in my heart sank away.

"I'm sorry," I said.

"I believe you," Egris nodded as I moved away.

"I will…"

"I still believe you are the one that will free us of this curse. It is not my place to allow a personal grievance to get in the way of the greater mission. We are all victims of the curse, of the King's wickedness. It would do no good to fight amongst ourselves."

"Thank you," I said.

"Arianna, I have one more thing to say."

"What is it?"

"Your father would be proud of you."

I buried my head in Egris' chest one more time as Chass woke up, stretching his arms wide into the air to take the last watch and I felt my eyes shut. I didn't have enough time to dream as dawn approached but if I had, I'm sure I would have dreamed of Manse village as it should have been.

How it will be after I'm gone.

ARGENTIS

Getting the Mayor to the ruins was the easy part. He believed our lie entirely. In fact, he seemed to think some recognition from the King was long overdue. We strapped our two fastest horses to the smallest carriage we could all three fit in and took turns driving while the others slept. The horses were pushed to their limit by the time we arrived, but they pulled through. Several other of the Mayor's guards escorted us on horseback.

Finding the Temple of the Storm Spirits within the winding ruins of Castle Kakara wasn't so easy. Even with spreading out and systematically making our way through the maze it took us most of the day. A few guards fell prey to traps and mimics that were still active. Amateurs.

We made it to the ruins first, and set up a signal fire to guide the King and his men to the temple. They would be arriving from the opposite direction as us, so marking our path wouldn't have done much good. So we waited.

There was a large, round platform at the center of the ruins, surrounded by stone pillars carved with runes and topped with the faces of mythical creatures. The floor seemed to have a coat of dark, dried out paint. I kicked at it and several flakes broke loose and blew off in the wind. Dried blood from a mass sacrifice, most likely. I wondered how long dried blood would last. This blood seemed old, sure, but hundreds of years? Not likely.

"Carine was right, after all," Mayor Talze remarked. "It's not surprising really, he was always a smart man."

Eldrad stepped up onto the platform next to me. "I wish I could just run the old man through right now," he said.

"Let him talk," I replied. "It doesn't mean anything."

"I wish I could have done more to help him," Talze continued. Easy to say, now that he'd had the man killed. "But I stand by my decision to fight the drought through hard work and sacrifice, rather than a hopeless fantasy. I'm glad the King has seen the wisdom in it."

It was only a matter of hours before Arianna and her gang of vagrants showed up. I was surprised to see the King wasn't with them.

"What's this? What's going on here?" Mayor Talze demanded. All of his guards pulled their swords out immediately, as did Chass and the Satyr. It looked almost identical to the one I had just killed. But then, I couldn't hardly tell any of the creatures apart.

Chass stepped forward. "We escaped the King and are here to end the curse once and for all!" He yelled.

"I was under the impression the King's plan was to break the curse," the Mayor said, confused.

"You really don't get it, do you?" Arianna interjected. "The King is not who you think. His plan is evil."

All the secrets. All the lies. It was really starting to get under my skin. I didn't even know whose side I was on anymore. "So what exactly is the King's plan?" I asked.

Talze didn't seem too happy with my outburst. "Silence, Argentis," he said. "Let me handle this."

"No," I said. "You know what? I'm tired of being lied to. Of being treated like a hired hand expected to obey without questioning. There's something more going on here, and I want to know what it is."

"It doesn't matter what the King's plan was," the satyr said. "Any minute now this place will be flooded with an army of Faun, and we will win."

I knew he was right, but until they arrived, we needed to keep the advantage. "You mean like Arctis?" I asked.

The satyr's ears perked up. So he knew that name.

"You'll be happy to know he fought well. A real brute, right up until the end."

"Liar!" The creature screamed. The fear on his face gave me a deep sense of satisfaction.

"And what did he say the other's name was?" I asked, looking at Eldrad. "Miev? No, I don't think any of your friends are going to be joining us today. The King, on the other hand, was likely right on your tail all the way from the castle. There is really no point in continuing the charade, so just tell us what's going on!"

"Never!" Chass yelled as he raised his sword. A brave fool, but a fool nonetheless. Arianna stepped up beside him and placed a hand on his shoulder.

"No, Chass, he's right," she said. "We have no choice." Finally, someone was seeing reason. "King Drevon is the one who started the curse," she said in an unexpectedly authoritative voice. Talze and many of the guards gasped.

"Impossible," The Mayor muttered. After everything I had seen, I honestly wasn't surprised.

"His plan was to use the Rain Spirit to make the entire Kingdom dependent upon the capital, while using the Spirits of Lightning and Thunder as instruments of war."

All of the pieces were falling together now. The mines, the ruthless training the knights had been going through, Eldrad and I being sent to keep tabs on a seemingly dead-end village. It was all part of the plan.

"The King has allowed himself to be possessed by the Rain Spirit, just as I was possessed by the Spirit of Lightning on the day I was born," Arianna said as she raised her hand and allowed sparks of electricity to swirl around it. "The day the curse was put in place."

Mayor Talze stood with his mouth agape, stunned. "So you're not just an elemental?" he asked.

"We've had one of the most powerful forces in the world right under our nose, and never knew it," I said.

Eldrad chuckled, "The runt who was bullied was actually a god who should have been worshiped." He bowed in mock humility, "Your Majesty." Several of the guards laughed.

I stepped forward, swinging my sword casually. "So when the King promised me the power of the gods as reward, I suppose he meant I would be taking on the Spirit of Thunder."

"That's right," A booming voice called from somewhere in the ruins. We all looked to the source of the sound, and there, from under an ancient stone archway, King Drevon emerged, riding on the back of an armored praeg. The creature's scaly skin was darker than any praeg I had seen before. Scorched with fire, no doubt.

The King's guards emerged from all corners of the ruins. They quickly surrounded Arianna, Chass, and the satyr. The King certainly knew how to make an entrance. Behind him on a black stallion rode in a mage who I immediately recognized as the hooded figure who had tipped Eldrad and I off about the location of the Thunder Temple. Of course the King would never have been able to put such a far-reaching curse in place without an immensely powerful magic user.

The King's beast sauntered into the center of the ruins on its two hind legs and the King deftly dismounted.

"Allow me to give you a bit of a history lesson," he said as all eyes were on him. "The true history of the war with Alahara."

I almost dropped my sword. I had on many occasions personally heard him deny that the Kingdom of Alahara had ever existed. And now I was about to learn the truth about my people's downfall.

"A secret history," the King continued. "Passed down from father to son, King to King, until it was told to me by my father." He stepped up onto the stone circle at the center of the ruins. "As the siege of Castle Kakara was coming to an end, when the people of the mighty Kingdom of Alahara had no hope of continued resistance, the elders came here, to this very temple, to make one final plea to the gods. They begged the Spirits of the Storm to join their war. To fight on their behalf. But the gods do not take sides.

"Their request angered the spirits so much that they abandoned the Kingdom altogether. Their avatars left the temple and retreated to a cave far beyond the Chasm of Fire. In their fury they sent a terrible storm like none that had been seen before. They laid waste to the Castle of Kakara, and decimated all the lands of the once-prosperous Kingdom of Alahara."

So it was never the viciousness of Idril that turned our kingdom into desolate wilds, but our own arrogance. Our own foolishness.

"In their vain attempt to win the war, they made their defeat all the more complete. Now, some five hundred years later, I began to see the weaknesses of Alahara infesting our own Kingdom from within. Their naive reliance on peace, economic prosperity, and the misguided practice of democracy was threatening the stability and security we hold so dear. The Royal Bloodline has protected the Kingdom of Idril for millennia, and I wasn't going to be the one to let it crumble. And so I had an idea.

"I assembled the Relics of Vel from the corners of the earth and I brought them here, not with a request for the gods, but with a demand." His voice was growing louder, more resonant. I glanced over at Arianna. Her fists were clenched and lighting was arcing around her, but the guard's sword across her neck was keeping her contained.

"I spilled the blood of hundreds of my own people to summon the spirits here and enslave them within the relics, but there was one among them who eluded my grasp." He stepped down from the platform and marched toward Arianna, his deliberate steps emphasizing each word. "The Spirit of Lightning slipped through my fingers, and chose to funnel itself into a poor, pitiful, pathetic peasant girl instead." He was practically spitting the last few words in Arianna's face. "It took me years to locate the spirit's new host." He turned away from her and walked toward Eldrad and me. I felt uncomfortable as everyone's attention shifted my direction. "When I heard rumors of a young girl with elemental powers, I sent my two most trusted knights to keep tabs on the situation."

Most trusted knights? That was news to me. It would have been nice to know my true mission at the time. Had Eldrad known? Had he been sending messages to the King behind my back?

The King was approaching me now. It took everything I had to keep my back straight, my head held high, and to meet his towering gaze. "And now as recompense for your years of faithful servitude, I offer you the chance to join me as a god on earth. Kill the traitor Chass, and I shall bestow upon you the power of the Spirit of Thunder, and you shall take on the mantle of Champion of the King of Idril."

The guards holding Chass back pushed him forward. Eldrad shifted awkwardly beside me. "But your Majesty, I —"

"Not now, Eldrad," the King interrupted. "You shall receive your reward soon enough."

So there was something more going on between them. Had I been nothing more than a puppet in their game this whole time?

Chass was moving toward me, his sword raised. I stepped forward to meet him.

"Father, tell them to stop this!" Chass called out. "It's not too late!"

The King's gaze shifted to Mayor Talze, gauging his reaction.

The fat coward stammered out, "I, I'm sorry son. There's nothing I can do. The King's orders must stand."

The King smirked with a satisfied chuckle.

"I should have known you were taking orders from the person who started the curse!" Chass yelled.

"Oh, not at all," King Drevon replied. "Your father was simply an opportunistic pig who took advantage of a desperate situation. Quite impressive, really."

I looked over to Talze. His face was conflicted. He couldn't decide whether to stand tall with pride at the King's backhanded compliment, or to hang his head in shame at the realization that he had betrayed his own people, his family.

I raised my sword toward Chass and crossed my blade with his.

"You don't have to do this," he said through gritted teeth.

"Oh, I think I do," I replied. I pushed his blade away and swung my sword around to slash down at his left arm. He quickly recovered and parried my attack. He knew exactly where I would strike first. I took a step back. After years of sparring, we had memorized each other's moves. If I was going to win, I would have to do something unexpected.

He charged at me and I knocked his blade away, leaving his chest open. We had been through this routine a hundred times before. I raised my foot as if to kick him, and he positioned himself to catch my leg. Smart. He was finally catching on. At the last second I shot my foot downward, slamming into his knee. He crumpled to the ground.

I swung my sword over my head to slash down at him, but he rolled out of the way and my blade stuck in the dirt. I pulled it out of the ground as he jumped to his feet and we squared off. I circled around him, and as he turned to track me he couldn't hide his limp. Good.

"You've seen what the curse has done," he said. "You've seen how the people suffer." Was he trying to reason with me? "Do you really want to be on the side of monsters?"

"I've seen true power," I replied. "I'd rather be on the side of the winners." After everything I'd been through I wasn't going to let myself waiver now. I was finally getting the recognition I deserved. The reward I had fought so hard for for so many years.

I lunged at Chass, and we sparred back and forth for several minutes. I would feign an attack one way, then pull back and strike from another direction, but Chass always predicted my moves. No matter how I maneuvered, he was always one step ahead of me, ready with a parry and a counter-attack. He even got in a few hits against my armor, but never enough to do any damage.

I pulled in tight and took hold of his wrist with one hand, locking our blades at the hilt with the other. We struggled against each other, pushing and pulling, until I was able to swing my foot behind his good leg and sweep it out from under him. With all his weight on his injured knee he stumbled and fell flat on his back.

I slashed down at him again and again, but he deflected every time as he scurried backward along the ground. He finally managed to kick my own feet out from under me, and we rolled away from each other and pushed back up to our feet, breathing heavily.

"Your ancestors once believed in peace and equality," he said between labored breaths. "If you join with the King, you'll only be helping him destroy everything your people stood for."

"What do you know of my people?" I yelled as I launched another volley of attacks at him. I hammered into him with all the force I could muster. He only just managed to deflect each of my advances as he hobbled backward, careful not to put too much weight on his injured leg.

My attacks slowed as my energy began to wane. I swung at his side, and rather than deflecting the blow he hooked his blade underneath mine, carrying it over between us and pinning it to the ground on the far side. He stomped on the hilt of my sword, ripping it from my fingers. Within an instant he brought his blade level to my throat and was guiding me away from my fallen sword.

"I know they were wise. They sought to work with the spirits, not enslave them."

"They were fools! Weak! They trusted the spirits and what did it get them? Look around! Our people are scattered and our legacy is nothing more than a forgotten pile of ruins!"

I could see his resolve weakening. His eyes fell to the ground, and his sword drooped ever so slightly. In his moment of weakness I made my move. I deflected his sword with my gauntlet and took hold of the blade at the base of the hilt. I could feel the blade digging into my skin between the creases of my armor. I swung my other arm around and my fist connected squarely with his jaw. The force of the impact caused him to lose his grip on his sword, and I tossed it behind me.

I swung at him again, but he ducked under my arm and kicked at the back of my knee. I stumbled slightly, but recovered and spun around to meet him, swinging my arm behind me. He jumped backward and my fist flew within inches of his face. With his smaller size and light, leather armor, he would have the advantage of speed, but it didn't matter. Even with his sword he couldn't break through my armor. He didn't stand a chance in hand-to-hand combat.

He ran toward me and jumped, feet first. Just like that little brat from the village we burned down. I braced myself for the impact, and took the full force of it to my chest. I barely budged as Chass bounced off and slammed to the ground. I swung at him again but he scrambled to his feet and ducked around behind me once again. This time he jumped on my back.

I could feel him trying to wrap his arms around my neck, but he couldn't get to it through my helmet. I tried to reach for him to throw him off, but my restrictive armor prevented me from raising my arms high enough. He managed to get his fingers under the edge of my helmet and rip it off, tossing it to the side as he clenched his legs around my abdomen for support.

Just as he finally managed to get a choke-hold, I lurched my torso forward and he flew over my head, landing on his back right in front of me. I brought my fist down toward his head but he rolled away just before I cracked his skull open. He pushed up onto his hands and knees, but before he could get to his feet I kicked him in the stomach. He rolled several times and lay there, clutching his gut.

I stepped over to him as he squirmed, helplessly, at my feet. He raised his eyes to meet mine, and wheezed out, "Their legacy… can be restored…" he coughed and spit up blood, which splattered across my boot. "…through you." I froze and stared down at him. "Be the hero your people deserve."

Hmmph. What people? They were scattered and forgotten. I had given up on being a hero a long time ago. I was there to follow orders. To make a name for myself in the King's service. Still, I didn't move. I didn't press my foot into his scrawny neck and suffocate him like I had imagined doing so many times before. I just… stood there.

"What are you waiting for, south-dog?" The King's voice called out from behind me. "Finish him!"

Chass laughed, and more blood spattered out. "South-dog," he said. "That's all you'll ever be to him."

"That's all I'll ever be to anyone," I said as I placed my foot on his chest. The thought of crushing his rib cage filled me with adrenaline. Stomping on his heart over and over until it finally stopped beating. I could feel my own heart pounding inside my chest.

"Not to me," he whispered.

"What?"

"You were the one who trained me. You taught me discipline, perseverance. Without you I would be a fat slob like my father." I couldn't help but chuckle. He had a point there. "You taught me to protect myself, but more importantly, to protect others. I saw you split your rations with the workers when there wasn't enough to go around."

I could feel my chest heaving in rapid, shallow breaths. "They were exhausting themselves in the mines," I said. "They deserved to eat."

"Then let them," he replied. "Help us break the curse, and there will always be enough food to go around."

I dug my heel further into his chest, sparking another blood-filled coughing fit. "Shut up!" I yelled.

But deep down I knew that he was right. And that made me hate him all the more. Would this be my legacy? The man who followed orders. So I would gain the power of gods, but it would only be used to squash the innocent. To attack those who couldn't defend themselves. I was only a pawn in the King's game.

As a child I once saved my mother from a jackal by fighting it off with my bare hands. Even then I had a strength and ferocity that couldn't be matched. My mother always told me I would find true greatness someday. That I would be the bravest protector the world had ever seen.

She had fought and scraped and did whatever she had to do to make a life for us in the Kingdom. But somewhere along the way I had forgotten who I was. Why I was doing all of this. I had to work twice as hard as my peers for the same recognition. Fight without mercy just to have a chance. That had made me calloused. Resentful. I went from protecting the innocent to killing for spite.

It was time for that to end.

I took my foot off Chass' chest and turned to King Drevon. "This isn't right," I said.

"It's right because I say it is," the King replied. "If you aren't strong enough to do what must be done, I'll just have to find someone who is."

I suddenly felt a sharp pain in the back of my neck. I tried to scream, but the sound was caught in my throat. I took a deep breath in, but no air would come. I fell to my knees and reached for my throat. I felt the tip of a knife sticking through the front of my neck.

Eldrad stepped around from behind me and walked up to the King. He knelt to one knee before him. "Have I earned your respect now, father?"

Father? So Eldrad wasn't just an ambitious knight trying to make a name for himself. He was a crown prince who had been forced to prove himself to a cold and heartless father.

I watched as the King pulled the Thunder Relic out from his robe and extended it to Eldrad. "You have done well, my son. Now go, take the blood of your enemy, and receive the power of the gods!"

Eldrad took the relic, and I heard a long, low rumble as darkness began to overtake the corners of my vision. Eldrad walked back over to me and pulled the knife from my neck. Cold air rushed into my lungs and I grew dizzy and fell onto my side.

As the earth shook in a violent earthquake, my world went black.

·36·
ARIANNA

I watched in disbelief as Chass and Argentis continued to duel. They were both fighting harder than they ever had in training. Only one was going to walk away alive. I thought back to all the mornings on our quest where I woke up to find Chass already training. All the times he insisted Egris or I spar with him, even at the end of a long day of traveling. He had been preparing himself for this moment. To protect me. To protect the Kingdom.

"Your ancestors once believed in peace and equality," I heard Chass yell. "If you join with the King, you'll only be helping him destroy everything your people stood for."

Even after everything Argentis had done, Chass was trying to turn him. I had saved the man's life, now Chass was trying to save his soul. I couldn't help but admire Chass' optimism. His unwavering faith in humanity that had somehow managed to survive everything we'd been through.

Unfortunately it only seemed to provoke Argentis even more. He continued to wail into Chass without giving him a moment of respite. Every time Chass gained an advantage, Argentis managed to turn it around in his favor. Before long they were both unarmed, kicking and punching and choking each other out.

Finally, Argentis gained the upper hand. Chass was on the ground, wheezing. Even after all of his training, he couldn't beat Argentis' raw strength and enhanced armor.

I wanted to run to his side, to unleash a blast of lightning that would take Argentis out of the fight for good, but I could feel a trickle of blood as the blade across my neck dug deeper.

I saw Chass say something, too soft for me to hear at this distance. Argentis paused, but the anger on his face never abated.

"What are you waiting for, south-dog?" the King yelled. "Finish him!"

I could see Chass and Argentis continue talking, but it didn't seem to be doing any good, as Argentis placed his heavy boot over Chass' heart.

I couldn't bear to watch. I clenched my eyes shut, but for several moments nothing happened. No cries of agony, no snapping of ribs, nothing. The silence was almost unbearable.

Just when I thought my teeth couldn't be clenched any tighter, I heard the last thing I expected. Argentis' voice called out, loud and clear, "This isn't right!"

My eyes shot open. Argentis had turned to face the King. Chass rolled over and crawled away as fast as his injured body could manage.

"It's right because I say it is," the King said in answer. "If you aren't strong enough to do what must be done, I'll just have to find someone who is."

I could see Eldrad moving toward Argentis, his knife drawn. Everything in me wanted to scream out, to warn him. At the same

ROBBIE BALLEW AND STEPHEN LANDRY

time, everything in me wanted to watch it happen.

He killed your father! He deserves much worse than this.

I had saved his life once, before I knew the truth. Would I be willing to do it again? Chass seemed to think he was redeemable, and apparently he had been right. But it didn't matter now. There was nothing I could do.

I watched in horror as the knife was thrust into the back of Argentis' neck, and burst through the front of his throat. Argentis fell to his knees, his mouth opening and closing as though gasping for air that refused to come.

But even after all this, nothing could have prepared me for what happened next.

"Have I earned your respect now, father?" Eldrad asked as he marched toward the King.

It was almost too much to take in. The quiet, stoic figure standing vaguely in the background of so many unpleasant memories was actually the crown prince?

"You have done well, my son," King Drevon said as he pulled the Thunder Relic from his robe. "Now go, take the blood of your enemy, and receive the power of the gods!"

Stop him! You cannot allow my brother to be made subject to his will!

But there was nothing I could do. As the ground shook beneath our feet, I could feel the unsteady blade at my neck digging deeper into my skin. One false move and it would slice through me like butter.

Eldrad took the relic and moved toward Argentis. The King and Cypress followed along behind him, chanting an ancient ritual.

Eldrad pulled the knife from Argentis' throat, and let the blood flow onto his hand, holding the relic. Argentis fell to his side, and

I knew he would be gone within seconds.

A deafening boom shook the ruins. The guard holding me back dropped his sword, and in his moment of disorientation I turned and blasted him just hard enough to knock him on his back. I ran to Chass' side and let a surge of electricity run through him, healing his wounds. He jumped to his feet, said a quick, "Thanks," then grabbed his sword and ran toward Egris who was quickly being overpowered by a handful of the King's guards.

I turned my attention back to Eldrad. He had fallen to his knees as his armor was denting in on itself. I almost worried it would crush him alive.

The resounding crashes of thunder were suddenly replaced by an eerie silence. Eldrad sat hunched over, and the dim clashing of blades ceased as everyone looked on breathlessly. After several long moments Eldrad pushed himself up to his feet, looked around, and extended his arm toward a tall stone pillar. A shockwave of thunder blasted out from Eldrad's hand. It distorted the air in its path, knocked Eldrad back several feet, and turned the stone pillar into a pile of gravel.

Eldrad turned his gaze toward me. I took hold of the bow that was still miraculously slung around my shoulder, and quickly strung an arrow. I closed my eyes and felt a surge of electricity charge up the bolt. I opened my eyes and unleashed the arrow toward Eldrad's extended hand just as a crash of thunder filled the air.

His blast and my electrified bolt met mid-air, and unleashed a shockwave that knocked everyone to their backs. I blacked out for a moment, and even when I came to I couldn't seem to shake the ringing in my ears. When I finally managed to sit up, I saw that the

King and Cypress were the only ones still standing, and they were heading right for me.

I scrambled toward my bow, but a wave of water from the King sent me sprawling across the ground. I jumped to my feet and saw Chass and Egris running toward me, but they were too late. Cypress was right in front of me, and his knife was thrust into my stomach. He had a hand on my shoulder, supporting my weight, and his golden, reptilian eyes were locked on mine.

"I'm going to enjoy being the God of Lightning," he whispered.

He pulled the knife out and as my body collapsed I felt Chass' arms wrap around me. He fell to his knees and I lay helplessly across his lap. "Arianna, no…"

Suddenly, a massive bolt of lightning shot out from me, and I watched as its tendrils spread out across the ruins, seemingly in slow motion. I looked around and realized all of the people were standing completely still, as if frozen in time.

"*What's going on?*" I asked the Lightning Spirit.

I've had enough, it replied. *It's my turn now.*

With what felt like a massive gust of wind, my spirit was ripped free of my body. I found myself standing in the center of the stone ruins. I could see Chass and Egris hovering over my body while the King and his men stood around them. They were all frozen in place.

The ruins looked different somehow. Less ominous. As if they weren't ruins at all, but had been restored to their ancient glory. It was like I could see the walls that had once stood tall around the Temple of the Storm, but at the same time I couldn't.

My mind raced to tell me I wasn't really there. I couldn't even feel my heart beating, my chest was locked in place. I didn't panic.

The ruins around me were glowing, illuminated by the arcs of lightning that slowly spread across the whole area. There was a soft blue hue as wisps of energy flowed out from the cracks in the stone.

The runes that were once damaged were restored. I still couldn't read them, but I doubted anyone had for a thousand years. Several yards away from me I saw two figures emerge from behind ruined pillars. My parents! My father Carine, looking just as he had the day he left Manse Village, and my mother Solph, like an adult version of me with long brown hair, green eyes, pointed ears, and a smile that glimmered. As she moved closer I could see her pale skin sparkle and shine and I realized without a doubt she was the most beautiful woman I had ever seen.

I didn't hesitate.

I didn't even question whether this could be one of the King's tricks. I ran up to my father and wrapped my arms around him and he embraced me. I felt the warmth of my mother's hand as she joined in. I felt her tears touch my face and mix with my own.

"I always knew you had the spirit of the storm in you," my father said.

"This is the end, isn't it?" I asked in a serene voice.

"That is your choice to make," my mother's voice. It was soft. Well-spoken. I'd never heard her speak before, and yet it was completely familiar. Comforting.

I turned and looked toward my fading body. There, among the frozen crowd, stood another figure I hadn't seen before. It wasn't an elf, though it had vaguely the same shape. Its body seemed to be made entirely of electricity. I knew at once it was the avatar of the Lightning Spirit.

"I can heal myself, can't I?" I asked the spirit.

"Yes. If you choose to," it answered. Its voice was oddly familiar, almost a distortion of my own.

"And what happens if I don't?" I asked, looking back to my parents.

My mother and father glanced at one another lovingly.

"Death isn't so bad. It's very peaceful," my father said.

"You could stay with us. Forever," my mother added.

I let go of their arms and walked over to Chass and stroked his hair. I stared at him for what seemed like an eternity.

"Why can't we have that peace while we are still alive?" I asked, staring at the heartbreak in Chass' eyes.

"Perhaps you could. If you succeed," my father answered, standing beside me, my mother behind me. She knelt down beside me. As I stroked Chass' hair I looked over and saw Egris. I remembered seeing him when I was a child wandering into the woods. How far I'd come. How strange the world was.

"You've done your part, Arianna. No one could possibly expect any more from you," my mother said gently.

"Nevertheless, more must be done," the Spirit interjected. "If you allow the King to control all three spirits, he will be unstoppable. Everyone you love will be enslaved and tortured. The very land will be warped into an abomination of his evil will. It may be hundreds, even thousands of years before the natural order is restored."

I looked to my father. He was always so wise. My source of direction when nothing else made sense. "What should I do?" I asked him.

"No one can make that choice but you, Aria," he replied. "I

trust you'll make the right one."

I closed my eyes and let out a sigh of determined resignation. I knew what I had to do.

"This burden has been placed on me. I alone carry it. If I don't break the curse now, no one will be able to stand against the King."

"You are my daughter, aren't you?" My father said with a warm smile.

"I'll be with you soon enough," I said, hugging both of them.

"We'll be waiting," my mother said as they both moved toward a massive wooden door in the ethereal ruins. Just before they opened the door, my father paused and turned to the battlefield. It was only then that I noticed a strange man standing over Argentis' body.

He seemed to be in a daze, broken only when my father called out to him, "Come, Argentis. It's time to go."

Argentis? I suddenly realized his strange robe must have the ceremonial garb of the ancient Alaharan people. In his final moments he had honored the memory of his ancestors, and now they were ready to welcome him home once and for all.

"But, how can I?" Argentis asked. "When I —"

"I don't blame you for what you did," my father interrupted him. "You were deceived, the same as the rest of us. I am no more without guilt than you are, but that is all behind us now. Come, let us find peace."

I watched as my father and mother, the two people I'd loved more than anyone in the world, together with Argentis, the man I had hated more than anyone, passed together into the void beyond the veil.

My father's spirit was gone, but I could hear his voice echo through the temple, "Go, Aria, my little songbird. Save the world."

I crouched down next to my lifeless body. Hovering a hand over the hole in my chest. "But you must know that if you survive, you won't be the same."

I paused and let my father finish. "The spirit has been part of you since the day you were born. It has molded you into who you are."

"Once it is removed," my mother added, "that part of you will be gone forever. You will be a different person."

I looked up to the avatar of the spirit, still hovering over me.

"Then I will find out who I truly am. I hope I like me."

I smiled and pressed my hand into the wound on my chest.

Everything went black.

I wasn't standing near the ruins anymore. Chass, Egris, everyone disappeared and I stood in a void. The avatar of the Spirit of Lightning was all that remained.

"Before we go back, I think you and I need to talk," she said.

"Yes, I think we do," I replied.

"You have to let me take control," she said. "The only way to free my brothers —"

"No," I cut her off. "Our only hope of winning is to fight side by side. Not as master and slave, but as sisters.

"Sisters?"

"I've spent my entire life trying to suppress you, control you. As if you were a part of me that I could keep quiet, if only I had the willpower. But you're not a part of me at all."

"Sisters," the spirit repeated, mulling the word over.

"It has always been your anger, your impulsiveness that has pushed me to act when I was too timid, too afraid."

"And your compassion," the spirit said, catching on, "that has kept me in check. Preventing me from killing everything in our path."

"So it's settled then. We're a team."

The spirit's sparking eyes seemed to narrow. "It's settled."

I jerked awake, gasping for air. Chass was startled and nearly dropped me from his arms. Egris leapt to his feet. The King spun around and I heard him shout, "What!" as I rose to my feet.

"You didn't think it was going to be that easy to kill me, did you?"

ARIANNA

A distant noise echoed through the stone ruins, like a faint whistling of wind through the trees.

Egris' ears perked up, and he took a hopeful step forward. He seemed to brace himself, as if for impact, then let out the most ferocious noise I had ever heard him emit.

His cry was answered by a symphony of howls from the forest. The echoes sounded like the drums of war, reverberating off the stone walls and almost causing the ground to shake as Egris towered over the guards and held out his arms. He looked like a warrior. Even despite our many battles this was the first time I had seen him rise. He had been waiting for this moment.

Moments later a swarm of Fauns and elves, even dwarves and others I didn't recognize rushed out from the woods. Egris grabbed hold of me and the two of us moved away from the guards. I saw one of them strike Egris' shoulder, but he didn't even flinch. I felt his fur, his arms wrapped around me protecting me from the arrows flying in our direction. Egris was too fast for the King's archers, who changed targets and tried to attack the newcomers.

They were too late. The swarm was already attacking the King's guards. Among them I saw Chrysalis riding an armored Emery, Miev, and even Scyenna.

Miev. So Argentis had been bluffing. I looked around for a sight of Arctis, but I couldn't make him out in the fury of fur and swords. Perhaps Argentis' lie was based on a half-truth, after all.

Egris let me go when we were far enough away to not get caught in the crossfire. I watched as Scyenna took on three guards at once. She was still as graceful and precise as I had ever seen her, but I could see the rage burning behind her controlled face.

From my perch atop the stone platform at the center of the temple I could see the whole battle playing out. The King's guards were hopelessly outnumbered, but they were quickly proving that their ruthless training had been well worthwhile. Each one fought with the strength of ten.

As I examined the faces in the melee there were many that I recognized, but at least as many I had never seen before. Yet it all felt somehow familiar, as if the vivid descriptions and sketches in my father's journals had come to life before me. The family crest on a shield that deflected blow after blow. The thick braid of dark hair that sat perched in a tree with a crossbow.

As I made eye contact with each one of them, they all seemed to know exactly who I was. All of my father's old friends reunited for one final mission.

I noticed Miev had several arrows stuck in her arm, but they weren't slowing her down. I had no idea the Faun could be so strong. A part of me wondered if this was why the King had tried to turn them into monsters. They were peaceful creatures, but when it came down to it they fought with all their hearts in battle. I realized a guard had a crossbow trained in my direction, but Emery tackled him from behind at the last second. Chrysalis dismounted and dispatched the guard as Emery bounded toward me, snuggling her armored muzzle into my chest.

The stone pillars around me cracked as Eldrad's thunder rang out around us. The ground shook. Several of the Fauns stopped in their tracks. As they stopped Chrysalis jumped forward with a golden longbow and fired three arrows towards the King. Eldrad clapped again and the arrows shattered into a million splinters. Chrysalis fired again. This time one of the arrows almost hit him. Chass stared at her with amazement. Just as hopelessly in love with her as the day we left. Maybe more so now. Miev grabbed hold of her just as she began to pull another arrow from her quiver. A blast of distorted air rushed over them. A crumbling stone pillar burst like broken glass as my ears went deaf from the sound of thunder.

Miev used her body to shield Chrysalis. Her hair standing up on end. Her horns broken. I could see the blood flowing out from her arm. She turned her face towards us. I could see the sadness in her eyes as she realized what this place had once been. Despite the pain the two of them stood back up and continued fighting as Emery leapt back to Chrysalis' side.

More of the King's guards were rushing in. They must have been hiding out nearby as reinforcements in case things didn't go as planned. Some of them were mercenaries. Talze's men. Probably hired them along the way here to make sure Chass never made it home. I wanted to strike him down for what he did to Chass. Chrysalis reloaded her bow with another three arrows.

Chass had followed close behind us. Shadowing Egris. I could still feel the presence of my mother and father as we stood at the center of the ruins. King Drevon and Cypress marched toward me. Eldrad, still covered in the blood of Argentis, was following behind them. The two piece-meal armies were all fighting one another, evenly matched despite the sheer power of the Fauns and Chrysalis' archery skills.

I looked back to Chass and Egris. "Take out Mr. God of Thunder and I'll hold off the King as long as I can," I commanded, promising myself it was a good plan. I reminded myself I had the spirit of lightning inside me like an older sister watching my back. Chass and Egris immediately moved toward Eldrad. The three of us had been through everything together and had come to reach an understanding. Despite our failures we'd still grown close as a family; friends bound by blood, bound by the fate of the world.

As Egris and Chass pressed forward they were spotted by two guards, who engaged them. They dispatched the two guards easily enough as two more appeared. I could see Eldrad had broken off from guarding the King and was waiting for Chass and Egris to reach him.

The King approached me. Still grinning like he'd won. He waved his hand and streams of water emerged from his fingertips and floated in front of him. Cypress was moving around to my left, flanking me. I closed my eyes and took a deep breath.

"It's time. Let's do this."

I opened my eyes to find the King and Cypress stopped in their tracks, staring aghast. There, next to me, stood the avatar of the Spirit of Lightning.

"Side by side," I said.

"Like sisters," she replied in a buzzing voice.

I tightened my fists. Bolts of lightning formed spikes protruding from the backs of my wrists. Lightning arced around my palm to form a gauntlet. I could feel the energy of lightning surrounding me like armor. Solid white with specks of blue.

The King summoned several more balls of water and hurled them in my direction.

I raised my arm and formed a small shield around my forearm in the shape of an arrowhead. I imagined the shield as a recreation of one I had once seen my father use. The one with our family crest. Another artifact he had to sell to get food on our table. The blasts of water hit the shield and evaporate in a puff of steam.

"Impressive," the King grinned as he formed two spikes of ice, mimicking my own weapons of lightning.

Slowly and deliberately the Lightning Spirit and I forced our way between the King and Cypress, standing back to back as we fought. The King didn't let up. Each time an ice spike shattered against my shield or was sliced off by my own spikes, he would simply generate a new one and strike again. Any blows I managed to land glanced off his enchanted armor.

I could sense, more than see, Cypress engaging with the Lightning Spirit behind me. I was aware of her movements, almost like watching through a second pair of eyes in the back of my mind. Cypress was wielding his staff, casting spell after spell to ward off her attacks and launch a few of his own. He may have been more powerful than any other living mage, but this level of magic use was bound to take a physical toll on anyone.

We were slowly moving away from each other as each of us pushed our respective opponents back. While it seemed we had the upper hand for the moment, I knew this close-quarters combat would only end in a stalemate, and wasn't allowing any of us to make full use of our powers.

I glanced to the side and noticed an entrance to a staircase, now half in ruins, that must have once led to the top of a mighty tower. As I pushed the King nearer to it I slipped past him and ran up the stone steps. I projected a force-field of lightning behind me, completely blocking the entrance. I knew it would only take a few seconds for the King to blast his way through, but those few seconds would be enough.

EGRIS

Chass and I flanked Arianna, swords drawn, as the King and his twisted mage advanced toward her. She had to be protected at all costs.

"Take out Mr. God of Thunder and I'll hold off the King as long as I can," Arianna shouted.

Did she really think she could handle the King and Cypress at once? Chass and I exchanged glances. We had no way of knowing what happened during those few brief moments we had thought she was dead, but clearly something had changed. She had a confidence in her bearing, an authority in her voice that couldn't be ignored.

Chass and I broke off and made to cut off Eldrad, who was lagging several steps behind the others. Two guards jumped at us, seemingly out of nowhere. A blade swung down toward me, and I knocked it to the side with my sword. The guard stumbled from the force of his deflected momentum, and crashed into his companion. Chass' sword came down on the disoriented guard, and I threw a knife at the one who had been knocked off balance. My knife found its mark in the small gap just below the guard's helmet.

No sooner had those two guards been eliminated than two more appeared to take their place. I could see Eldrad standing by, watching us. Taunting us.

These two guards were better prepared than the first. That, and I was beginning to feel the fatigue of battle set in. Their attacks were coming too swiftly, my parries not swiftly enough. Chass and I were switching back and forth between them, forcing them to keep their guard up in all directions, not knowing where the next attack was coming from. They caught on soon enough, and tried to draw us apart from each other.

All around, I could see the battle raging in the corners of my vision. This contest wouldn't be won by the strength of either army. It all came down to Arianna. But even if she miraculously defeated both the King and Cypress, it would be a moot point so long as Eldrad held the power of the Thunder Spirit.

It didn't take long for the guard I was engaged with to disarm me. I had let myself become distracted. Worried about things beyond my control instead of focusing on the fight in front of me.

As the guard pulled back to thrust his sword toward my gut, I dug my hooves into the dirt and summoned all of the strength I could muster. I let out the most vicious, guttural howl I had ever unleashed, and launched myself at my assailant. I deflected his sword with my horns and pounced on his chest. An instant later he was flat on his back, my claws piercing through his breastplate and into his chest.

I jumped to my feet and squared off toward Eldrad, who seemed visibly shaken by my display of raw ferocity. Chass stepped up to my side, having finished off his own attacker. Eldrad extended his hand toward us, and we jumped in either direction to avoid his blast. I rose to my feet and rushed toward Eldrad, knowing that without my sword there wouldn't be much I could do against his cursed armor. With his attention fully trained on me, I saw that Chass had a window to assault him from behind.

I maintained my charge and took the full brunt of one of Eldrad's blasts, giving Chass just enough time to make his attack. Eldrad barely reacted in time, and pulled out his sword as Chass' blade came down toward him. With their blades locked Eldrad tried to send a thunder blast into Chass' stomach, but at such close range Chass had no trouble dodging it.

As I recovered my breath from the impact, I noticed my sword lying on the ground nearby. I swooped it up and rushed toward the dueling Chass and Eldrad. "Keep close!" I yelled as I advanced. "Don't let him use his power!"

Unlike his father, the King, Eldrad didn't have the wherewithal to master his newfound ability so quickly. As our swords clashed it almost felt like we were dancing. I stepped off to the right, Chass moved in from the left. Without his new powers to protect him, Eldrad was no match for the two of us. When we thought we had the upper hand, Chass swung down toward a dent in Eldrad's armor just as I knocked his sword from his hand. It wasn't enough.

A blast of thunder that shook even the ruins burst forth from Eldrad. We were both knocked to our backs. The blast was so powerful it ripped Eldrad's armor to shreds, leaving several gaping holes. Eldrad turned toward me with his hand held high. As I braced for the impact, Miev interceded.

Clutching Eldrad's arm, she tackled him to the ground. Eldrad blasted her off of him and retrieved his sword. Miev launched another attack, ignoring Eldrad's blade as it glanced off her broken horns, her blood-soaked arms. She was using the deep magic. Magic passed down through her family. Forbidden to use in battle unless necessary.

Miev caught Eldrad's sword in her hand and pressed forward, the blade tearing into the muscles inside her fingers. She didn't back down. She clenched her fingers around the blade and pushed forward until she was neck and neck with Eldrad. With her free hand she formed a fist and punched through a gap in Eldrad's armor. She pulled back a bloody fist as the jagged edges of Eldrad's shredded armor tore through her skin.

"That was for Arctis!" She yelled as she let go of his sword and readied herself for another attack.

The thug stumbled back as he tried to catch his breath. Even with the power of the Thunder Relic he was no match for Miev's rage. There was a price. Using the deep magic like that was only temporary. Unnatural. Miev's body began to give way. She launched herself toward Eldrad, but he was ready this time. He regained his composure just in time to swing upward and take Miev's arm off.

He allowed himself a quick smile in his victory, when an arrow caught him in the back of the neck. Miev made her retreat toward one of the Faun priests waiting for her. Eldrad, surprised by the attack, turned toward Chrysalis and ripped the arrow from his neck. He held out his hand. A wave of energy formed from the compressed sound of thunder.

Chass moved in front of Eldrad.

"No!" he shouted. The blast hit his chest and knocked him back.

Chrysalis quickly mounted on Emery's back and the pair bounded toward Chass.

Eldrad was laughing in his temporary victory. He had fended off every attack we had thrown at him, but I knew his luck was running out.

I glanced over to where Arianna had engaged with the King and Cypress, but nothing prepared me for what I saw. Rather than Arianna, the avatar of the Spirit of Lightning was locked in combat with Cypress, who was clearly being pushed to the edge of his ability as a mage.

I couldn't see Arianna, but after a moment I spotted the King staring up at a tower at the far end of the temple. I looked up just in time to see Arianna rush out onto the top of the tower and turn back toward the top of the stairwell. Only the King didn't follow her up the stairs. Instead, he shot a jet of water at the ground beneath him, and propelled himself up over the edge of the tower.

"Arianna!" I shouted as loud as I could, but I doubted my voice would carry over the cacophony of the battle.

ARIANNA

I spun around just as I heard my name ringing out from somewhere in the battle below. I turned just in time to see the King being propelled over the edge of the tower and launching a fresh round of ice arrows at me. I threw up my shield just in time to catch the projectiles, but the impact sent me stumbling back against the parapet.

I grabbed onto the edge to keep myself from toppling over the side. From my vantage point just above the trees, I could see for miles in every direction. Distant mountains glowed red in the light of the setting sun. The temple rested atop a slight hill, though I hadn't noticed the uphill climb as we had approached.

"You'll never win," King Drevon taunted as his quiet footsteps crept up behind me.

I surveyed the chaos below. Swords clashed. Arrows flew. Bodies were strewn throughout the ruins. So many people had sacrificed so much for me.

No, not for me. It was for their families. For their children. For a better world. I just happened to be the only one who could make that better world a reality. "Return to me, sister," I whispered to the Lightning Spirit. "I need your strength."

My gaze found Chass cradled in Chrysalis' arms as Eldrad dueled with Egris nearby. Chass' eyes met mine, and he gave a slight nod. He rose, took up his sword, and hobbled toward the unsuspecting Eldrad.

"I have to win," I muttered as I could feel the King's shadow looming over me. "I have no other choice."

As I felt the full power of the Lightning Spirit flow through me once again, I channeled it all into my fist, spun around, and launched a massive bolt of lightning through the King's chest just as his own blade of ice pierced my heart. King Drevon looked down to the smoking hole in his armor in shock.

A boom rang out from below, and we both turned to see

Eldrad on his knees in a cloud of dust, sitting at the bottom of a small crater. Anyone near him had been blown clear across the ruins, and the rest of the battlefield had fallen silent. Chass' sword was protruding from his back, and Egris' sword was lodged in his stomach.

I felt my mother's voice whispering into my ear, echoed by my father's. Another voice, the Lightning Spirit, telling me to repeat what I heard, "apsene pice húta lya marta," As I recited the last part of the ancient spell I coughed up blood, "mettanyë húro."

A low rumble shook the ground, and the King's blade of ice, still stuck in my chest, dissolved. A wind blew up from between us and we both fell onto our backs. From the ground I gazed up to the sky to see a bolt of lightning travel across the clouds. It was followed by a loud crash of rolling thunder. I pulled myself up over the edge of the parapet. In the distance, over a golden plain of withered grass, a black cloud was moving toward us. The cloud seemed to stretch from the sky all the way down to the earth. As it moved closer I began to hear a low rumble; not like thunder, more like a pattering sound.

Below I could see everyone looking up as droplets of water were falling all around. Could this be rain?

My question was answered a moment later as the black cloud overtook us, and a torrent of water gushed from the heavens, soaking into my clothes and turning the hard ground below into a slick mud. I could see the King's guards struggling to keep their traction as they scattered into the ruins around the temple. The Fauns, as if remembering how much they loved traveling in these conditions, wasted no time chasing after them. I collapsed and slid down the edge of the parapet.

Nice going, sis.

Cypress rushed out onto the roof of the tower and saw the King lying motionless at my feet. He ran to the King's side, and in an instant they both vanished into thin air.

I smiled as the rain flowed to my wound and sealed it up. I closed my eyes and let myself be lulled to sleep by the comforting sounds of the first storm I had ever experienced.

ARIANNA

I didn't choose to be born into this world cursed; the vessel for a spirit of lightning. I didn't choose to be a hero. I didn't choose my own fate.

Rain fell down on the grave where I buried my father's ashes. A small tombstone sat with an ancient rune. Rebirth. For the first time since my mission began I finally had a chance to mourn him. Not just cry but actually mourn the loss of the life I once had. The life I once resented having.

As the embers burned out they swallowed the last pages of my father's journals, and I was left wondering. Feeling a sense of hope. Everything had not yet been made right with the world, but it was a start.

King Drevon still ruled from his throne in Fennox Castle. It must have taken Cypress every ounce of dark magic he could muster to keep the king alive. King Drevon had proclaimed to the citizens of Idril that he was the one who had broken the curse, and that it was, as he had always suspected, Fauns who had started the drought for their own nefarious purposes. He said we would no longer tolerate their hatred, their wickedness, their feral appetites. He had effectively declared war on the entire species.

And so my father's legacy would live on in secret.

His mission was complete, but my own journey was only just beginning.

I looked out over the lush green fields that stretched beyond the graveyard. In just a matter of weeks the crops had shot up faster than I ever imagined they could. Emery hadn't left my side since the ruins.

I was wearing a dress for a party at what used to be the Mayor's mansion. No one lived there now. It had become a center for trade and council. That night, it was to be the venue for a wedding. Chass and Chrysalis. Their union would signify a new friendship between elves and Fauns. The celebrations were sure to last all through the night.

My leather armor had been locked away in a box in my home. Maria insisted she could fix it but I didn't want her to.

I felt strange without the Spirit of Lightning inside me. Alone. I could sometimes hear a voice calling out to me in my dreams. It was far away from here. Sometimes I woke up in the middle of the night. My bags were packed. I was ready to run away again.

Maria was more than happy to have me back. She said the mine workers rebelled against the foreman and Talze hadn't been back to the village since the first storm. A part of me hoped I would never see him again.

In his absence, Chass and I helped establish a small ruling council, though neither of us wanted to be a part of it. It was only a matter of time before an all-out civil war broke out, and we had to be prepared to do what was necessary.

In the meantime, Manse village had become a refuge for the oppressed, a shelter for troubled times.

Chass approached me from behind.

Since being freed of the spirit I had refused to touch a weapon. I couldn't stomach the thought of violence, much less inflicting it myself.

"We may have broken the curse, but this is far from over. The King is going to come down on us with the full force of his wrath," Chass said, standing beside me. I took a deep breath and stared into the distance. My flowing dress flapped in the wind.

"My part in this war is over, Chass. The next battle is going to be yours."

I turned and walked away, leaving him alone with his thoughts.

My own destiny lay on a different path. I had to answer the call of the spirits. To return to the temple. And maybe, just maybe, I would find out who I truly was.

Want to stay updated on news about the Temple of the Storm series and more from author Robbie Ballew? Visit
https://bit.ly/3nB3rxx
to sign up for his newsletter and receive a free gift!

You are invited to attend the wedding of Chass and Chrysalis in…

Temple of the Storm Book 2: Chrysalis and the Fire of the Forge

ROBBIE BALLEW

Robbie is one of those introverts who loves to stay out late at parties or hanging out with friends, but then has to crash for three days afterwards.

He's been passionate about writing since he was 11 years old, when he started a cheesy novel about a group of medieval kids who were stranded alone in the woods and had to kill an elephant for food (Don't worry, all copies of that manuscript were destroyed with his old Gateway computer).

He peaked in his early teenage years when he posted emo poetry on Xanga, and now writes young adult novels to help him relive his glory years and pretend like he's not 30.

He lives in Arkansas with his talented wife, Amy, and their two head-strong daughters, Lucy and Hero.

STEPHEN LANDRY

Stephen Landry is the author of the LitRPG series Star Divers, Sci-Fi series Deep Darkness, and multiple award winning short stories. After graduating from Nossi College of Art in 2012 with a degree in Graphic Design, he discovered a new passion for the creative process and started working on his first series. Deep Darkness released at #1 on Amazon in Cyberpunk in 2016. In 2019 Stephen released his first GameLit short story titled HUSK in the anthology Game On! A GameLit Anthology which reached #1 New Release in Virtual Worlds and followed with a full length novel from LEVEL UP PUBLISHING called Star Divers: Dungeons of Bane, a brand new LitRPG series that combines Stephen's love of science fiction, video games, and survival horror.

Twitter: @AstralStrikes
Instagram: Stephen.Landry
Website: www.stephen-landry.com

Thank you for reading Arianna and the Spirit of the Storm.

Please don't forget to leave a review!

Made in the USA
Coppell, TX
07 May 2021